SPECIAL MESSAGE TO READERS

This book is published under the auspices of

THE ULVERSCROFT FOUNDATION
(registered charity No. 264873 UK)

Established in 1972 to provide funds for research, diagnosis and treatment of eye diseases. Examples of contributions made are: —

A new Children's Assessment Unit at Moorfield's Hospital, London.
•
Twin operating theatres at the Western Ophthalmic Hospital, London.
•
A Chair of Ophthalmology at the University of Leicester.
•
The establishment of a Royal Australian College of Ophthalmologists "Fellowship".

You can help further the work of the Foundation by making a donation or leaving a legacy. Every contribution, no matter how small, is received with gratitude. Please write for details to:

THE ULVERSCROFT FOUNDATION,
The Green, Bradgate Road, Anstey,
Leicester LE7 7FU, England.
Telephone: (0116) 236 4325

In Australia write to:
THE ULVERSCROFT FOUNDATION,
c/o The Royal Australian College of
Ophthalmologists,
27, Commonwealth Street, Sydney,
N.S.W. 2010.

Love is
a time of enchantment:
in it all days are fair and all fields
green. Youth is blest by it,
old age made benign:
the eyes of love see
roses blooming in December,
and sunshine through rain. Verily
is the time of true-love
a time of enchantment — and
Oh! how eager is woman
to be bewitched!

THE ROSE BOTH RED AND WHITE

Margaret Tudor, the elder daughter of Henry VII, made the hazardous journey north to marry James IV, King of the Scots, a man she had never met. As his Queen, she vied for his affection against the counter attractions of several mistresses. At last, with the birth of a son and heir, she began to experience a tremulous happiness, but James denied its fruition on the field of Flodden. Widowed, beautiful and only twenty-four, she rushed headlong into a foolish union and quickly discovered that she had chosen the wrong man.

Books by Betty King
in the Ulverscroft Large Print Series:

WE ARE TOMORROW'S PAST
THE FRENCH COUNTESS

BETTY KING

THE ROSE
BOTH
RED AND WHITE

Complete and Unabridged

ULVERSCROFT
Leicester

First published in Great Britain in 1970 by
Robert Hale Limited
London

First Large Print Edition
published September 1995
by arrangement with
Robert Hale Limited
London

British Library CIP Data

King, Betty
    The rose both red and white.—Large print ed.—
Ulverscroft large print series: romance
I. Title
823.914 [F]

ISBN 0–7089–3377–7

Published by
F. A. Thorpe (Publishing) Ltd.
Anstey, Leicestershire
Set by Words & Graphics Ltd.
Anstey, Leicestershire
Printed and bound in Great Britain by
T. J. Press (Padstow) Ltd., Padstow, Cornwall

This book is printed on acid-free paper

Acknowledgements

I wish to thank the following people for their kind assistance in the preparation of this novel: Miss O. E. Bunting and Miss T. J. Ash; the Staff of the Enfield Central Library; the Staff of the British Museum Reading Room; Mr. Daws and the Staff of Guildhall Library; Mr. John Robertson, Chief Librarian of Stirling; the Staff of Linlithgow Palace; and my family for their forbearance and encouragement.

Bibliography

Lives of the Princesses of England.
  M. A. E. Green (1849 – 55)
The Queens of Scotland.
  Agnes Strickland (1850)
King James of Scotland.
  R. L. Mackie (1958)
Henry VIII.
  John Bowle (1964)
The Divorce.
  Marvin H. Albert (1966)
Henry VIII.
  J. J. Scarisbrick (1968)
The Dictionary of National Biography
The Early Tudors.
  J. D. Mackie
Memoir of Margaret.
  Cooper
Lady Margaret.
  E. M. G. Routh

Prologue

THE procession formed in the Whitehall Chamber close to the royal suite where, on the previous evening, the Queen had been safely delivered of a daughter. To the King's Chamberlain, Sir William Stanley, who tried in vain to stem the excited chatter and instil some order into the richly clad men and women who thronged the hall, the Christening seemed an unnecessary, tedious matter which could have been marked by a much less formal ceremony. He heaved almost visible sighs of relief as Lady Berkley, flanked by the Earls of Arundel and Shrewsbury, with the child on her arm and supported by a knot of nurses, came from the Painted Chamber and made her way to the head of the untidy mass of waiting courtiers.

As if drawn by invisible strings the company formed into lines and those who held unlit candles looked about them to make certain they were close enough to

1

the pages who bore the flint and tinder boxes. The women near to the head of the procession craned to catch a glimpse of the infant princess closely wrapped in swaddling and fine silk against the biting chill of the November day which penetrated even the thick walls of the Palace of Westminster.

At a signal from the Chamberlain the company moved in the direction of the great doorway leading into the Church of St. Margaret. Here, in the shadow of the Abbey Church the King with his mother, the Lady Margaret Beaufort, Countess of Richmond and Derby, waited beside the silver font brought especially from Canterbury.

Henry Tudor, thirty-three years of age and losing a little of the grace of figure and dull gold hair that he had brought to England four years earlier when he had wrested the crown from the head of Richard of Gloucester, looked round the church with pleasure; seeing in the fine embroideries hung from the ceiling and the countless tapers guttering on the great silver chandelier a mark of the prosperity he was striving to give to the realm that had suffered for so long beneath the ruinous altercations of the Houses of Lancaster and York. He smiled at Archbishop Morton who had done much to make his accession to the throne possible and thought with a sense of gratitude of God's goodness in blessing his union with Elizabeth of York in this latest addition to the royal nurseries. Early in his married life Elizabeth had presented him with a son and heir, whom they had named Arthur in proud recognition of Henry's Welsh ancestry; but since then she had miscarried rather too often to please her physicians and it had looked as if the Tudor lineage would hang on the slender thread of the three year old Prince of Wales.

It was not by chance Henry had commanded the Christening should take place on the day immediately after the birth for the thirtieth of November was St. Andrew's day, the feast of the patron saint of Scotland and it was already in his mind that the crumpled-faced baby should heal the running sore of unceasing distrust between England and her northern neighbour. Henry gave no heed to the seventeen years dividing James IV, King of Scotland and his new-born daughter for differences in age were as nothing when a country's future was at stake and he had himself been betrothed to Elizabeth of York without as much as a glimpse of his bride to be. This marriage, despite the warring influences of the opposing houses to which they belonged had been tolerably happy and his wife was docile and pliant enough to his will. He did not flatter himself that this ease which existed between Elizabeth and himself was all his own doing for he was an extremely busy man who looked with minute attention to the smallest detail of his Kingdom's business and was on constant watch for the treasonable acts of discontented nobles who might at any moment ferment loyalty to the dead House of York and threaten the stability he strove to bring to England's glory. Henry knew in his heart Elizabeth's support and tolerance, if not her love, had been fostered for him by the devotion of his mother for her son's happiness which had made the Lady Margaret befriend the heiress of the White Rose of York and with gentle handling train her in the arduous task of consort to the King.

Henry looked towards his mother as she stood now beside Lady Norfolk and Jasper Tudor, former Earl of Pembroke and Henry's uncle, created Duke of Bedford to mark Henry's coronation out of gratitude for the loving aid and succour he had bestowed upon his nephew since he had been born in his Welsh stronghold of Pembroke. Thirty three years in which Jasper had sacrificed fourteen at the height of his own man-hood to accompany Henry to exile in Brittany as the Yorkist hounds bayed for their blood across the fields of England. Thirty three years in which Jasper had supported the Lady Margaret in her widowhood following the death of his brother Edmund, Henry's father, and had acted as the parent the King had never seen.

Glancing from one to the other Henry saw they were both looking outwardly calm and selfpossessed but suspected they were sharing some of the pleasure he was experiencing for they felt his successes and failures as keenly as if they had been their own. The Lady Margaret was dressed in an elegant gown of fine white blanket furred with pure miniver and did not appear over burdened with the forty-eight years her son knew she would readily admit as her age. Jasper, eleven years her senior, was more sombrely clad in dark red with the red dragon of Cadwaldr emblazoned on his chest and, Henry noted with the perceptive eye of affection, although he held himself as proudly as ever his lined weatherbeaten face betrayed a certain fatigue and unusual pallor.

Henry had no time for further speculation as the Bishop of Ely came into the tapestry-hung porch and led the Christening procession around the silver font. In the light of the chandeliers the white chrisom and the gold salt cellar gleamed in dulled splendour while the cold church warmed a little with the press of silk and velvet clad bodies.

As the company settled in their allotted places the choir sang from the body of the church and Lady Berkley handed the child to her nurse, Alice Davy, who saw to the removal of the swaddling clothes before handing the now naked infant to the Lady Margaret. Enclosing the babe within the fur of her sleeves she waited until the Bishop leant forward to take her godchild and immerse her in the silver font.

When called upon to do so she named the child, Margaret, and with one accord the court lit the tapers held in their hands and the new baptized infant squalled lustily as the water washed over her and the candle-glow haloed her with light.

1

THE pale winter sunshine filtered through the casements of the Queen's apartments at Richmond and fell on the gathered Court as they watched the betrothal ceremony of the King's daughter and James IV, King of Scotland.

Henry Tudor stood close to his Queen, her figure distorted with the child soon to be born and her face taut with the strain of this, her seventh pregnancy. Elizabeth of York had smiled little since the death of her first born, Arthur, in the previous year but had made it plain she wished to attend the fiancels of her elder daughter. For this reason the King had chosen his new Palace at Richmond rather than London or Westminster to celebrate the union; but no effort had been spared to underline the importance of the occasion and most of the noble families of England with Ambassadors from Spain and Venice together with the Pope's Orator clustered behind the bride and the proxy bridegroom, Patrick Hepburn, first Earl of Bothwell, sent by James to betroth her.

Patrick wondered as he stood beside his sponsors, the Archbishop of Glasgow and the Bishop of Murray, if the fair-haired child close to his elbow had any conception of the man to whom, in a few moments, she would be binding herself in matrimony.

A loyal and faithful servant of his sovereign Patrick knew that while James recognized the necessity of this marriage, his heart, if not his body, was entirely given to the beautiful Margaret, daughter of Lord Drummond of Stobhall in Perthshire. For the last six years James had been deeply enamoured of this young woman and had taken her into his household where she lived, to all outward appearances, as his wife. First at Stirling and later at Linlithgow she had awaited his frequent visits and in 1496 had presented the King with a daughter, the Lady Margaret Stewart. It was Patrick's private belief that the reluctance James displayed in the final signing of the marriage treaty with Henry VII had been caused as much by his devotion to Margaret Drummond as his support of Perkin Warbeck, the Pretender to the English throne whom he had welcomed to his Court in Scotland and given in marriage to one of his own cousins, the Lady Katherine Gordon. When Perkin had finally paid the price of his folly and had been hanged at Tyburn in 1499 James had raised the question of the consanguinity between himself and his proposed bride and thus delayed his own wedding for a further eighteen months.

Not that James, virile, handsome and charming, had always been faithful to Margaret Drummond. He already had a son by Marion Boyd and had recently been attracted to Janet Kennedy who had also given birth to a boy prior to his Ambassadors setting out to contract this wedding with Henry's daughter. Bothwell was relieved to know that before they had begun their long journey south James had seen the wisdom of presenting an appearance of domestic stability to his future father-in-law and had dismissed his paramours and their offspring to an honourable and, he found himself hoping fervently, permanent banishment.

The Earl of Surrey interrupted the flow of Patrick's thoughts as, straight-backed and with hardly a wrinkle despite his sixty years, he came up to speak to Henry and at a nod from the King addressed the Court and asked the Secretary to set forth the purpose of the proceedings.

"Does your Grace know any impediments on your part in this wedlock?" the Archbishop of Glasgow asked Henry.

"None," said the King, firmly.

"Does your Grace?" the Archbishop turned to Elizabeth, the Queen, who shook her head, smiling slightly as she gestured towards the fourteen year old bride.

"And you, my Lady Margaret — you know of no impediments to your marriage, nor have any reason to mistrust the alliance?"

Margaret raised the eyes which she had kept downcast until this moment and Patrick Hepburn was surprised by their depth and a swift glint of what he could only describe as coquetry. He had felt so certain the yellow, flowing hair and the pale, guarded face had spoke of submission and pliancy that he was thrown off his guard at this unexpected sign of spirit. Perhaps Margaret Tudor would prove more mettlesome than James anticipated and give Margaret Drummond serious reason to mistrust her hold over her royal lover.

Hepburn almost missed the low, murmured assurances of the Princess and found himself listening with irony to the King asking gravely of the Archbishop if James were free to engage the affections of his daughter; with an effort he controlled himself from snorting aloud as the churchman solemnly declared his sovereign was completely disengaged and ready to espouse his bride.

"You will endorse this, my Lord Bothwell?" Henry asked raising an eyebrow at Hepburn.

"Yes, your Grace," Patrick said loudly.

"Very well," Henry said, "Come, my child, kneel to your mother and ask her blessing."

"I, Patrick," Hepburn heard himself saying a little later as Margaret returned to his side and he was prompted by the

Archbishop, "Procurator of the right high and mighty Prince, James, by the Grace of God, King of Scotland, having sufficient power to contract matrimony per verba de presenti with thee, Margaret, daughter to the right excellent Henry, by the Grace of God, King of England, do here contract matrimony with thee, Margaret and take thee unto and for the wife and spouse of my said Sovereign. All others for thee he forsaketh," Hepburn raised his voice to counteract any inward trembling that might undermine his confidence and finished with a flourish, "In and during his and thine lives natural and thereto I plight and give thee his faith and troth, by power and authority committed and given to me."

He took a deep breath and gripped Margaret's hand as she turned to face him and repeated after the Archbishop her own vows. Her voice was expressive, deeper than he had expected, with a throaty catch that matched the glint he had surprised in her eyes. Not a little disturbed he was glad when the trothing was done and trumpeters blared, from somewhere above their heads, in strident

14

cadences of triumph. Bowing to Margaret he handed her to the Queen who rose stiffly from the raised chair where she had watched the proceedings. Elizabeth led her daughter, ceremoniously, to an adjoining room where a banquet was laid ready.

During the days of rejoicing that followed Patrick had ample opportunity of learning more of the new Queen of Scotland and saw she had much in common with her more obviously extrovert brother, Hal, whose sturdy frame and good looks already singled him out despite his twelve years. Together they would sing the haunting Welsh airs they had been taught by their nurses and dance, with abandoned fervour, the taxing set pieces of the Court.

The courtly manners and deportment of both Margaret and Hal were impeccable and the girl-bride deferred to her husband's proxy with a charming grace Patrick found irresistible. Hal was more distantly polite with him and it was rumoured he did not look with favour upon his sister's betrothal to James and had flown into a high rage when he had been required to salute Margaret for the first time as Queen of Scotland.

The children were surrounded by excellent tutors and were given ample opportunity of partaking in the rich, new feast of learning now sweeping through Europe. Hal grasped at this teaching with both hands but Margaret found lessons tedious and although she could read and write a tolerable hand preferred walking in the open air or riding one of the beautiful horses her father provided for her use. Since her elder brother, Arthur's death, in the previous year, Patrick's confidants told him, she was subjected to fits of melancholy when she would shut herself in her room and lie, face down, on her bed for hours on end.

There was not much time for private feelings in the days following the fiancels for joustings and feastings were held in a succession of dazzling brilliance. At one particularly magnificent supper presentations were made between the two companies and cups and ewers of gold passed hands. The Queen of England, propped on her husband's arm, gave her personal thanks to all those noblemen who had graced the occasion and later the new Queen of Scotland spoke in a clear, accomplished little speech, her gratitude for the efforts made, in both the tourneys and pageants, to mark her marriage with splendid happiness.

This happiness was brought to an untimely end when it became known Elizabeth of York was in labour and experiencing some difficulty in bringing the expected child into the world. The long corridors and great halls which had so recently rung with laughter and gay music became hushed as the Queen of England was eventually delivered of a stillborn girl and lay in a state of semiconsciousness between life and death.

She died on the eleventh day of February and the Palace of Richmond was plunged into gloom. Bothwell felt deeply sorry for the child who had just pledged herself in marriage to a man she had never seen and then found herself within a few short days bereft of her mother's counsel and comfort. The lying in of Elizabeth of York had taken place in the Tower and she had been surrounded with notable physicians but they had been helpless in the face of the weakness that robbed the Queen of any power to fight. Bothwell was grateful to Henry for his wisdom in removing his Queen from Richmond where it would have been all too easy for the impressionable new bride of the Scottish King to witness her mother's sufferings.

At the funeral Margaret bore herself with fortitude but the pale face was ashen and the stark, hard head-dress covering the abundant hair gave the girl a nunlike appearance. She had been devoted to her mother and before Elizabeth had left for the Tower had sat with her, playing softly on the lute, to help her forget her ungainly body and the ordeal before her.

Margaret received Bothwell in audience before he quit Richmond to begin his journey into Scotland to report his completion of the mission assigned to him by James. He longed to comfort the grieving girl who, such a short time before, had been enjoying the celebrations of her wedding; but Margaret sat in a backless chair, her hands crossed on her lap, and kept her swollen eyes downcast. She received his protestations of sympathy with monosyllabic courtesy and he withdrew with an uneasy sense of having accomplished nothing. He felt his lack of touching her grief more keenly as he had come to her straight from receiving messengers who had posted from Scotland with the extraordinary tidings of the sudden death of Margaret Drummond.

It appeared James's mistress had been staying with her family at Drummond Castle and she, with two of her older sisters, had died after eating porridge at breakfast. The most strenuous efforts were being made to discover the perpetrators of this wicked deed but so far, the couriers from Scotland had reported to Patrick, there had been no success. It was whispered the Kennedy family, jealous of Janet's position with the King, had found means of entering the kitchens at Drummond and mixing a deadly potion with the cauldron of cooked oatmeal; other people believed, however, that it was not Kennedys but the King's own advisers who had seen fit to do away with the lovely Margaret, seeing in her a stumbling block to his intention to carry through the marriage with the King of England's daughter. Patrick found this latter theory impossible to support and shook his head, refusing to listen to speculations that cast aspersions on James's ability to keep his word; he was certain James, having promised to marry Margaret Tudor, would not change his mind. After all he had had plenty of time to make the lady of Drummond his wife if he had so wished and now he had taken the binding step of the proxy marriage with the daughter of the King of England it was most unlikely he would run the risk of alienating his fellow sovereign by jilting this child for the sake of his former mistress.

Patrick had made guarded enquiries about James's reception of the news of Margaret Drummond's death and had heard he was prostrate with grief without surprise; the messengers told him the King of the Scots had gone immediately to Drummond to look into the tragic affair and make provision for his daughter to be brought into his keeping when she could be spared from her sorrowing grandparents.

It seemed a strange quirk of fate that made James and Margaret sorrow at the same time; Patrick found some comfort in the knowledge that the two deaths threw the new Queen of Scotland into greater prominence. Her mother's demise removed the possibility of further heirs to the English throne while Margaret Drummond's untimely murder gave her a greater chance of making her husband happier without the risk of James being tempted to return too often to his former love.

Bothwell left for Scotland haunted by the disconsolate face of his new young Queen and the foreboding of ill that had marred the start of her married life.

2

IN Richmond Palace Prince Hal came to bid farewell to his sister before she set out for Collyweston, the Rutland seat of her grandmother, the Countess of Richmond and Derby.

They greeted one another affectionately, each thinking the other very dashing in the new clothes they had chosen for this important day. Margaret's riding dress of rich red velvet showed up her delicate complexion and enhanced the golden lights in her fair hair, while Hal's yellow doublet matched the curls clustering close to his well shaped head. It was a moment of tense emotion for they were both aware of the years that might elapse before they would meet again and the omnipresent risk of being parted for ever.

Neither of them knew why the day of departure to Scotland had been put forward by several weeks but accepted it as part of the strange life that had been theirs since the death of Arthur and their mother.

"Do you think it is true," Hal asked as they stood at the window and gazed down at the river flowing beneath, "that Father really did write to Ferdinand and Isabella and ask their permission to marry Katherine of Aragon?"

"I hope not," Margaret replied suppressing a shudder, "for I do not like to think of him contemplating a marriage with our brother's widow when Mother had been dead so short a time. Katherine is supposed to be betrothed to you, anyway, isn't she?"

"Yes." The reply was noncommittal and Hal went on to speak, quickly, about Margaret's forthcoming meeting with James. "When you talk about the difference in Father's age and Katherine's don't forget you are eighteen years younger than your husband! What are you going to do if you find he has paramours?" Hal's innocent, speedwell eyes regarded her with curiosity tinged with malice.

"Hal!" Margaret cried, shocked. "Where do you learn about such things?"

"My ears are long and servants gossip."

"You have heard no mention of James and — other ladies?"

"No," said Hal rather reluctantly, "but you surely cannot expect to find a man of thirty has not been in love!"

"From what I am told James is a man of honour; well read, also, and with the interest of his country at heart. It is said he does penance every day for his part in the death of his father and is a patron of the church and the poor!"

"All very noteworthy and undoubtedly reported to you by your proxy bride-groom, Patrick Hepburn, who would have hesitated to mention his sovereign's love life! But I tease, Meg, and would not wish you ill for the world; I shall find life tedious here with only Mary to keep me company and I confess I look forward to the day when I am a grown man and can live a life of my own — "

"Married to Katherine of Aragon?" Margaret could not resist the sly dig.

"I find the fair Katherine very attractive but it is not for her sake alone I would grow to adulthood. You women," he said with mock despair, "you can think of nothing but love and marriage!"

"That's not true!" Colour glowed in the pale cheeks.

"Well, tell me what else interests you!"

"Dancing and singing — oh, Hal, I shall miss our songs together — do you think there will be ballad makers and poets at the King's court in Scotland?"

"I believe the Scots are as keen as the Welsh and the English in story making and with the long hours of darkness during the winter months they would have ample opportunity of perfecting the art. Will you write and tell me what you find in your northern kingdom?"

"I'll write as much as I can, but you know I am not good with the quill and find writing tedious." She moved away from him and stood at another window. "Do you believe the Scots are more civilized than they were?"

"You are thinking of the affairs that led up to the death of James's father?"

"Yes; it would seem the Scottish nobles are for ever at each other's throats."

"From what the Earl of Bothwell had to tell us I should imagine your James has gone a long way to heal the breaches fostered by his father. It is true, Robin Skelton tells me, that the Highlanders have never submitted to the yoke of the Scottish King and regard themselves outside his dispensation and authority and he says, also, the Borders are not a healthy place in which to reside when trouble brews between Scotland and England — but of course, I forget — you are going north to prevent just that very thing! You know, Meg, for all you are a romantic woman I can't help admiring you for going those hundreds of miles to patch up the quarrels of the two nations."

Pleased, Margaret, came back to his side and put a sisterly arm about his waist.

"Whatever turns out I shall always have you at the back of me, won't I, Hal?" The catch in the throaty voice was accentuated by the tears threatening to overspill from her eyes.

"Of course, dear Meg, you can rely on me."

The royal entourage with Henry personally escorting his daughter took ten days to come to Collyweston. It lumbered its stately and brilliant way through the lanes of Hertfordshire and Huntingdonshire in perfect June weather and came to the manor of Collyweston on the twenty-seventh of the month. Here, in the stone house which had once belonged to the Cromwell family the King's mother received her son and granddaughter with lavish hospitality and great affection. She spared none of her vast fortune in entertaining them with the best furniture, food and bands of tumblers she could obtain.

Margaret, who had not seen her grandmother, for some time, was struck by the simplicity of her gowns and the air of aesthetic living that clung about her in marked contrast to the splendour of her surroundings and the welcome she afforded. The Countess of Richmond and Derby had always seemed to be the most royal and elaborately dressed woman Margaret had known and she was at a loss to understand why her grandmother now chose to wear the habit of a lady abbess; she wished her mother was alive to ask her if she had any explanation of this volte face. There was, however, nothing different about the Countess's kindness and tender counsel and she spent several hours a day talking with Margaret and giving her the benefit of her long years of experience.

They sat together, on the last afternoon before Margaret left for Scotland, in the walled garden where tansy rioted and gilly flowers filled the air with heady sweetness, talking of the long journey ahead and the responsibilities Margaret could expect to encounter as Queen of Scotland.

The Countess spoke of the various houses and hospices that had been chosen for the lodgings on the way and drew a quick portrait of the men and women who would be receiving the girl and her retainers. Margaret listened, fascinated, to the anecdotes her grandmother recalled, laced with humour but devoid of malice. The young Earl of Northumberland, Henry Percy, who had been a ward of the Countess' when his father had been killed soon after Henry had come to the throne, seemed the most colourful of those who would play host and Margaret discovered she viewed the coming separation with less apprehension than had plagued her since she left Hal at Richmond.

There was one question she longed to ask her grandmother and at length she summoned sufficient courage to blurt out: "Do husbands and wives always love one another? Did father and mother? Did you love grandfather?"

Once she had spoken she was paralysed with terror for her temerity and looked down the length of the garden to a pair of swallows, flashing blue and white in the sunlight.

Her anxiety deepened when the Countess did not answer straight away and she glanced hurriedly to see if she had given offence but her grandmother was smiling.

"Which question shall I answer first? Shall I take them in order?" Margaret nodded, dumb. "Well, then, husbands and wives do not always love one another and this fact has caused much misery and suffering; a great deal of which could have been dispensed with if the couple had been sensible and not cried for the moon. You are asking me this, I know,

29

because you are given in marriage to a man you have never met, but take heart and remember that your mother had not set eyes on your father before he arrived in England from France and claimed her as his promised bride — and I think they were happy, don't you?"

Margaret nodded.

"So it must be possible to live in harmony with a man unknown until one is wedded with him, isn't that so?" the Countess asked gently. "For the last part of your question, I did love your grandfather and I was fortunate in being able to choose him — within a little. My father, John, Duke of Somerset, died when I was only three and this fact made me a good match for any of the Lancastrian families; my guardian, Duke of Suffolk, was the first to ask for my hand for his son but he fell into disgrace and King Henry VI gave me in wardship to two of his half-brothers, Edmund and Jasper Tudor with the wish I should marry Edmund when I reached the suitable age."

"How then did your choice come into the matter?" the girl sat forward, her mouth slightly parted.

"When I was about nine years old St. Nicholas came to me in a dream and told me I must marry none other than Edmund and when I related this strange occurrence to my mother she took it as an omen and would hear of no other suitors!"

"Had you met my grandfather before this?"

"Yes, I had," the Countess replied softly, "and dreams are often wish thoughts of our hours of sleep." She stopped and took the slim young hand that grasped the stone arm of the seat. "I was very fortunate, my dear, and I shall not deny I have every sympathy for you in the ordeal ahead — but you are born a king's daughter, where I was not, and as such you are called upon to make sacrifices — indeed, as your mother did — unknown to those of humbler birth."

"But suppose I do not like James?" the cry was wrung from the slender throat.

"You will have to interest yourself in the life of the court about you as many

31

another woman has done before you and make prayer to God to sustain you. Don't look so cast down, my little Meg, Beaufort women have married Scottish kings before this and from what I can hear of it your husband is a talented and charming man!"

"My lady grandmother," Margaret hesitated, "Hal teased me with tales of mistresses and paramours and such like; would you think James was likely to have had affairs of love?"

The Countess regarded the earnest young face turned upwards to her and longed to smile and turn off the question with a light reply but knew she must answer truthfully and with as little hurt as possible.

"James," she said gently, "is over thirty years of age and doubtless has been attracted to many women of the court who have been eager to give themselves to him in the hope of becoming his wife or at least reaping much reward for themselves and their children — "

"Children?" This incredulously and a little faintly.

"Yes, I think it is kinder to warn

you that there are several — by various mothers."

The pale faced girl snatched away her hand and knuckled her mouth, her eyes dilated.

"I hate him!" she cried fiercely, "hate him, hate him — I shall not go to Scotland and become just another of his women! How could my father sell me to such a man?"

She walked up and down in front of the stone seat, her breast heaving.

"Calm yourself." The Countess did not raise her voice or move as she watched the velvet shod feet pace the flagged terrace. "Do not forget James could have married any of these ladies over the years but he waited for you — "

"He was handfasted to every Yorkist heiress there was before I was born!"

"Yes, quite right, he was — but he did not marry them and now you are betrothed to him it is your sole concern to be a good wife and see him happy."

"Does he wish to make *me* happy?" the throaty voice was heavy with scorn and the Countess gave her granddaughter a sharp look.

"I am sure he does! He is eager to make lasting peace between our two countries and Patrick Hepburn spoke much of his Master's wish to concede you every privilege and honour your rank demands."

"So he told me, while, fortuitously, he forgot to mention his sovereign's penchant for amorous dalliance. Oh, grandmother, could you love — or even, like — a man who had bedded other women before you became his wife?"

"Yes, I am past sixty years of age and have known two husbands since your grandfather died and I did not query their lives before we were married."

"But you took a vow of chastity before you wedded with the Earl of Derby!"

With difficulty the Countess suppressed a smile.

"True enough, but I have known, also, what it is to be loved by and love a man who had had a mistress who gave him a child before we discovered our mutual devotion."

Margaret stopped her restless pacing and sank down again beside her grandmother looking at her for the first time as a real person rather than a respected and aged parent.

"And you found it in your heart to forgive him?"

"For what? He had not sinned against me! It was with God he had to make his peace."

"And you married him, knowing this?"

"No, I did not marry him — "

"Ah," the triumph could not be concealed, "then, you have proved my argument!"

"Not at all," the Countess told her calmly, "for I would have done had we both been free to do so, for I loved him more than life itself. But that is enough for the moment and I would beg you to be both tolerant and kindly disposed towards James for most women have some cross to bear in their married state and you have many blessings for which to be deeply grateful. Come, tell me of all your splendid new dresses and robes, are they packed ready for your journey?" The Countess tilted the oval face, so like her own, and smiled until Margaret responded.

"Yes, the ladies of the bedchamber

were seeing to the matter with the tiring women while Alice Davy fussed over them and bewailed the fact she had not been allowed to do all as she had wanted."

"I am sure they will be as fresh when they come out of the chests as when they were made and you will look very beautiful in them."

"Do you really think James will find me pleasing?" Gone now was the rebellious mood and the Countess detected an uncertainty that was touching.

"He cannot fail to think you so," she said warmly.

"You do not believe he will find me callow and uninteresting?"

The Countess shook her head.

"You will charm him outright with your good manners. I would not hide the fact I consider a man likes his wife to be intelligent and accomplished and you have talents that are sure to please and have been well schooled for this purpose."

"You do not think he will chide me for my lack of book learning?" Margaret's expressive eyes were troubled.

"He will not expect you, at fourteen to be a scholar but I am sure you will find it worthwhile to study and glean wisdom from those who have had more experience of the world than you have yet had time to gain."

"I wish I liked reading more than I do!" The full mouth was pursed in a straight line, "but it always seems such a pity to stew in the house over a heavy book when the sun calls one to sit in its warmth and soak up the summer air."

"There is no need to spend tedious hours like an insect beneath a stone but a little of each day spent in the acquisition of learning will prove an enduring pleasure, I do promise you!"

The Countess broke off as the Controller of the Household came to summon them to the Hall where supper awaited.

On the following morning the company met again in this well appointed place and watched Margaret as she knelt to her father and grandmother and asked their final blessing.

When Henry had delivered this benediction he spoke privately with his daughter and those standing near enough saw he had tears in his eyes; he presented Margaret with an illuminated book of prayers and opening it she saw he had written in it for her:

'Remember your kind and loving father in your good prayers and I will give you at all times God's blessing and mine. Henry R.'

In an uprush of emotion Margaret embraced her father, grown stooped and emaciated since his two bereavements, and clung to him unwilling to depart now the irrecoverable moment had arrived. Sobs wracked her and the Countess comforted her, disengaging her from Henry's arms and leading her to the courtyard where her large escort was assembled.

Three footmen, dressed in green and white with the Beaufort portcullis embroidered on their jackets, helped her mount the white palfrey she was to ride. From the horse's broad back Margaret looked round on the familiar manor, remembering for future comfort each gable and slated roof. The royal household crowded the steps and waved until Sir David Owen gave the signal for the procession to move off up the steep lane outside the gates.

The quiet village was filled with spectators who hung out of casements and gaped from outside stairways to watch the glittering assembly as it wound its way to the highroad to the deafening accompaniment of the trumpeters and the Queen's own band of musicians. Since the King's mother had lived in state at Collyweston the dwellers within the neat stone houses were used to the yearly visit of Henry and his Court but there was a slightly different interest for this procession which took an English princess to meet her bridegroom. The shouted encouragements to the gorgeously arrayed girl were as much in sympathy for her courage in leaving behind her family as admiration for the brilliance of those gathered to escort her to a distant country of which the majority had but a faint conception. Used as Margaret was to receiving the acclaim of her father's people she found the snatches of good wishes she heard a balm to the misery surrounding her and she did her best to smile and acknowledge them.

Her grandmother's husband and Lord Essex rode with the procession for a mile and then took their leave, reining in their mounts until the dust had settled behind the rear guard. With this last link severed Margaret set her face towards the north and concentrated on the physical task of becoming used to the constant motion of the horse beneath her. Around her she was dimly aware of the excited chatter of her ladies and the deeper voices of the squires who formed her bodyguard. With tact the two Bishops who rode at her elbow spoke little but when the Master of Horse came up and asked her if she were tired and would like to transfer to the litter they added their concern for her comfort. Margaret thanked them for their courtesy but claimed she was not tired but enjoying the pleasant sunshine of the July day; she realized also that within the confines of the elegantly hung litter she would be at the mercy of her zealous governess, Mistress Denton, and the other ladies of the bedchamber who would smother her with attention and fuss. She needed the privacy given her by the wide open countryside to think of the new life ahead; the first repulsion she had experienced when her grandmother had spoken of James had worn away but she found she still regarded her betrothed in a distasteful light. She saw the glowing praise Bothwell had for his royal master as nothing but trickery to convince her of James's accomplishment while he hid from her the man's real nature. She could not conceal from herself, however, that she was intrigued and quite impatient to meet this man who, for so long, had been such an important part of her life. With conscious effort she forced herself to dwell on this future occurrence rather than the painful scene in the Hall of Collyweston.

The company was to spend the first night at Grantham and rest there for the Sunday which followed. Four miles out of the town they were met by a happy concourse of inhabitants led by the aldermen and burgesses. It was obvious by the ale barrels and the singing and dancing that hardly stopped as Margaret's procession came into their midst that the event was proving a good excuse for a revel. The squires and footmen were hard pressed to keep at bay the young men, laughing and dressed in their best doublets, who pushed forward in an attempt to offer their drinking cups to the young Queen. Far from being frightened Margaret discovered she enjoyed the frank stares of the youths who tried to come near her.

"God's teeth, I wish I was the King of the Scots!" she heard one lad, broader and swarthier than his companions, exclaim over the heads of the green and white clad footmen.

"Mistress!" another shouted, "Call off your journey to the heathens over the border and you'll find your loyal subjects here are as lusty as any Scottish king!"

Margaret longed to make some reply but the two Bishops who stayed close beside her recalled her sense of dignity and she contented herself with bestowing her most winning smile upon the gallants before the company moved off in the direction of Grantham. Much comforted by the knowledge she could command admiration, even if it were from the populace in a holiday mood, she gave her attention to the more sober reception awaiting her at the lodging where priests sang lauds at the College gates.

3

FROM Grantham to Newark, from
Tuxford to Doncaster and thence
from Pontefract to the outskirts of
York it was the same story. Everywhere
the fairytale procession halted it was
surrounded with a crowd of wellwishers
who jostled and elbowed their way
to catch a glimpse of the King's
daughter. While mayors and dignitaries
spoke rehearsed speeches the populace
gave spontaneous demonstrations of their
interest in the girl who went North to
create peace between the kingdoms.

Her ladies of the bedchamber, Lady
Nevill, Lady Lisle, Lady Stanley and
Lady Guildford attended her evening
retirement and gave her details of the
day's events beyond the immediate circle
of her own experience. They told her of
the Sheriffs who vied with one another
to provide the best dressed escort while
the civil authorities dug into their coffers
to load the boards with exotic food

and drink. Lady Stanley spoke of the problem facing Sir John Milton and his companions when they had planned her visit to Pontefract and wished to cause her no pain by asking her to lodge in the Castle there which had, not so long before, been witness to the murders of two of her Mother's uncles at the hands of Richard III.

"So this is why we are staying here in this private house!" Margaret cried as she looked round the small room where the setting sun gleamed on the much polished floor.

"Yes," Lady Stanley told her, "so anxious are those who are looking to your well-being that you should not be afflicted with unhappy memories they leave no possible avenue unexplored that might open up some best forgotten incident."

With a flourish Lady Surrey swept into the chamber.

"How is your Grace? Not overtired before the great festivities that await you on the morrow?"

"I am very well, I thank you."

"Are all preparations in order for the state entry into York?" Lady Surrey next enquired of Lady Guildford.

"Quite ready, Lady Elizabeth; we think it best her Grace should wear a simple robe for her journey to Tadcaster and beyond and then stop in some convenient place to put on the state robes for her entrance into York."

"That seems an excellent idea!" Lady Surrey, over thirty years the wife of the man who was in charge of escorting the Queen of Scotland, was relieved to find she was not required to settle disputes between ladies of the bedchamber and tiring women or even between the Queen and her women. It was not unknown for the daughter of the King to have distinct preferences for the gowns she wished to wear on particular days and Lady Surrey had been summoned more than once to act as arbitrator when tempers waxed high after a trying day on the road.

It was particularly important that the visit to York should be marked with great ceremony and harmony among the royal party. For it was here that Richard III had been held in the greatest esteem and it was here that the northern lords, Scrope and Northumberland, were to take over the responsibility of the safe conduct of the Queen of Scotland.

Margaret did not admit to herself that her ready acceptance that the change of gowns should be delayed until the company was almost within hailing distance of the walls of York had anything to do with her wish to look her best when she met the Earl of Northumberland; but she knew this visit to the ancient stronghold of the Yorkists gave her a quickening of the pulse which was not due in any sense to prescient danger as a daughter of a Lancastrian King. Her ladies had spoken much of the dashing young nobleman who had once been ward to her grandmother and she, who had few friends among the splendid nobility accompanying her, looked forward with near eagerness to meeting Henry Percy. Only twenty-five years old, newly married and with a baby son, he had shared a common background during his boyhood in London and would have much to tell her of her family.

After they had eaten a mid-day meal at Tadcaster the procession, with no signs of lowered standards after a week on the road, was met by Lord Scrope with an army of knights, squires and retainers. Later the Sheriffs of the West Riding joined the growing throng and rode on ahead when the Queen's party drew off the road and the Queen entered her litter to change from her riding dress to a robe of deep green velvet with slashed sleeves and the lowest bodice she had yet worn. In the cramped and stuffy confines Alice Davy arranged her hair and set upon her brow a small circlet of peridots and pearls. When she had finished she handed Margaret a mirror and the girl could not restrain the smile of pleasure her appearance accorded; for the first time she realized that although she was not a beauty her colouring and her abundant, gold-washed hair gave her a claim to attention.

When the footmen had helped her to the ornate saddle of her palfrey she waited until Surrey trotted up to her on his horse and asked if she were ready to enter the city.

"I am sure," the kindly, efficient old soldier told her as he took in the appealing gown and the care bestowed on her toilette, "your father would be very proud if he could see you now." She thanked him with eyes sparkling with excitement.

The trumpeters pealed and the band of musicians struck up an air as, with banners streaming in the breeze and armour brightly polished and glinting in the sun, the Queen's party entered the gates of York.

Two parties greeted her; the citizens headed by the Lord Mayor and the nobles with the Earl of Northumberland. It was not difficult for Margaret to distinguish Henry Percy from the other knights and nobles for he was dressed in crimson velvet heavily bordered with precious stones. His horse, a sturdy beast standing taller than the rest, was caparisoned in red and cloth of gold while the harness and saddle-bow were embossed in the same precious metal. As Percy advanced towards the Queen, bowing low over the neck of his steed, she had time to take in the fact that he was a pleasant looking young man with a ready smile. He kissed her hand with a flourish denoting he considered her the world's Queen rather than a consort of an inveterate enemy of England. As he spoke formal words of greeting the corners of his eyes creased with a merriment belying the ceremony of the moment. Margaret discovered she was enjoying this welcome more than any of the stiff proceedings that had welcomed her into the towns and cities that lay behind her on the route from England and she replied with words that needed no prompting from the speeches she had conned by heart.

The narrow streets of York were hung with banners and at each corner pageants were enacted with white-robed maidens and choir boys depicting sprites and angels who showered the royal bride with flower petals. If anyone had doubted the warmth of the reception that a daughter of Henry of Lancaster might receive in this Yorkist stronghold they were completely disarmed by the display of affection and the lavish scale of the entertainment.

At the end of the fatiguing reception Margaret was lodged in the Palace of the Archbishop close to the pinnacled magnificence of the Minster and she went to bed happier and more relaxed than she had been since she left Collyweston.

She was up early on the following morning and lingered in the warmed and scented water put ready for her in a wooden tub. With pleasurable anticipation she stood while her tiring women dressed her in a gown of cloth of gold and hung round her waist a girdle of semi-precious gems. Alice Davy brushed her hair until it shone and twined it in thick coils about her shapely head.

As it was an especial occasion the Countess of Surrey carried the yards long train of the Queen and her ladies formed a double line behind them to escort them to the porch of the Minster where the Archbishop waited to lead Margaret to her place within the building. The sun struck jewel-bright through the myriad of stained glass windows, matching the brilliant robes and doublets of the many hundreds of people gathered to hear Mass.

Later it was Margaret's turn to give hospitality and she provided a feast for those who had received her into the City.

Percy brought his young wife, Catherine, to kneel to her and Margaret bade her rise and kissed her warmly on the cheek; later the Earl and Countess sat at table with her and they soon lost all trace of shyness and talked easily of shared backgrounds and common ancestries.

"Your lady Grandmother, she is well?" Henry Percy asked. "She was a wise woman and the Buckingham boys and I have much to thank her for — even if, while we were her wards we chafed at the hours we sat at lessons with our tutor, Maurice Westbury!"

"I fear I am a great disappointment to her for I am not bookish in the least," Margaret said, slightly guilty and uncomfortable at the thought, but to her relief Henry Percy threw back his head and roared with laughter.

"I am glad to hear it for I am made devilish uneasy when in the company of learned females! Tell me what do you like?" Percy leaned forward to look into the pale, oval face.

"Riding and sitting in the sun," Margaret told him lamely, wishing for the first time in her life she could lay claim to some attribute which would enthral this splendid and elegant being.

"What a pity your stay here is not to be longer for I have just the mount that would carry you safely over our moors and I could take you to see some of the waterfalls and hamlets that lie hidden in the folds of our heather-covered hills! Do you think we might persuade our venerable Surrey to delay your progress for a few days at Alnwick so that we may chase the hart over the Cheviots?" While Percy asked the question his eyes paid her court, glancing from her jewelled head-dress to the curve of her bosom.

Margaret shook her head with a pout that did not escape her companion.

"You find the Earl of Surrey a dull companion?"

"He is well enough and his wife is kind but he is apt to forget sometimes that we are not his troops and urges us forward when my ladies and I are dropping with the fatigue of the day's journey." It was good to have a sympathetic ear and Margaret embroidered the difficulties of the travel which, to be fair to those in charge, were eased out for her in every conceivable way.

"I expect Surrey is anxious to see you safely delivered to the fortunate James and return to England before the winter sets in and delays him," Percy told her and could have bitten his tongue when he saw the pout change to a droop.

"He is fortunate to be going back," Margaret said sadly, "I wish I were accompanying him."

"What desolation for James if that were to be the case!" Henry Percy cried. "We have it here on good authority that his Grace is making great preparations for his bride."

"Think you so?" she asked eagerly and then sank back against her chair, "I do not think he is anxious for me to come to him, for from what I know he is enamoured of another."

The impetuous Percy thought more deeply than his wont and gambling on the likelihood of James's affection for the daughter of Lord Drummond being the cause of Margaret's discomfort told her quietly she had nothing to fear on that score for the young woman had died at the turn of the year and left James heartfree. The look of joy that illuminated the delicate young face made him hope fervently that this was still the case and James had not reverted to the company of Janet Kennedy.

"I am sorry for the lady but glad I shall not be called upon to outrival someone who already held my husband's esteem."

"Well spoken," Percy said warmly. "Will your Grace honour me with partnering me in the next dance?"

Next day, outside the North Gate of the city Margaret said her farewells to the English lords who had accompanied her so far on her journey, assuring them of her gratitude for their devotion and protection. If possible, an even larger crowd than that which had welcomed her, came to wish her Godspeed on her way and she accepted their goodwill with a charm that brought acclamation from the townsfolk.

The days until her party came to Northumberland's own castle at Alnwick were the best of the journey; to match the fine splendour of the young Earl,

Margaret had herself dressed in her more lavish gowns and took trouble to be pleasant and attentive to all those who paid her court. This was in no way difficult, for basking in the obvious admiration of Henry Percy, smiles and witty sayings came easily. The countryside also played its part in this gayer mood and the wooded slopes of Durham and Northumberland were enchanting as the warm sun sparkled through the trees and bathed the tender ferns and brackens in amber light.

Margaret's ladies congratulated themselves upon the change of mood in their mistress and looked forward with a new eagerness to the ever-approaching meeting with her betrothed; if Percy could work this miracle then James, renowned as a romantic captor of feminine hearts, should have an easy victory.

Northumberland was as good as his word and persuaded Surrey to allow two days of rest and merry making at his stronghold. He sent messengers to Alnwick giving orders for the Queen's reception to be the most brilliant the grim walls of the castle had yet witnessed. He put at Margaret's disposal the pick of his stables and rode beside her through the park-like country of his estate in chase of the roe deer. As the excitement combined with the crisp air to bring colour to her pale cheeks he found himself envious of James and hoped the girl would be able to overcome the obvious reluctance she had for her marriage and allow her betrothed to glimpse the charming companionship that awaited him.

For Margaret the two days went by so quickly that she had no time to dwell on the fact that once through the border fortress of Berwick she would be on Scottish soil. With the rest of her entourage she danced and feasted, dropping into her bed and falling asleep as her head nestled in the pillows. Northumberland, without his wife, accompanied her to Berwick and watched with a wry smile the bear fights that were provided for the Queen's amusement. Margaret sat upright with wide eyes and a polite upward curve of the mouth as the dogs yapped and snarled round the lumbering creatures; she longed to look away and forbid the spectacle but remembered she had been schooled since the cradle to register no emotion in public and contented herself with an occasional glance in the direction of Henry Percy who she was well aware was cognizant of her discomfort.

Her party lingered in Berwick while clothes were washed and refurbished and armour and trappings polished. No dancing or singing wiled the now tedious hours but the battlements rang to artillery salutes and the baying of hounds set to follow a captured stag as it ran for its life around the grassed sward within the walls. Margaret's ladies sent for her musicians when twilight fell but the girl was restless, pacing the floor of her chamber unable to enjoy the familiar tunes and airs. Northumberland was occupied with the men of the party as they arranged the last details of the handing over of their royal charge to the Scottish Borderers who would take up their duties from Berwick.

It was almost a relief when the time came for departure. The vast concourse left by the north gate with the armed escort preceding the Queen's own party which, in its turn was headed by her band of trumpeters. Margaret sat within her litter in a dress of silver-threaded gauze, composed but unable to dispel the slight thrill of combined fear and enjoyment that clutched the pit of her stomach. She was well grounded in the history of Berwick as it stood sentinel between her father's kingdom and that of her husband's and she knew that it was more often in warlike vein the soldiery set their faces towards the north. On this bright morning nothing could have been further from the thoughts of those who had made such effort to present the future wife of James in shining brilliance to the Scots people.

On the cavalcade's right hand the sea shimmered into the distance while the road rose sharply through the hills of Lammermuir. Overhead larks twittered, joining their song to the tinkling of the thousand small bells decorating the elaborate dress of the English noblemen; close to Margaret the musicians strummed their lutes and played softly on the stretched skin of the drums hung from the saddles of their mounts. It was a peaceful and auspicious entrance into Scotland.

At Lamberton, in front of the church, the Archbishop of Glasgow and a host of Scottish nobles, awaited the Queen. Margaret saw them from a distance as the van of her party were received and she was struck by the simplicity and sombre colours of their clothing; the uprush of pride for the magnificence of her entourage was followed by a dampening reminder that her new subjects might consider her flippant and too worldly. She was not given long to worry over this before her litter stopped opposite the Archbishop and he, and his companions advanced towards her and knelt on the grass to pay homage. Margaret thanked them for their courtesy and accepted their invitation to come with them to the pavilion put up to provide her with shelter and refreshment. Willing hands helped her to alight from her litter and she sat in the high-backed chair set slightly aside from the other few stools. A woman, dressed in scarlet and attended by several handmaidens, came forward and after curtsying handed the Queen a basket of fruit from King James. Spiced wine and white bread was offered to all the travellers and an air of festivity marked the delicate moment of transition. Margaret did her best to prolong the happy meeting but all too soon it seemed Northumberland was at her side come to bid her a private farewell before he and Lords Scrope and Dacre took their formal leave.

"You will visit me in Scotland?" she asked of him anxiously.

"If circumstances permit and your husband will allow me!"

"You do not think he will keep me as a nun?" she cried.

"No," Henry Percy reassured her. "King James would not impose harsh restrictions on his bride, I am quite sure."

"If you go South you will give good reports of our journey," she said and added wistfully, "and do not forget to tell my father that I miss him sorely and wish I were on my way back to him."

"Your Grace will soon have Scotland eating out of your hand," Percy told her warmly, "and James will cherish and spoil you so that you will forget your homesickness."

She did not answer but the pupils of her eyes dilated with the misery that lay ever-present below the surface of her self control and he took her hand and held it to his lips with a comforting gesture that eased her pain more than his words.

The other nobles came to assist her to the saddle of her palfrey and one by one paid their homage and led off their troops as she watched from outside the pavilion. Alice Davy, still serving the Queen since the days of the nursery, saw the droop of the young shoulders and the tense whiteness of the mask-like face and prayed the rest of the day's journey to the stronghold of Fastcastle might be especially interesting to divert Margaret from the wrench of parting with her trusted friends. Alice was not to be disappointed for she, coming from Wales as she did, had not seen a countryside to equal that through which the entourage now passed. The road, often uneven and in places giving the appearance of being newly made, lay across desolate moorland and was bordered with bogland where the white puffs of the bogplant warned travellers against venturing on the treacherous ground. To the west the Hills of Lammermuir grew steeper and more bare and with the approach of evening the sky was fretted with bars of flame that deepened into blood. The ladies of the English suite were glad of the tough looking Scots who were now acting as their guardians for although they were not dressed in any livery or carried lances gave a comforting sensation of immovable protection as they rode in front and behind, sitting stolidly on their shaggy ponies and blending with the browns and rusted heather of the moorlands. Only a small party accompanied the Queen to Fastcastle and the majority rested at the Abbey at Coldingham; this proved to be a wise move for the way to the forbidding fortress, perched high on a rocky headland beyond St. Abb's, was reached by a tortuous and difficult path that plummeted downhill and threatened to unseat those who were bold enough to remain in the saddle.

Margaret shivered as she crossed the ledge of rock separating the castle from the mainland but could not help looking below to where the sea rushed in to crash against the rocks and recede with a sucking intake of loose pebbles that shook the unfenced natural bridge on which she rode. She could only marvel that the race of which she had come to be Queen was made of stern stuff that for generations no one had seen fit to put so much as a flimsy railing-wood between themselves and the ocean boiling below. She was not surprised when later, drinking an incredibly good Claret and eating an indifferently cooked meal, she was told the castle had once been the stronghold of pirates who had ravaged the seas and terrorized those people who scratched a scanty living on the formidable coast; but the strong air and the day's excitement sent her straight to sleep when once she had gained the privacy of her bedchamber and her women, composing themselves about her, blessed the Providence that gave her no opportunity to brood.

In the morning Lord and Lady Home, castellan and mistress of the Fastcastle, stood and wished her Godspeed as she rode off to rejoin her escort and she thanked them for the generosity of her first night on Scottish soil.

Two days later, having passed through Cockburnspath and Haddington, the royal party came to the Castle of Dalkeith where the Earl of Morton received the Queen with great respect and attention to detail. It was expected she would remain within the house for several days while messengers came from James announcing his plans for his first meeting with his bride.

Lady Morton took Margaret to a suite of rooms that had been specially hung with tapestries and refurnished and left her to rest, telling her she would send her Steward to await Margaret's pleasure in ordering a midday meal. She had hardly closed the door behind her when strident trumpets pealed in the courtyard below and the Ladies in Waiting hurried to the narrow casement to peer out.

"Some great Lord," said Lady Nevill, "to judge by the number of attendants."

"Let me see!" commanded Lady Surrey, elbowing the others out of her way. "Some great Lord indeed!" she snorted as she turned from the window and hastened to Margaret's side, "No less than the King himself!"

Margaret felt herself blush from her bosom to the crown of her head and her heart beat in turgid waves that left her breathless. She gripped the arms of her chair to prevent herself running from the chamber. It was Alice Davy who saved the day, hurrying forward with a bottle of sweet-smelling stuff that she stroked onto Margaret's brow and nape.

"You look very beautiful, my lady," she said loudly, "and no Tudor ever showed faint heart in the face of fear!"

4

IN the short interval before James presented himself in her suite and while she and her ladies stationed themselves within the doorway to receive him a thousand thoughts jostled and pushed themselves around in Margaret's brain. Supreme was the knowledge that the meeting she both dreaded and awaited with curiosity was almost upon her and there could be no turning back. She could hear herself telling her grandmother of her hate for the man to whom she had been betrothed and the Lady Margaret's calm recital of the life James had led; somewhere also Margaret recaptured the conversations she had had with Patrick Hepburn when he had extolled his master and begged her to regard her future as safe within his keeping. Safe! How could she be safe with a man who spent his time in furtive entanglements with any willing woman? What safety was there for her tied to a man of gross appetites who doubtless resembled Bluebeard with an unwieldy paunch and a number of double chins? Margaret found her palms moist and her breast tight with the agitation that refused to be allayed. When a young man, not over tall but well built and pleasantly arrayed in an informal doublet of velvet, came quietly into the room she opened her mouth to command Lady Surrey to beg the gentleman to retire as she was expecting the arrival of the King at any moment. Margaret closed her lips on an exclamation of astonishment as she saw the Earl's wife make an obeisance to the auburn-haired man who graciously acknowledged her salute but came straight to where she was standing and bowed deeply. Speechless, Margaret curtsied, gathering her shattered wits; this — this comely personage, clear complexioned and bright-eyed, could not possibly be the King! This must be some cruel deception to lull her into accepting him who now took her hand and raised it to his lips until the bloated lecher of her imagination entered the chamber to claim her as his bride. Before she could wallow deeper into this morass of muddled thinking James was addressing her.

"So you are the little Margaret of whom I have heard so very much! Welcome to Scotland! I am happy indeed to meet her who has done me the honour of consenting to become my wife."

Drawing her closer by the hand he still retained within his own he kissed her lightly on the cheek and Margaret murmured a conventional greeting.

"Will you present me to your ladies?"

Glad of the opportunity to be occupied Margaret led him first to Lady Surrey and then to all the other women who remained standing at a respectful distance but yet craned forward in order not to miss any nuance of the historic meeting.

James kissed each of the ladies and then spoke with Surrey who had come into the chamber with him; as the two men talked James held his arm for Margaret to place her hand upon it and from time to time glanced at her and smiled.

Lady Morton returned to the chamber with her Comptroller and a bevy of servants who set up the trestle tables and covered them with bleached linen and silverware. Margaret watched them while she recovered slowly from the shock of her meeting with James; darting quick looks from the busy men preparing the room for supper she saw her future husband was all and more that Patrick Hepburn had promised. His voice was pleasing and melodious, his manner courteous and the merry glance of the hazel eyes outshone even the playfulness of Northumberland's. He wore, she noticed with some pleasure, a hawking-lure over his shoulder, which meant that, at least, he shared her passion for hunting. Margaret found her heart softening towards him until she happened to catch a glimpse of one of her ladies eagerly pressing forward in an effort to be noticed by James; at once she stiffened and the hand on his velvet covered arm curled until the knuckles glowed white. Almost as if her tenseness conveyed itself to James he politely drew his conversation with Surrey to a close and turning to Margaret asked her to come with him to an alcove where they could speak together alone. She accepted his invitation in a scarcely audible voice and went with him to the far end of the stone-walled chamber.

Afterwards she could not remember everything he said but when, at last, she found her tongue and replied to his questions about her father and grandmother he astonished her by revealing an intimate knowledge of her family history.

"You know that we are related?" Margaret nodded. "Your great-great aunt married my great-grandfather and made him the happiest man alive."

"Was he not a poet?" Margaret asked shyly.

"He was, most certainly; do I take it that you like poetry?"

"Very much — but I am not skilled in the writing of it," she added hastily.

"There is no need for that; in my court are several men only too willing to write polished verses on the slimmest of excuses. With you here," James said gallantly, "I am sure the pens of William Dunbar and Gavin Douglas will leap to cover the paper I provide to indulge their art!"

"I think I have heard my grandmother speak of William Dunbar — was it he who came to London when — when first our marriage was mooted?" The words came quickly with a breathy note that troubled the attractive natural huskiness.

"It was indeed Master Dunbar and he wrote lines about the city of London which make me envious. Do you remember?

'London, thou art of townes A
    per se.
Soveraign of cities, seemliest in sight,
Of high renown, riches and royalte;
— London, thou art the flower of
    Cities all.'

Had you heard them before?"

"My governess, Mistress Denton, had read them out to me, but somehow they did not sound as pleasant as they do now."

James, recognizing the small spark of warmth he had kindled, nursed it with impersonal talk about the poet who had wandered the courts of Europe as first a cleric and later a threadbare pilgrim before returning to Scotland to become the King's laureate. With an older, more worldly woman James knew he would have gone on to quote some of Dunbar's robuster lines but he was pleased that, for the moment anyway, his young and apprehensive betrothed was content to converse with him in the informal fashion he had initiated.

"Do you like music also?" he asked.

"Oh, yes! Hal and I often sing together."

"Then I shall look forward to hearing you for we make much music to spin away the long, dark Scottish evenings. Tell me of your brother and sister."

On the other side of the chamber Lady Morton and the members of the royal suite waited for James to bring Margaret to sit at the table where all was now ready for the supper; no one cared to interrupt the couple as they stood, framed by the narrow window, and talked together. It was obvious to Patrick Hepburn, who had accompanied James, that his master was exerting himself to charm the young Queen and Bothwell guessed by the heightened colour of Margaret's cheeks that she was enjoying the delicate wooing.

At last James glanced towards their hostess and taking Margaret's hand placed it again on his arm and brought her to the table where pages held ewers and silver bowls for the ceremony of hand-washing. James allowed no one but himself to hold the towel for Margaret and waited until she was seated before taking the chair beside her. Throughout the courses of roast venison, hare and partridge he was attentive to her wants, eating and drinking little himself and when the meal was finished persuaded her to dance with Lady Surrey. James leant back smiling and clapping his hands as his bride glided through the stately measures to the accompaniment of the minstrels who played from a gallery. When she curtsied on the final chord he escorted her to the table and told her he must take his leave. Margaret, considerably more relaxed than when the King had arrived some two hours earlier, thanked him for his courtesy in coming to Dalkeith and wished him a safe journey in the soft twilight.

James did not speak as he and Bothwell ran down the stone stairway to the courtyard where a groom awaited them but once on the Edinburgh road confessed he was delighted with his future wife.

"What think you of the lady, Patrick?" Bothwell was a long time in replying.

"I think the Lady Margaret is malleable metal, my lord," he said at last, "time alone will tell if the fusion of Tudor and Yorkist elements produces pure gold."

"A strange answer," James's voice was tinged with amusement. "I am not so certain, on reflection, that I am anxious for any woman in my life to resemble that rare commodity my advisers tell me I waste time in attempting to manufacture!"

"Exactly!" Bothwell's tone was dry and he refused to be drawn further.

At Dalkeith Alice Davy persuaded the other ladies to withdraw and alone helped Margaret, pale with the strain of the meeting, to bed. She too, was anxious to know what others thought of her husband-to-be but could not bring herself to ask straight out for Alice's opinion. The nurse helped her by saying bluntly she thought the King of the Scots was a fine, handsome young gentleman who conducted himself in a manner that might well be the envy of other sovereign lords.

"Do you really think so?" Margaret asked, sitting up in her canopied bed and hugging the silken sheets to her shoulders.

"Yes," Alice said stoutly. "The king seems to me to be the kind of man, once having given his word will not revoke it."

"I hope you are right, Alice; my lord has a certain charm of manner that reminds me of Hal. I do not think he is very much like my father, do you?"

Alice glanced at the girl quickly, but in the half light of the chamber her expression was void.

"You cannot compare your father who is old and stooped with care to a young man at the height of his power."

"No, you are probably right. Good night, Alice; have you had your bed put close to my door?"

Assuring her charge she had had her truckle placed across the threshold of the bedchamber Alice blew out the candles and retired. She was awakened after what seemed a very few minutes from the depths of much needed sleep by the smell of burning and loud shouting from the courtyard below; as she struggled to collect herself she heard a frightened cry from the Queen's room and stumbled in to find the walls lit with a sharp orange glow. Margaret, a bedrobe about her shoulders, was silhouetted against a mass of flames soaring heavenwards from the building on the east side. Alice hurried to join her.

"Saint's bones deliver us! Here, my lady, put on some hose and shoes and we'll go downstairs while there is still time."

"Do you think we are in danger?"

"Nothing immediate but it would be foolish — " She was interrupted by several men and women who pushed into the chamber without knocking and urged the Lady Margaret and Mistress Davy to go below with all haste.

"Where has the fire started?" Margaret asked as she bundled into some clothes.

"Someone thought it began in a loft over the stables." This from a sleepy-eyed waiting woman whose hair straggled from under a bonnet sitting askew on her head.

"The horses! Are they safe?"

"I do not know, my lady, but you may be certain the grooms will look well to their charges."

"It is to be hoped they have all been led to safety; I cannot bear to think of harm befalling the poor things; they are frightened enough at the mere smell of smoke."

The husky voice registered more concern than royal dignity usually allowed. Lady Surrey, composed and dressed, quietly despatched a page to discover what had befallen while she shepherded the motley company down the stone stairs to an outbuilding detached from the rest of the castle. The boy did not return for some time and when he came his face was blackened with soot and his legs and feet were wet from the water which had slopped over them while he was helping the chain of men plying pails from the moat. He opened his mouth to speak but Lady Surrey took his arm and went outside with him.

"The Earl and his household think the

conflagration is well under control and are sending bedding for us to remain here for the rest of the night. He assures us there is no cause for alarm." Lady Surrey spoke briskly and shook her head when Margaret asked for news of the horses.

"Young Owen could not come near enough to discover what had befallen and I think we shall all be of more use if we take Lord Morton's advice and snatch some sleep." She turned gratefully as the page came into the outbuilding with a roll of blankets and a small goblet. Alice Davy took the bedding and laid it in one corner of the room as Lady Surrey gently persuaded the anxious girl to lie down and drink the warmed milk she had requested. Surprisingly obedient, almost as if she shied away from hearing any ill-tidings, Margaret allowed them to cover her and settled down in curled repose.

Lady Surrey took Alice outside and told her nearly all the horses had been destroyed, among them the palfreys Margaret had used throughout the long journey from England. Alice gasped when she heard the sad news for the Queen doted on the beautiful little beasts and took a deep interest in their wellbeing.

"It was very wise, my lady, not to tell her of this misfortune until the morning for her Grace will be desolate. Oh, misery, we could have done without this misfortune just when my lady seems to be accepting her lot with more grace than I thought possible."

But the loss of the palfreys could not be kept a secret when once the day broke and the disturbed household set about remedying the disaster. As Alice had expected Margaret was heartbroken when she learned the horses had perished and sobbed inconsolably. The waiting women were at a loss how to comfort their mistress when a panting messenger came from James, who had quickly been told of the fire, expressing his sympathy and the hope that Margaret and all her train would remove themselves instantly to the castle at Newbattle. This fortress was not far from the ill-fated Dalkeith and James was already having it prepared to receive his bride. He ended his message by announcing he intended to visit Margaret in Newbattle when she had had a chance to settle there quietly.

Blessing the King for his kindly thought Lady Surrey hustled the women and her royal charge into preparations for the move. As soon as a litter could be summoned Margaret was handed into it and her personal procession set off; what remained of the drawing horses would be eked out by the steeds promised by James and these could bring the mountainous piles of baggage later in the day.

Newbattle, set in woodland and pleasant meadows, aroused admiration from Margaret's ladies although she could hardly see for her red and swollen eyes. Alice Davy, once inside the castle, sent maids for hot water and a tub and persuaded Margaret to lie in it. Margaret was sufficiently recovered after this relaxing treatment to choose one of her prettier informal dresses of an open skirted robe above a petticoat of similar tone embroidered with pearls; pads of linen wrung out in cold water had done much to reduce the puffiness of her eyes and a judicious amount of claret had restored colour to the pale cheeks.

At the same time as the Earl of Surrey,

accompanied by the Archbishop of York and some of the other Englishmen, had set out to meet the King as he rode to visit Newbattle, Margaret sat down with some of her ladies to wile away the waiting with a game of cards. They played Tarot with a new-painted pack thoughtfully provided by the Countess of Richmond and Derby as a divertissement for her granddaughter to ease tedious or difficult hours. Only three hands had been finished when James came into the Queen's chamber with a few close friends. Margaret scattered the cards as she rose swiftly to greet him, her hands held out with her cheek upturned for his salute.

"Well met, my lord, I am right glad to see you come! Did my lords meet up with you on the road?"

James smote his forehead with his open palm and looked slightly abashed.

"God's Grace," he said with a grin, "I came by the Craigmillar road and never thought to tell them. Patrick, would you go and bring in these poor, misled gentlemen?"

Bothwell bowed and went out smiling;

it was as well it was high summer for in winter the Edinburgh road could be bleak and unfriendly. By the time he came back with Surrey and the others he found the musicians playing and the Queen dancing with Lord Gray. James came immediately to apologize for any misunderstanding and servants brought in wine and baskets of white bread; when the Archbishop and the Earl were served James took wine to Margaret and they drank together from the same cup. Those who had been apprehensive about the outcome of the marriage between the two — and there had been many in both England and Scotland — saw with pleasure that Margaret's face had taken on a new radiance. It was obvious the hurt of the loss of the loved palfreys had been forgotten as James paid her court and when he sat down to play for her on the clavichord she stood at his side, listening with rapt attention. All her Celtic blood leapt to enjoy this demonstration of his true understanding of the nature of music making; for a long time a gentle magic held the hall in its power and even the sceptics and the sophisticated confessed afterwards that they were enthralled. Eventually the dying light of the day warned James he must start out for Edinburgh and the court accompanied him to the yard where his courser awaited; he delighted those who watched by leaping to the saddle without assistance. Less speedily Surrey went after him on horseback and rode with James until they reached the outskirts of Eskbank.

For the next three days Margaret and her train stayed at Newbattle, the King visiting her each evening. On Monday, 7th August, Margaret stood in her bedchamber while her women dressed her in cloth of gold for her state entrance into Edinburgh. Mistress Denton sniffed her disapproval when Alice produced a vial of precious scent she had been harbouring for this day and ostentatiously removed herself from the bedroom to find her own cloak; she had already expressed distress when whalebone corsets had accentuated Margaret's bosom and exposed an unusual amount of comely flesh and she thought the perfume the final straw.

"Poor Mistress Denton does not realize her charge is about to become a married woman and will no longer be needing her schoolroom ways," murmured Lady Lyle to the Countess of Surrey as she lifted a great necklace of pearls from a velvet covered box and hung them about Margaret's neck where they gleamed softly against the young breast.

"Let us hope her charge realizes the same thing and acts accordingly," replied the Countess a trifle grimly, "I must confess I find the King of the Scots utterly charming but I'll wager my new gown to yours that he'll need every ounce of that quality to overcome her reserve when once they are bedded!"

"Think you so? Truly? I should have thought, having known so many women he would find the task easy." Lady Lyle's plucked eyebrows almost disappeared beneath her pleated coif.

"In that sentence you have the key to his difficulty; you do not imagine, surely, that the bride is unaware of his past misdemeanours?" Lady Surrey stooped to pick up her trailing skirt and followed the Queen as, unaware of her ladies speculation, she went down to take up her position in the small procession that waited to escort her to her litter.

At the great doorway she gasped with pleasure as she saw two white palfreys, splendid enough to match her own lost ones, held ready for her inspection. Each of the horses was hung with new harness and Bothwell's nephew, who had brought them from Holyrood, told her they were the King's gift to his bride. She thanked him with real pleasure, the words stumbling over each other in her excitement and it was some time before she could tear herself away from their soft nuzzles and liquid eyes.

Not far from Dalkeith the King followed his first present with another; this time a tame hart so that Margaret could disport herself on the road if she so wished. Almost as she accepted the beast Surrey saw dust rising on the road ahead of him and guessed the King was approaching. They were not kept long in doubt for James came at breakneck speed reigning in his great charger in a flurry of loose stones. With consummate grace and skill he threw himself from the saddle and knelt beside Margaret's litter. He also had taken great pains with his dressing and had attired himself in a jacket of cloth of gold edged with fur, with hose of scarlet and shirt banded with pearls. Bothwell, who dismounted with the King, recognized the look on James's face as he bent over his bride's hand and saw that James, probably for the first time, was attracted by the girl who lay shyly within the half-drawn curtains of the litter. Momentarily, before taking up the sword of state, carried until now by an usher, Bothwell closed his eyes and prayed the tenderness he had espied would be reciprocated and sustained; he recalled his own faint sense of surprise when he had realized, during the betrothal ceremony at Shene, that Margaret had an unexpectedly sensual streak. "Heaven help them both," he prayed silently.

Outside Edinburgh, where curious townsfolk swarmed to catch sight of their sovereign and the King of England's daughter, James called for the enormous charger, hung with cloth of gold and red velvet, that he had ordered to carry Margaret and himself into the city. He rode up and down a little on the grass beside the road and seemed quite content with the behaviour of the horse. However, when one of his gentlemen sprang up behind him at his command the charger bucked and almost threw them.

"I am sorry, my lady, but we shall have to use one of your palfreys," James said coming to the litter.

"There will be no hardship in that; I cannot thank you enough for your kindness in sending the palfreys to me and while I am cast down for you that we may not ride upon your splendid horse I am, nevertheless, glad of the opportunity to try out my new mare."

James helped Margaret from the cushioned palanquin and mounted the palfrey, holding the bridle while gentlemen ushers joined their hands for her to mount behind him. Gingerly Margaret placed her hands around James's waist, keeping herself as distant as possible from the straight back in front of her. As the cavalcade moved off he turned to her, sniffing appreciatively, "My English rose smells as sweet as she looks!"

Margaret blushed and imperceptibly

slid her hands away from James's side; laughingly he grasped the reins through two fingers and reaching behind imprisoned her small fist and drew her nearer to him.

"Don't be afraid," he said softly, "I'll not eat you, you know."

Warily, as Arthur's Seat came into view, she allowed herself to sway against him and found his warmth strangely comforting and reassuring. Used as she was to the staring of her father's people since she was a child it was yet heartening to be close to this man who understood these strangers who gaped at her from such close quarters.

Pageants marked their progress to the gate of the city where another vast concourse of citizens waved and shouted greetings and a procession of Greyfriars came to hold a Cross for the King and Queen to kiss. To approving shouts from the townsfolk James declined the honour of being the first to salute the Holy staff and waited until Margaret had touched it with her lips. Trumpeters sounded at their entry beneath the turreted gate where white-robed angels sang hymns of joy and presented the Queen with symbolic keys to Edinburgh.

At the Church of St. Giles priests held up a relic of the Saint for their reverence and James himself broke into a Te Deum; soon all the company joined in and then at the conclusion rushed to drink their fill of the wine pouring from a fountain near the Mercat Cross. Margaret shook her head when James offered to dismount and bring her a drink and told him she would refresh herself later when the feast of pageantry was over and they were safely arrived at Holyrood. From the overhanging windows carpets and banners fluttered gently in the warm air and small stages, wherein were enacted both Classical and Religious tableaux, wore garlands of thistles and roses.

Margaret had never seen a city such as Edinburgh before and she asked James why he did not use the Castle set high on its rock above the narrow streets.

"It is too grim to live in all the time; now I intend to make Edinburgh the capital, the house I live in must be less foreboding than that great fortress towering above us. You will like Holyrood, I hope; it is not yet completed but we have done all we can to make you feel welcome and at home. From what my ambassadors tell me your father and grandmother keep great state and I should not like to think I had failed their trust by asking you to live in second rate rooms."

Within the Church of Holyrood there seemed small chance of this discourtesy for when Margaret alighted at the porch into James's upheld arms she found the interior lavishly decorated and cushions of cloth of gold for her and James to kneel upon. Apart from her waiting women she was the only lady in the place and all the nobles bowed to her as they took their ways to stand in the nave for the blessing given by the Archbishop of St. Andrews.

From the service James and Margaret walked through the cloisters to the great hall of the palace where the ladies and lesser members of the Scottish Court waited to greet the Queen. James put his arm about her waist as they went through the dim passage and she moved as imperceptibly nearer to him as she had earlier moved away. Before the doors were opened to admit them to the expectant company James kissed her lightly on the forehead.

"Courage, my sweet, from tomorrow I shall always be at your side."

5

IN the city of Edinburgh the bells of the churches rang out in gladness for the forthcoming marriage. Down Canongate to St. Giles, the Tolbooth and Mercat Cross the peals filled the summer evening with gladness while the wine still flowed and the people danced for joy and the unspoken hope that, at last, peace might be sealed between the Scots and the English. The fair young girl who had ridden into Edinburgh on this momentous day brought not only a wife for their lovelorn King but an instrument by which one day the crown of England might come to rest on a Stewart head. It was well enough for Henry VII to believe the lesser kingdom would always follow the greater but he had only one heir now, and who knew but that one day divine providence would not intervene to make the offspring of James and Margaret Tudor a king of England? The very thought was intoxicating and the townspeople drank deep of the red wine and — when they remembered it — toasted the cause of their celebration.

At Holyrood Margaret was suffering with a devastating attack of nervous exhaustion. Now that the long and tiring day was over the rooms she had been given as her own seemed, by comparison, horribly quiet and remote and Mistress Denton, unwisely as it was to turn out, decided that early to bed was the best thing for her royal mistress. She had overruled Alice and insisted upon Margaret retiring and taking a light supper in her bed. Despite the Queen's protests she had banished all the waiting-women as soon as they had helped Margaret disrobe and when Margaret sent away her supper, petulantly claiming she had no appetite, the curtains had been drawn and the candles snuffed.

Some hours after this Margaret still tossed and turned on the soft mattress unable to lose herself in blissful sleep while her brain was afire with the day's events. When at last the sun's light faded from the sky and the church bells ceased there came over the Palace a quietness that was more disturbing than the half-heard noise.

Margaret dozed and awoke sweating as she imagined herself in the arms of some strange beast with a dozen limbs that crushed her in a deathly embrace; the bed-curtains swayed, threatening to fall in and engulf her and when she attempted to cry out she discovered she could summon no voice.

Afterwards she was never able to separate fantasy from reality during this pre-nuptial night and the apprehension James had sought to dispel returned to dog her as it had done when she first left her father in Collyweston. With the excitement of the long journey and its attendant pomp now behind her the life her royal parent had chosen for her to lead began in earnest on the morrow and she would be faced with endless years of dwelling among strangers. She tried to comfort herself with the knowledge that she was to retain twenty-four of the women who made up her own entourage who would be able to speak with her of the days at Richmond and other palaces in the distant, lamented England of her birth. When she thought of James she could not face up squarely to her feelings for him; she was prepared to believe in his undoubted charm but an obtuse resentment kept her from accepting with complete accord his kindness towards her. She knew, although she could not have put it into words, that she feared this man who was to become her husband in a few hours almost as much for his obvious attractiveness as for the revulsion she had had towards him before their first meeting. When he smiled at her with the skin crinkling round his hazel eyes she could not rid herself of the mental picture of James bending over other women with exactly the same expression on his face. It was only an extra irritation that these unnamed females were always older and more accomplished than she.

She must have slept for when her women came to rouse her she was heavy with the sleep that followed the wakeful hours of restlessness. She was quiet while maids brought in warmed water and lavender-smelling towels for her tub and submitted to the ministrations of Alice in a detached state where her mind refused to take part. The Welsh woman had brought with her some milk and white bread and when the fire she had begged was kindled in the hearth she wrapped Margaret in a blanket of fine wool and sat her in a chair beside it.

Margaret drank and ate and began to feel the slow return of life to her brain and limbs. She was now aware that it was a beautiful morning and although the sun was hidden by light mists they would soon disperse and leave the sky cloudless. The bedchamber was a scene of constant movement as women brought in robes and undergarments from the garderobe and set out the complicated articles of the Queen's toilette.

Margaret was standing while Lady Guildford, who from this day would be lady-mistress, supervised the fastening of the robe of white and gold damask, when a waiting woman came to tell her Lord Bothwell awaited an audience. She received her proxy bridegroom solemnly but could not restrain a cry of delight when he presented her with the crown James had had made for her by an Edinburgh goldsmith named John

Currour. It was a magnificent piece of work, light and delicate and it became suddenly the focal point of interest, symbolizing as it did the day's meaning. Margaret thanked Bothwell with genuine warmth; as he turned to leave her she felt the first stirring of pleasurable anticipation and submitted to the rest of her dressing with a good grace.

The Countess of Surrey, herself richly gowned, coming in to take up the duties of train bearer complimented the Queen on her appearance.

"I am sure the King will be delighted with his bride; the white and gold becomes you and blends perfectly with your necklace of pearls and the crown."

"If you were to ask me," whispered Alice as she dabbed more of the precious scent behind Margaret's ears, "it isn't the dress or the crown — and I'll give you they are handsome enough — that will give him the most pleasure, but the sight of your hair!"

It was true that the long tresses, falling below Margaret's knees, gave her an air of fragile beauty and the girl was glad she had submitted to the early awakening and the washing and tedious brushing of her hair which had followed. She asked Alice for a mirror and smiled her gratitude when she saw how the cloud of gold enhanced both her jewels and gown.

Surrey entered the chamber and the bridal procession fell in behind him as he took the hand of the Queen and placed her between himself and the Archbishop of York. Close to them walked Lady Surrey, the Nevills, Lady Lisle and the Countess of Guildford with Mistress Denton.

In the chapel of Holyrood, Surrey led the bride to stand beside the font, there to await James and his gentlemen. They had not long to settle themselves in their allotted positions before trumpeters announced the arrival of the King and James walked into the church and stopped on the right of the font. He was accompanied by his brother, the Archbishop of St. Andrews and attended by a large number of heralds and the nobility who, to judge by the magnificence of their dress, had been subsidised for the occasion out of the royal coffers. This fact did not escape

Bothwell and he thought back to the conversation he had had with the King when they had ridden home to Edinburgh after the first encounter with Margaret at Dalkeith when James had commented wryly upon his experiments to make gold from quicksilver and other strange chemicals. If the King of the Scots was to keep up his efforts to impress the Princess of England and those who accompanied her he would need a bottomless treasure chest and none knew better than James how difficult it was to keep the Exchequer Rolls with a goodly balance in hand.

As Bothwell pursued his thoughts the Archbishop of York and the Archbishop of Glasgow read the Papal Dispensation necessary for the marriage of the distantly related bride and groom and with this formality completed James took Margaret by the hand and led her to the high altar to kneel on cushions of gold. The crowded chapel had a brief glimpse of the royal pair, as both dressed in white and gold, they made their way through the mass of people.

Halfway through the ceremony the Queen was anointed and presented with

100

the sceptre of the realm at which the choir sang a Te Deum and two priests came forward to hold a canopy of cloth of gold above the heads of the King and the bride. This remained in position during the most solemn part of the service and was only removed when the mass was finished and members of the household moved among the congregation distributing bread and wine. In the ensuing hubbub James bent down and kissed Margaret's cheek.

"No King ever had a more charming bride or was so entranced by such a mantle of golden hair!"

So Alice had been right. Margaret gave James a hesitant smile and a hurriedly veiled glimpse of eyes dilated with an unnamed emotion and when he began to move towards the doorway of the church and the cloisters beyond followed him meekly.

They dined together with a few of the company and then went together to the hall where musicians were already playing. James and Margaret sat side by side in red velvet chairs and listened to the airs until a band of singers took up their positions directly before them.

"If I am not mistaken you are now going to hear the epithalamium William Dunbar has composed especially in your honour," James told his bride.

"Oh, is Dunbar here?" Margaret looked about the great place.

"Yes, he is standing over there to the right in that press of people — can you see him? — a tallish man, thin-faced and wearing a gown that almost certainly came out of my wardrobe to judge by its antiquity!"

Margaret did not have much difficulty in finding the poet for Dunbar wore the expression of one who dithered between pride that his work was to be given and doubt as to the manner in which the singers would do justice to his genius.

"You shall meet him," James promised, "perhaps not today, but later when the festivities are over."

"I shall look forward to the occasion, my lord." She stopped talking as the musicians struck a chord and listened intently as they sung the words Dunbar had written in her honour.

"O fair, fairest of every fair
Princess most pleasant and preclare,
The loveliest that ever has been,
Welcome in Scotland to be Queen!"

Margaret felt herself blush; she was fairly used to panegyrics but the words surprised her and in the confusion lost the opening lines of the second verse.

" _____

Fresh fragrant flower of fairhood
   sheen,
Welcome in Scotland to be Queen!

Welcome the rose both red and
   white,
Welcome the flower of our delight,
Our spirit rejoicing from the spleen,
Welcome in Scotland to be Queen!"

"I am not the only one to be overcome by your beauty," James told her laughingly, "for I see you have enslaved Dunbar as well!"

"He does not know me!"

"Of course he does; there is not one man or woman in the Court who could not describe in minute detail your every feature and you can be assured Master Dunbar will see more than most."

"I am at a loss to know whether to be flattered or put on my guard by that declaration."

"In the case of Dunbar I should accept his praise as coming from his heart, he is not the type of man to spare his pen either to approve or condemn — when he thinks that necessary."

James and the Queen danced for a little while until he asked her if she were tired and would care to rest until supper. Margaret gratefully accepted his thoughtful offer and he summoned her ladies and she left the hall to the curtsies and bows of the assembled company.

In the privacy of her bedchamber she stepped out of the heavy robe and put off the crown, whose light appearance had belied the weight that seemed to press further on her brow with each successive hour of the ceremonies. With a satin bedrobe about her she stretched out on the canopied bed and asked to be allowed to sleep in peace.

She was not awake when the hour

of Evensong approached and Mistress Denton told Alice she must rouse the Queen and prepare her to accompany the King to church. Alice refused and stoutly stood her ground even when Denton went to fetch Lady Guildford to endorse her belief that Margaret should go with James. Lady Guildford drew back the heavy curtains of the bed and looked at the young face, mercifully relaxed against the silk covered pillows.

"My lady will have plenty of time to go to chapel with the King; let us leave her in peace for now."

Mistress Denton sniffed and Alice turned away to stir the fire and hide the smile of triumph she could not suppress.

Supper was an intimate meal held in the King's chamber where red and blue hangings covered the walls. James sat close to Margaret and saw she was served on every occasion before he was. The food was less ornate than the sumptuous banquet of the morning when the bride and the groom had eaten from gilt plates Wild Boar and Roast Swan with side dishes including one where the arms of

England and Scotland were moulded in a jelly, but Margaret had more appetite and enjoyed the meal. As it was almost ended James called his squire who stood behind his chair and the young man returned after a short absence with the poet Dunbar.

"My lady," Dunbar bowed and at a nod from the King brought out a roll of parchment from his robe and handed it to Margaret.

"Do not attempt to read it now," James said, "but keep Mr. Dunbar's poem until daylight when you may appreciate his verse more easily. What have you called it, William?"

"The Thistle and the Rose, my lord." Dunbar's eyes were expressionless in the light of the flares against the wall and he smiled at Margaret, quite unabashed by her rank. To a Tudor, used to the protocol of court life in England, this was a novel experience and Margaret returned his greeting shyly.

"Do I take it from the title you dwell as much upon the emblem of Scotland as upon the Rose of England?" James asked.

"Read it, my lord, and you will discover," was the enigmatic reply.

"I shall most certainly do that!" James promised as Dunbar took his leave.

"Mr. Dunbar is a most interesting man, is he not, my lord?"

"Interesting indeed and not above taking his royal patron to task."

"For what?" Margaret asked innocently.

"Oh, mostly for omitting to raise his benefit to the high level he thinks his talent commands," James told her, a trifle hurriedly and beckoned for Bothwell's nephew to bring the silver basins for Margaret and him to perform the ritual washing of their hands. He dried Margaret's hands himself and when the task was completed asked her quietly if she were ready to retire; he almost hated himself for the look of anguish she gave him, extinguishing in a second the pleasure conjured by Dunbar.

"If you would delay — "

"My lord, I have been instructed that when a husband commands his wife she obeys him." The stiff speech touched him and he rose from the table and without fuss took her out of the chamber and went with her to the door of the room that was her own.

"I am going to play at cards with Surrey and the others; if you are still awake when we have finished I will come and bid you good night."

The room seemed full of women when she came into it; most of whom, Margaret knew, would not have been present on an ordinary evening. The petulance that asserted itself when she was at a loss to deal with a situation caused her to say more loudly than she meant that she was tired and wished to go to bed. She did not miss the knowing glances that passed swiftly between her ladies.

"My lord is to play cards with the Earl of Surrey — " she began.

"What a good idea!" Alice bustled towards her mistress. "See, we have built a fire against the evening chill and if you wish I'll bring you a hot posset."

"Thank you."

"Well, Mistress Davy, what keeps you?" Lady Guildford beckoned Elizabeth Barley, one of the maids of honour, and curtsying to the Queen began the ritual of disrobing. Margaret gave Alice a near-despairing look as the nurse went reluctantly from the room but stood quietly enough while the women helped her from the heavy robe and brought a chamber-gown. She sat on a stool while her hair was brushed and saw Mistress Denton officiously remove the heavy silken bedcover from the enormous bed and hover nearby to assist her climb in. Margaret was suddenly determined that when Surrey and the English party returned to England and her father she would beg of James that her governess should be among those who left Holyrood. Denton seemed, in a moment, to have become a symbol of the childhood she was now anxious to forget and while she realized Alice was also part of this past life the kindly Welsh woman represented all that was comfortable and consoling against the schoolroom discipline of the governess. Denton too, could be relied upon to convey letters to King Henry without opening them to read their contents; this, added to the fact that she would be most useful to Henry in the schoolroom where the six year old Princess Mary would be beginning her lessons, convinced Margaret her motives were entirely justified. If she were sent to Scotland to become Queen she would show them all she intended to act as one! Comforted by this resolution she submitted to being led to the canopied bed and huddled quickly beneath the covers.

"Thank you," she said, mustering all the dignity she could, "you may leave me now!"

"All of us?" Despite her exalted position as Lady Mistress, Lady Guildford could not conceal her disappointed surprise.

"Yes, thank you; the anteroom where you and Elizabeth are to sleep is close enough to call and with Mistress Davy in the truckle bed against my door I am well enough protected."

"But, my lady — your Grace — " Joan Guildford began.

"You are all very kind but my most urgent need at this moment is rest and quiet after this exhausting day; be well assured I shall summon you if the need arises," she added quickly, unwilling to offend this wife of Henry's trusted Comptroller of the Household.

Slowly the ladies filed from the room, obviously unwilling to forgo their privilege of being present when James came to bed his wife. Margaret did not breathe properly until the last one had closed the heavy oak door behind her. Alice entered shortly afterwards and brought a pewter mug with hot, sweetened milk; she did not tell her young mistress that she had mixed a few drops of distilled poppy juice with the sugar and stayed only long enough to see Margaret settle back among the goosedown pillows. At Margaret's bidding she left two candles burning in their silver sconces.

Alone, without the cluster of excitable females, Margaret was able to think over the day's events and admitted she had enjoyed them more than she had anticipated. The Scottish nobles and their ladies still remained a jumble of half-remembered names; Douglas's, Hamiltons, Drummonds, Grahams and Kennedys and while they differed from their English counterparts they were by no means as alien — or as ignorant — as she had supposed. If Dunbar's verses spoke of the measure of Scottish learning there was no lack of it at James's Court. With the thought of James came the remembrance of the reason for her vigil in the close-curtained bed and Margaret felt a chill strike from the soles of her feet to her neck. With an effort she controlled the shivering that accompanied the cold and concentrated on the gentle manner in which her husband had treated her since their first meeting. She thought of James's skill on horseback and his accomplished singing and playing of the clavichord; surely there could be no harm in a man who enjoyed both the outdoor life and the making of music! Tomorrow she must ask him if he could obtain the music of the song sung in her honour at dinner so that she could play it for herself. Margaret found herself humming the melody and relaxing into the feather mattress almost at the same moment she heard the latch of her door lifted and swiftly replaced. Her eyes, which had drooped momentarily, opened wide and she strained to see in the close darkness of the four poster. As she looked the curtains were drawn back softly and James stood at her side.

"Are you asleep?"

"No," she murmured.

"Good," said her husband and threw himself down beside her, his face next to hers and one arm thrown across her body. Margaret lay very still, hardly daring to breathe; the limbs that had been icy cold began to flame with an unknown heat.

"Does your apartment please you, little Margaret?"

"It does, my lord, I thank you."

"If there is anything you want you know you have but to ask it of me."

James stroked the side of her neck and the bared shoulder with a caress that would have gentled the most highly wrought mare in his stable and Margaret discovered a delicious sleepiness creep over her shutting out the strange mixture of emotion she had suffered while she awaited his coming.

"You are not afraid, are you, my little Margaret?"

"No, yes — I do not know, my lord," she whispered.

"Go to sleep and I shall stay with you; but will you do one thing for me, before you drift away?"

"My lord?" She was more awake now. "My name is James; will you not call me so?"

Within the safe, reassuring circle of his arm she would have found it difficult to refuse him anything. Her acquiescence communicated itself to the experienced man who lay beside her and for a moment he was tempted to throw away the scruples he had for her youth and consummate the marriage; but he hesitated because the protectiveness she aroused in him left little room for passion and reminded him, uncomfortably, of the trust his various children gave him.

"James — James," she murmured and with infinite tenderness he kissed the rounded cheek, so close to his on the pillow.

6

BELOW the stark cliffs the sea broke in wavelets on the smooth sands; seagulls wheeled in a sky of unclouded blue and now and then a kittiwake darted to the placid ocean and momentarily disturbed the surface to fly up with a fish crosswise in its beak.

It was a day of unruffled tranquillity and Margaret was strangely happy; with two or three of her women and an informal guard of her own knights she was leaning against the towering rocks and absorbing the sight and smell of the sea. Her ladies could not understand her craving to watch the movement of the water and the play of the sun on the lazy diminutive breakers; they stood apart from her talking quietly and now and then glancing at Margaret who seemed oblivious of the young men who were practicing golfing shots with sticks for clubs and stones in place of the usual leather ball.

Margaret liked Dunnottar and the fortress built into the cliff above her and had been glad when James had sent her to stay in the castle while he dealt with the second uprising in the Western Isles since their marriage almost two years before. Dunnottar, home of the hereditary Earls Marischal of Scotland was situated on the east coast near Stonehaven and was well away from the wild, roadless highlands where clansmen constantly rebelled against the King's authority and bickered among themselves for superiority. Margaret knew James blamed himself for much of the lawlessness that existed among the scattered, proud peoples of the north, for early in his reign he had visited them, hearing their problems and bestowing favours upon them but had delegated his authority too early to the Earl of Argyll who had not always honoured the trust bestowed upon him. This youthful idealism had given James many anxious hours and in the summer of the previous year he had fitted out ships of war with the Barton brothers who were devoted captains of his fleet and sent them to patrol the waters around the deeply indented coastline of the western seaboard. Even this show of strength had not halted the restless tide of revolt and later James had sent an army which had smoked out some of the miscreants from their castles on the lochs and inland seas but had not secured a lasting peace. Now that summer was again melting the snows the highlanders were pledging their support to Torquil Macleod, brother-in-law to Argyll himself, who was setting himself up in defiance of the King and his authority. James had gone north to win allegiance from those clansmen who expressed their loyalty while at the same time he tried to catch Macleod and bring him to justice in Edinburgh.

Dunnottar could not compare in comfort with elegance with Linlithgow or Holyrood where James was rebuilding and refurbishing with unceasing energy, or even Stirling which had been bestowed upon Margaret as part of her marriage settlement, but its impregnability and boundless vista of seas was endearing enough and brought an ease of mind that was in itself a blessing.

The two years of her life with James had not been easy; he had treated her always with the punctilious kindness and courtesy which he had shown her from the beginning but had spent very little time with her. She had discovered within a short span of days after her marriage that James was possessed of a demoniac energy that would not permit him to stay in one place for any length of time. Coupled with this he was able to spend hours together in the saddle and could ride vast distances in a single day without tiring. Margaret had been inclined to grudge his protracted absences but her upbringing had taught her it was necessary for a monarch to be out and among his people and she knew, without question, from those about her, that James was popular and had the common weal of his people close to his heart.

She had also the comforting companionship of her women and the strange adoration of the poet William Dunbar who treated her with a devotion akin to the selfless love of a parent. He would sit with her, singing or reading her his latest verses, during the long summer

118

days or in the equally tedious winter evenings and charm her boredom and homesickness away.

James also saw that she lacked nothing to help her during her enforced loneliness and sent musicians and entertainers to amuse her. The letters she wrote home to her father in England were less plaintive than the missive which Mistress Denton had borne for her to Richmond and in truth she could find no real cause for complaint; if James saw any of his mistresses no word came of it to her ear and if she had been forced to accept the little Lady Margaret Drummond at court she had at least, the satisfaction of knowing her mother could not trouble her now. She was, in many ways, a different person from the frightened, overdressed girl who had travelled north against her will to marry a man she had not met. Although she still trailed her waggons of dresses and household goods behind her wherever she went she had learnt much from the people with whom she lived and shot of the restrictions of Denton's schoolroom ways had come to enjoy the search for knowledge. Not only Dunbar but Gavin Douglas, a son of the great Earl of Angus, Archibald Bell-the-Cat, wrote poems in her honour and took time off from his duties as provost of St. Giles in Edinburgh to read her his own works. Both poets had taken clerks orders but Gavin was more orthodox in his ways and had already been parson of Prestonkirk; idealistic also he yet made no attempt, veiled or otherwise, to take the King to task. It appeared to the average hard riding, hunting and hawking noble of James's court that Dunbar and Gavin Douglas were enchanted with the Queen and thankfully, if a trifle shame faced, allowed them to amuse her.

With a small sigh Margaret eased herself away from the hard rock face and stretched her arms above her head. At once two or three of her women came to her.

"Shall we go in?" Elizabeth Barley asked quickly.

"Let us take a walk across the strand and then begin the climb," Margaret said, unwilling to relinquish the magical quality of the summer day. She set off towards the edge of the receding sea and oblivious of her velvet-clad feet struck out across the damp sand, stopping now and again to pick up a gleaming shell. The waiting women, not so adventurous, hovered beyond the seawrack where the tide had not washed and hoped she would not long delay; but umber shadows were already bringing the chill of evening before the Queen had apparently had her fill of the gentle ocean and reluctantly signalled she was ready to mount the steep path to the stronghold above.

Margaret took her supper early, alone in her bower; she waved away offers of singing or games of cards and said she was sleepy with the fresh air. Gratefully the women, all older than she, helped her prepare for bed and took their leave to pursue the assignations of their choice, accepting with alacrity Alice Davy's offer to remain on duty with one of Margaret's own bodyguard and young Archibald Douglas, grandson of the great Earl and nephew of Gavin. This youth, of an age with the Queen, was also a nephew of the late Margaret Drummond; his other grandfather, Lord Drummond, was much at court and had had little difficulty in finding a place for the young Archibald. Archibald was pleasant mannered and popular with the entourage for he was always willing to run errands and make himself generally useful.

When the last of the women had walked past him with a flurry of trailing skirts and he had sat for a while with Alice listening to some of her stories of far off Pembroke where she had spent her girlhood, before she also, bade him good night and went to her rest in the adjoining room he took up his position outside the Queen's bedchamber. Here, perched on a high wooden stool he watched the darkling sky fade from apricot to a grey-green where stars glimmered feebly; although he would have loved to be with his father, George, Master of Douglas who accompanied the King he was quite content to do his bidding and serve the Queen instead. Like Margaret he was attuned to the sea and liked nothing better than to find some deserted cove with some of the other pages and strip off to bathe in the stringent water.

Family pride — which had hovered in the generations between loyalty and open rebellion to the Stewart on the throne at the time — coupled with a boyish shyness prevented him from regarding the King's wife as any other than a young woman who commanded his duty and his respect. There had been occasions when he had seen expressions on her mobile face which had aroused instincts of which he had been previously unaware and he had wished, with a strange inconsistency, that she was other than the King's wife and more accessible. All too conscious of the ribaldry such admissions would invoke in his companions he kept his thoughts rigorously to himself and concentrated on fulfilling with proper care the job he had been given.

At intervals he heard bursts of laughter and the high scraping of fiddles from the great hall and wondered who would be the first to slip beneath the long trestles in a stupor of wine or which knight would succeed in luring the lady of his heart to a trysting place among the warren of chambers in the castle. He was nodding slightly when he heard the music come to an abrupt end and sprang from his seat, drawing his dagger while he ran to the head of the steep stone staircase. A few steps down a man-at-arms unbuckled his sword and called to a companion some distance below. Archibald strained every nerve to listen for a clash of steel or voices raised in anger but could hear nothing but the clatter of the soldiers on watch preparing themselves for action. Torn between a desire to know the worst and not desert his post he hovered at the head of the stairway.

"What's that?" he heard the man-at-arms shout to the man below, "The King is here? But he is — "

"The King? Here?" Archibald echoed.

"So it seems, young Douglas. Best put away your dagger and return to guard your lady mistress! Could be you'll have to defend her against a very unexpected visitor this night!"

Returning to his post, crossed between disappointment and a guilty relief Archibald, grinned in the semi-darkness. If James did seek his wife's chamber this night he would be bombarded with the curiosity of his fellow pages on the following morning; but even as his chest rose at the thought of his coming importance he exhaled on a long breath and knew he would keep his counsel and the Queen's secrets to himself.

Within the chamber Margaret lay unsleeping and oblivious of the various noises from the hall; despite the languor brought on by the day on the beach only her limbs were relaxed while her mind was flaringly awake. The transparent half-dark was disturbing, making her a prey to memory and a new awareness of herself. Alone in the soft bed she found she was lonely; not, she discovered for the life in England which had faded long day after long day from the forefront of her remembrances, but for James and the tenuous bond he had striven to create between them. She was bitterly cognizant that at their last meeting she had failed his need of her; when tenderly he had endeavoured to make love to her she had raised barriers out of a sheer perversity she could not understand herself. She had parried his skilled advances with a frigid politeness that had sent him ruefully away; not even the thought of him finding solace in the arms of a willing mistress melting the ice of her revulsion. Every excuse she could muster came to her rescue — she was too tired, her head hurt and always beneath it all was the lurking fear that she might miscarry as her mother had done and die. It was now weeks since he had brought her to Dunnottar and ridden off for Inverness and the castles of the Highland chiefs and as the days went by she had come to realize he was angry with her for the first time and — although she hated to admit it — with good cause.

Unlike her grandmother Margaret was not particularly religious; she felt no desire, as the Countess did, to spend hours upon her knees in damp and chilly chapels. This evening, however, she found herself praying for an ease of the unfamiliar restlessness to which she had fallen victim. Little by little the kindling flame in her brain spread to her body and she was forced to pace the room. Standing momentarily at one of the windows which had been filled with glass for her visit she could hear the murmur of the sea in flood tide against the rocks beneath. She almost cried aloud for the emotion invoked in her breast and went to the door to summon Alice to bring lights.

James met her as their hands fumbled the latch and she saw him in the light of the flaring flambeaux behind him, crowned with an aura that singled him out from the others who followed.

Margaret caught her breath; James heard the quick, involuntary gasp and with a deft movement shut the door behind him, slipping the bar of the lock. Margaret went to the bed, agitatedly searching for her bedrobe, but James forestalled her, taking her by the hands and leading her once more to the window.

"This half-dark is garment enough," he said softly, "let me look at you after my long absence."

But she was unable to stand still as his words created havoc with the excitement which had been growing within her all the day and she twisted away from him. Not, however, before James had registered the parted mouth and caught the faint starlight mirrored deep in her eyes. With a sixth sense born of much experience in overcoming female scruples he knew this was the moment to make his wife his own; wordlessly he caught her by the waist and none too gently pushed her across the bed and imprisoned her with his body. For the space of a few minutes she fought against him, turning and heaving, crying upon anyone within earshot to come to her aid until James covered her mouth with his. The parted lips now clamped in bonds of steel but relaxed gradually as James, with practised skill, stroked the smooth young flesh and changed the rhythm of protestation into acceptance.

With acceptance came a response that surprised him in its liberality; gone now was every vestige of the timidity plaguing their marriage. When he possessed her her hands tightened about his shoulders but she did not cry out or draw away from him.

While he murmured endearments she fell asleep in the compass of his arms, her hair covering them both against the chill of the brief night. Eventually he slept but was awake early as was his custom to find Margaret regarding him with an expression he had not hoped to discover on the face of his apathetic bride; quickly he kissed the wide, dilated eyes and drew her close. Now it was her hands that caressed, waking him from a drowsy half-sleep in a manner far more positive than the embraces of most of his mistresses. With murmurs of pleasure she met his love making, giving of herself with delight until he took her to a climax of shared mutual passion.

Afterwards, when the sun rose and filled the chamber with flame, they lay talking in an intimacy they had not known before. When he said he had matters to discuss with the statesmen who had accompanied him she was reluctant to let him go but summoned sufficient good sense to realize that when he promised her he would come to fetch her to dine with him in the Great Hall he would keep his word.

"What would you like to do then?" James asked as he stooped to tie the points of his hose.

"I should like to walk on the sands — but I don't suppose you would be inclined to such childish pastimes."

"On the contrary there is nothing I

should care for more and I shall probably bore you to the death with talking of the creatures that live beneath the rocks and in the pools below the castle."

"May we go alone?" The wistful note in her voice did not escape him and he came to kiss her as she lay propped against the pillows.

"Of course! Today is ours and tomorrow also!"

"Will you have to be gone again?" Anxiety replaced the languorous ease and James stayed long enough to reassure her before he went to summon Hepburn and the others to confer on the outcome of his visit to the Highlands.

During the morning, when tempers were fretted and James was both praised and strongly criticized for his leniency and trust in the proud Chiefs who a short time before had been his bitter opponents, he found his mind wandering from the absorbing topic of the subjection of the rebels and dwelling with delicious delight upon the events of the previous night. He chided himself for his weakness and with considerable effort concentrated on the matter of bringing Torquil Macleod, who still eluded capture, to justice.

Despite this discipline he contrived to bring the meeting to an early conclusion and excused himself.

"What eats him?" George Douglas asked. "A new hawk?"

"I would think it was rather a bird he has already entrapped," Bothwell replied laughingly.

"But the Kennedy did not accompany us, surely?"

"You are wide of the mark — it is not anyone we brought with us!"

"Well, which of the Queen's ladies — ?" Then as a new thought struck him George Douglas slapped his leather covered thigh and rounded on Bothwell. "You cannot mean the Queen?"

"And why not?"

George raised his shoulders.

"I have never shared your enthusiasm for the cold little fish but, by God's teeth, I hope you are right, man!"

Covertly watching Margaret as they sat in the Hall Bothwell knew he was not mistaken. Perhaps more than any of James's other companions he knew the King suffered from the lack of the consummation of his marriage; realizing perhaps that the man's pride was touched in failing — where he had succeeded so many times before — to arouse the Queen's passion. While James's sensitivity would grant him patience and sympathy beyond the ken of his more ruthless nobles he would still be unhappy in his wife's reluctance and the lack of an heir was something he could not hide from his court and subjects however bold a front he put on his domestic affairs. If, as Bothwell, suspected the King had overcome the scruples of fear which kept Margaret aloof from him he would have more cause for jubilation than if he had, personally, caught the Macleod and brought him to answer the charges levelled against him at his public trial last year.

Bothwell knew also that he would not be alone in speculating upon the relationship between the King and Queen; but Margaret's demeanour would give little away to a casual observer. She sat, dressed with care as usual, on James's left hand holding herself in the somewhat rigid pose she had undoubtedly learned at her father's court. As was her custom also she listened with polite attention to her husband and the Bishop of Aberdeen, William Elphinstone, who was probably trying to interest her in the matters of his University. The seventy year old cleric did not notice, as Bothwell did, the hand that hovered near that of James on the polished board or the wide-eyed glance she gave her husband from time to time. Bothwell looked away with difficulty for he found Margaret an absorbing subject of interest; she was, in his opinion, growing into a woman who might well be, in the not too distant future, a beauty with considerable charm. The latent sensuality he had surprised in her on the day of her proxy wedding three years earlier was more apparent now than at any time before and he had it on good authority that the Queen was curbing her childish petulance and developing a dominant will of her own. Neither of these factors he found surprising for she came of a stock possessing both strong-mindedness and in the case of her maternal grandfather, Edward IV, tremendous physical attraction and prowess which promised in their amalgam a flowering of Margaret's personality that could leave its mark on the House of Stewart. He found himself praying unconsciously that all might now be well between James and his wife, each finding peace and fulfilment within their joint marital orbit.

Bothwell was not as unique in his appraisal of the situation as he believed and both Gavin Douglas and William Dunbar were aware of the subtle change in the Queen's demeanour.

But they, and Bothwell, were to be amazed at the King's behaviour for James lingered at Dunnottar for almost two weeks. This in itself was unusual for he had ships commissioning in Dumbarton preparatory to setting sail for the Isles and had guns being assembled at Edinburgh to carry on board and he liked to superintend these important matters personally; yet this departure from normal was small compared with the other changes in his daily routine. Instead of hawking and riding through the hills in chase of deer James walked on the beaches and took the oars of a small coracle to row Margaret in and out of the rock-strewn headlands surrounding the castle. At night he declined the invitations of his cronies to play at cards and listened with Margaret to the sweet singing and playing of her minstrels in the Queen's apartments.

At the end of the first week of enforced idleness the poets and Bothwell were not alone in drawing their own conclusions from James's protracted stay in Dunnottar and with well-hidden amusement the Court settled down to enjoy the unexpected respite. There were those among his intimates who marvelled at the hours he spent in his wife's company because they had too often been awoken with only the faintest trace of dawn to speak of a new day and been summoned by James, fresh from the bed of a mistress, to take horse and follow him to some far distant town.

In the warmth of the King's attentions Margaret bloomed with health; the long hours spent walking or sitting in the stern of the little boat brought a golden glow to her pale cheeks and bleached highlights in the masses of hair which she wore unbound at the King's request. She would lean back, face lifted to the sun and salty air and listen while James told her of his difficult childhood. For the first time he spoke of his mother, Princess Margaret of Denmark, who had brought with her as part of her dowry Orkney and Shetland and who had died when James was thirteen at the tragically early age of twenty-nine.

"Who took care of you after your mother was gone?"

"James Shaw; he had been made my governor when I was born and had looked after me even when my mother was alive. As you know full well, from the history of your own family, a woman has to have the strong backing of a man to protect her interests from any enemies her husband might have and in my case there was not only the threat of an English invasion of Scotland but the very real menace of my abduction by my father's brothers."

"Was your father popular as a monarch?" The question would not have reached her lips a week before but now Margaret felt her new-found intimacy with her husband gave her strength to speak.

"Not very."

James took up the oars which he had let fall across his knees while he rested his arms and looking over his shoulder began to row rather more quickly than before. Margaret sensed she had offended him and tried desperately to think of some other topic. To her relief James stopped rowing and once more leaned on the oars and looked towards her.

"I have not talked with you about my father's death because I am too deeply involved with the cause of his murder even until this day to speak lightly of it; but now, for the first time, I should like to tell you how I came to the throne nearly twenty years ago. Would it weary you to listen?"

"Of course not! I know that your father was killed on the Field of Stirling and that you were only fifteen at the time but this is about the extent of what I have heard."

"Small wonder, the needs of those early days were pushed fast from men's memories!"

As he spoke the sun went behind

a cloud and, involuntarily, Margaret shivered. James, noticing the hurriedly suppressed movement retrieved his cape from the thwart behind him and handed it to her telling her to put it about her shoulders.

"My father," he began slowly, "was not everyone's idea of what a King should be; he was more fond of books and learning than hunting and following the time-honoured sports of archery and fencing and he did not often go abroad among his people."

"Is that why you move so much among them?"

"Yes — a King must have the interests of all Three Estates at his heart if he would govern wisely. My father could not be persuaded to see this and his subjects turned, quite naturally, I suppose, to Albany and Mar who were more forthcoming and attractive. This would have been well enough if my uncles had been content to bask in the popularity they received and help my father govern but unfortunately it came to the ears of the King that his brothers were plotting against him to

138

overthrow him from the throne and set up Albany in his place. Rumour had it that the rebels had a considerable number of the nobles behind them and witches and devil-worshippers enlisted in their unnatural cause. Frightened, as much by this weird threat, as by the more tangible one of losing his throne Albany and Mar were imprisoned in the castles at Edinburgh and Craigmillar. Inexplicably, Mar died and Albany escaped, leaping out at his guards, killing those who tried to prevent him and slithering to safety on a rope tied to his barred window. One of his attendants hurt himself in following his master and Albany stayed long enough to lift him and carry him the entire way to Leith where he took ship for France. Both the death of the Earl of Mar and the heroic escapade of Albany turned the scales against my father and before long the plotting to overthrow him was intensified."

"But who was to lead them if your uncles were absent?"

"My father not only had trouble within his own kingdom but was harassed by England. Your grandfather" — the upward quirk of his mouth and his rueful expression broke the unusual look of severity on James's face. "Your grandfather seized the opportunity and made overtures to Albany and sought to bring him to England — "

"Did he come?"

"He did! And with your grandfather's brother, Richard of Gloucester rode North and lodged themselves in Alnwick. My father knew battle was imminent and he sent to his nobles to muster under his flag, but almost to a man they refused to come and the King marched out towards the Border with a handful of those whom he liked to have about him in an almost hopeless attempt to stem the tide of the English advance. As if this was not bad enough the nobles who had refused to come to his aid followed up behind the King and at Lauder bridge took him prisoner and hung on high all his favourites. Now, with the Earl of Angus in charge the other rebel lords took my father to Edinburgh castle as an ignominious prisoner and laid the way clear for Albany and the English to come up to the very gates of the same city."

"To Edinburgh? This seems impossible!"

"But it is true," James told her grimly, "and had it not been for the Scottish lords falling out among themselves you might not be sitting here with me as King and Queen of the Scots! We were fortunate in that not all of the Earls wanted Albany as their new King and he was wise enough to see that even if he succeeded in taking the throne from my father his kingdom would be divided. I think he decided he must bide his time and he made a show of releasing my father and even of visiting my mother and me at Stirling. For one whole year he lived amiably with my father protesting his loyalty while he plotted secretly to fuse together the dissenting nobles and confront the King once more. My father discovered the truth and for once acted quickly and decisively and summoned Parliament. Albany fled to his own castle and thence to England; here he found Richard of Gloucester on the throne with sufficient of his own problems to keep him from helping Albany to wrest that of Scotland from its rightful owner. Albany refused to be put off the struggle to oust the King and he once more gathered an army and headed for the Border. This time the King's forces came to the aid of their monarch and sent Albany packing; he escaped to France — "

"And lives there still?"

"No, he was killed in an accident at a tournament, but he has a son, John, by his wife Anne de la Tour, who lives in France and occasionally performs offices for Scotland by visiting the Pope for us."

"You do not hate him?" Margaret asked, wide-eyed.

"For what? It was his father, not he who sought to overthrow my father and there are few living now who could say their hands were free from the blood of King James III — including my own."

Margaret only caught the last words dimly as James muttered them inaudibly to himself but she made no comment.

"My father appeared to have learnt his lesson and when he brought Elphinstone in to guide him it seemed as if all would go well. A peace was patched up with England and it was proposed I should marry a niece of Richard's.

Then Richard was overthrown and your father came to the English throne. He had reason to be grateful to Scotland for during his long exile in Brittany and France he had received much succour from Scots and also, like my father, he was peace-loving by nature. For the first time for many years ambassadors moved freely between London and Edinburgh. If only his home policy had been as wise as his attempts to be friendly with his neighbouring kingdom all might yet have been saved — or it could be that it was this overture to England that the still unsatisfied nobles saw as a move to sell Scotland and it was this in itself which hardened the core of rebellion — I do not really know. Who can tell what sets the flame to kindling wood and starts the fire when revolution is in the air?"

"But without a figurehead who did the rebel lords choose as a leader — Angus?"

"Not Angus," James told her softly, "but me!"

"You?" Margaret echoed incredulously. "How could they?"

"Very simply; Angus, Hume, Patrick Hepburn and others came to Stirling and persuaded Shaw to give me up to them and I went with them to Linlithgow where they had set up a headquarters against my father. From here they blockaded my father in Edinburgh castle until finally he escaped and faced them at Blackness on the Forth. Here the rebels put their case and my father, playing for time, agreed to their requests and said he would take them into his Council in place of those whom they mistrusted and loathed. Regretfully, I must admit, he did not carry out his promises and went back to Edinburgh to gather an army. From here he marched to Stirling and called Angus and the others to join him in battle. This they did and taking me with them, went out to give fight."

"My poor lord!"

"Poor indeed and a weak cavilling knave that had not the guts to stand out against my father's adversaries but went with them to his murder! For weeks after the battle I still hoped my father had escaped but they took good care to see this was not possible for when his remnant of devoted followers saw they had no hope of winning through they persuaded the King to ride for Leith and take ship. In his headlong ride he was thrown from his horse and taken, dazed and hurt, into the house of a miller in Bannockburn. Foolishly my father told his rescuer he was the King and demanded the man send for a priest. A lurking enemy, searching for the King, quickly pretended to holy orders and bending over the wounded James, despatched him with five sword thrusts deep into his chest."

"How horrible!"

While James had been recounting the story the skies had darkened and now a scurry of wind brought huge, warm raindrops that discoloured the floor of the boat.

"Don't look so sad," James said, heading round towards the towering cliff and pulling at the oars, "I bear the guilt, not you — "

"But I suffer on your account, my lord!"

"Do you, little Margaret? If that is truly the case the burden will fall less heavily on my shoulders."

"James?"

"Yes, my dear?"

"Is it for this reason you wear the chain of penitence always about your waist?" She had seen the steel links next to his bare flesh and had wondered what sin he could have counted so deep to warrant such punishment.

"Yes, I can never rid myself of the responsibility I feel."

"But you went as prisoner of the rebel lords!"

"That is quite right but as son of the King I should have refused to accompany them when they rode out against him. It is true I had no idea they intended to put him to death but I was old enough to realize they meant to set me up in his place. For this alone I stand condemned."

"Not in my sight."

James looked at her with an expression she had never seen before. At last he smiled.

"Thank you — I do believe you have gone a long way to restore some of my self respect."

The boat ground against the shingle and Margaret jumped ashore with the aid of the squires and attendants who had gathered to help them beach the dinghy. As they began the climb up to the castle the rain lashed down upon them from leaden skies.

Later that night when Margaret lay within the circle of James's arms he told her he must be leaving at dawn.

"But I go to Stirling and will have all prepared for you to come to me within the week — I shall miss you if you stay longer from my side."

7

IN Holyrood Palace the Queen had taken to her own apartments to await the birth of her first child. This long-hoped for event laid a mantle of expectancy over the royal residence and its inhabitants found no other topic of conversation held as much interest. Even the dank haar, swirling outside in long veils that obliterated the heights of Arthur's Seat, lost its significance and much of its recurring terrors as the women spoke in hushed whispers of the Queen's approaching ordeal and the men gambled on the baby's sex. The pessimists shrugged their shoulders and spoke dolefully of the thousand and one perils that might yet rob Scotland of an heir while the more optimistic looked with hope to the future.

Margaret half lay, half sat on an improvised couch in front of the fire that was kept burning night and day in her parlour. She could find no ease for the burden of the child that swelled her stomach and made movement difficult. She chafed also against the close-curtained room where every crack of window and door had been sealed to allowed no passage of air that might bring sickness or disease to her or the unborn infant. Many times, when her head and back ached, she thought of the freedom of Dunnottar and the happiness she had shared with James in the poignantly brief two weeks they had spent together. Since then they had been allowed only the intimacy of snatched days when James could be spared from his overwhelming round of duties. Had he been less conscientious her life would have been easier and Alice Davy had rounded on her on more than one occasion when she had given vent to a return of resentful petulance. Naturally emotional but trained from the cradle to some sort of discipline she now discovered the two sides of her nature at war. Her task had not been made any lighter by James's nearness during the Christmas reveleries at a time when her pregnancy precluded any marital indulgence. The final burden had been the letters from her grandmother in England stressing the need for her to observe, with absolute rigour, the rules laid down by the Countess for a Queen's lying-in. Margaret had regarded with near horror the exclusion of daylight and soon felt stifled in the chambers where candles burnt from dawn to dusk.

Elizabeth Barley and the other ladies of the bedchamber spent hours playing cards and miming playlets for her but she could not keep her concentration directed towards their efforts. Battling to keep her eyes open she would force herself to make the necessary moves on the new ivory-inlaid board James had given her while she longed to be rid of the cumbersome weight of her unborn child. Strangely, as the time of her delivery came nearer, she was not afraid; terrified to allow herself to become pregnant she discovered a well-being she had not believed possible. James also was all attention and stayed within easy riding distance of the Palace coming each evening to sit with his wife and play for her on the harpsichord. Bothwell found him edgy and distrait and realized that although James had been a father on several occasions before this was the first time he had been hopeful of an heir born in wedlock or so close to the mother-to-be. A born romantic it was obvious James would be hyper-sensitive at this critical juncture of his reign.

On the eighth day of February Margaret told her attendants she could no longer stay mewed up in the smothering atmosphere of her chambers and begged her physician to allow her a walk in the cloisters. He shook his head, not daring to go against the stringent precautions laid down by the Lady Margaret of Richmond, and suggested instead the Queen should inspect the baby's trousseau for any deficiencies. Margaret waved away the proposition and paced the flagged floor.

"Bring me my steward!" she commanded.

"We cannot do that, your Grace!" Alice said, braver than the rest. "At this time only your physician may come to you!"

"A murrain on what I can and cannot do!" Margaret retorted while her women exchanged glances for the ill luck engendered by speaking an oath at this moment. "If I am not allowed to have a man come to me — send me his deputy, the housekeeper."

Elizabeth Barley quickly went from the room and returned with the woman who took charge of the linen and bed covers.

"You wanted to see me, your Grace?"

"Yes, mistress, I wish you to superintend the replacement of the hangings on the walls and the bed; I am forced to stay here and I can no longer endure to look upon these tapestries with their smirking nymphs and gloating satyrs. Bring me instead some with hunting scenes and devices of birds and hinds."

"A very good idea," said Alice, "you come and sit over here and we'll set about the changing at once; it'll be as good as going outside to look upon something different."

But when the women, staggering under the heavy rolls of canvas, returned and began to put up the coverings Margaret could not remain idle and more than once changed her mind about the positioning of each piece. Only by constantly applying the soothing oil of her abundant common sense was Alice able to keep frayed tempers becoming open rebellion.

"Bear with her," she told Agnes Hepburn, daughter-in-law of Patrick, "she is showing the signs of being brought to bed in the near future."

"All this fuss," Agnes snorted, "when it would be easier to slip away quietly and give birth as I have done on more occasions than I care to count."

"Be fair! Important as your children are to you, they are not future Kings!"

"And just as well."

At last the change-over was completed and utterly exhausted Margaret took some broth and retired to bed.

Before the eerie dawn was breaking her cries had brought Alice and the others running to her side. She went into a difficult and protracted labour while the atmosphere in the shrouded rooms became heavy and foul with the press of women who thronged from chamber to parlour. At last the physician dismissed them all except Alice and Elizabeth and in growing apprehension, as the Queen grew weaker, waited.

Throughout the day and most of the following night Margaret wrestled to give birth, screaming with the pain that she thought tore her apart. Alice, cap awry, and more frightened than she cared to admit, held the girl's hand while Elizabeth mopped the pallid brow with rose water. Now and again Margaret took a few sips of wine but refused any food.

The watch had called midnight when, with desperate effort, she gave birth to a son. Utterly exhausted, all energy spent she lay back and could hardly smile when the physician told her the child was sound and healthy.

Elizabeth Barley took the baby, wrapped in flannel and summoned the nurses to take care of him. With several of Margaret's ladies she returned to the bedside of their mistress. Alice, looking up as they approached, saw the lines of fatigue making deep furrows on Elizabeth's face and suggested she tidied herself and went to break the news of his heir's birth to the King.

"You are worn out with this vigil and if I'm not mistaken we are going to have plenty to do in the next few days; you have taken the brunt of the burden, I think you should carry the good tidings."

"That is kind of you, Alice, but what of yourself?"

"I'll stay with her Grace; no doubt she'll be glad enough to have her old nurse near for the remainder of the night."

Washed and made comfortable Margaret lay motionless among the down pillows, her cheeks flushed with a hectic bruising that contrasted oddly with the bloodless mouth and waxen forehead. Her women tiptoed about but Alice doubted if the young Queen would have heard them if they had been wearing the wooden clogs they used at home to cross the middens in winter for Margaret seemed unconscious of her surroundings. Now and again she murmured as a wounded animal and the heavy eyelids flickered in involuntary movement.

Elizabeth Barley returned from the King with no sign of the exhaustion she had shown earlier and told the eager women who crowded round that James had kissed her for joy and given her a cup filled with gold pieces.

"He wants to come and see the Queen and the child."

"Let the day wear on somewhat and her Grace will be able to speak with him." This from the physician who had snatched some sleep and now returned to his patient.

James came when the short February afternoon was almost spent and went immediately to the bed where Margaret lay, now drained of all colour and very still. He looked at his wife and then, with startled dismay glanced up at her attendants clustered by the doorway.

"She is not dying?" he whispered to Agnes who had taken over from Alice. The woman shook her head and forced an encouraging smile.

"My lady has had a difficult and troubled labour, your Grace, by the morning she should be completely recovered and ready to speak with you."

"I had thought to tell her of my great joy," James said slowly.

"Your felicitations will keep until later," Agnes said briskly and then added a trifle lamely, "and be richer for the waiting."

James was reluctant to leave but when he saw Margaret was completely unaware of his presence he kissed her, lingeringly, on the forehead where the golden hair lay damp, and went away. Twice before nightfall he returned to enquire anxiously if there was any improvement in her condition and on hearing she had not stirred went to the chapel and stayed praying for an hour on end.

She smiled, weakly, at him on the second day but could only whisper half formed words through her cracked mouth. The baby was christened and given the baptismal name of his father and she was still too weak to do more than indicate the place where she had put the christening gift she intended for her son.

James sent for the physician who confessed he was worried about Margaret's condition.

"It is not only the weakness which is to be expected but the low fever which appears to have the Queen in thrall."

"Have you tried all your remedies?"

"Everything that is usual under the circumstances."

"Would it be of any use to try any of the concoctions I have brewed myself?" James asked.

"We could try anything that we could be sure would not harm her Grace," the man agreed.

Together they went to the stillroom and selected from among the earthenware jars on the crowded shelves potions that were noted in the book James kept as being beneficial in fevers and agues. Anxiously they waited to see Margaret respond to the treatment but saw, with hopeless inadequacy, no improvement in her condition. True enough, she was sufficiently recovered now to speak with James for a few moments each day when her brain was clear enough to allow her to communicate with him, but she grew thinner and could swallow only wine mixed with a little water.

In despair James announced he was going to make a pilgrimage to St. Ninian's. This desolate hermit's cell was situated on the coast of Galloway not far from the monastery of Whithorn.

The King had visited the place before when he had some special favour to ask of God and this time he intended to walk the entire way to make certain He would listen to James's importuning. Those who had been prepared to accompany the King changed their mind when they heard this condition of travel for they knew only too well that James could cover vast distances in the day.

Only four minstrels, fresh from Italy, showed any eagerness for the journey and with James and his suite they set out for the western coast of Scotland.

Margaret, listless and still suffering, bore his going with resigned fortitude and tried not to show she cared if he stayed or went. She was so weak it was impossible to feel anything very deeply and her day consisted of pain and its attendant miseries lightened by bleak glimpses of her new-born son. With difficulty she held him in her arms for a brief time each evening but those about her could see she had no special joy in the lusty infant who suckled greedily from the wet-nurse who had been hurriedly summoned to the Palace.

James, greeted all the length of his journey across Scotland by cheering subjects who applauded his concern for his wife's health, had been gone about a week when Margaret took a dramatic turn for the better.

She had spent a most restless and uncomfortable night, calling piteously upon Alice to bring her some relief from her suffering until that poor woman confessed she was approaching the limits of her patience. She was spurred on to comfort the luckless girl only by overhearing a conversation among some of the women that Margaret would be better dead than condemned to the permanent invalidism which seemed to be her future lot.

She was lying among the pillows, her hands twisting and plucking at the air when, quite suddenly she had grown quiet. Alice, creeping to her side, was afraid she slipped into death but discovered the Queen was breathing evenly and freely. Calling silent thanks to the Almighty, Alice sent Archibald Angus who was stationed outside the apartments to the kitchens for a skillet of weak broth to keep heated at the chamber fire. Her foresight was rewarded for when Margaret awoke more than two hours later the first thing she said was that she was hungry.

From this moment her condition improved rapidly and by the time James came back to Holyrood she was able to sit in a chair at the uncurtained window of her parlour and watch the seagulls float on the thin fresh winds of Spring.

She greeted him with joy and announced she was also going to St. Ninian's to give thanks for her child and her safe deliverance. If James seemed somewhat hesitant to comply with her wishes he immediately put in motion the necessary preparations to depart as soon as she was sufficiently fit to undertake the long journey.

"There is one thing of which I am quite certain," he told her ruefully, "We shall not be walking this time! I had nothing but complaints from the Italians for every mile of the way until in the end I was forced to send them back by horse; bah, call themselves men — they are nothing but foppish fellows who can do little else but make music."

"You like music, James!"

"Of course I do, but I can walk and ride as well!"

"Perhaps it was because you had a special reason for making the journey that made all the difference."

"Yes, I expect that was at the root of it. How can I ever tell you how very grateful I am to you for my son and heir? Dear Margaret, you have made me the happiest and most fortunate king in Christendom."

Leaving the baby behind in Stirling Castle, James and Margaret set out for the Galloway coast. James rode but the Queen was carried in a litter; before them went their offerings for the Chapel and pack-horses laden with their clothing and furniture.

Once more in the fresh air Margaret regained her colour and fresh vigour in her limbs; she was happy because the intimacy between herself and James was renewed and they chatted happily of the future and the visits they hoped to make with their infant son to Dunnottar.

St. Ninian's was all she had hoped, a

chapel set on a peninsula of land that was hazy in the warm winds of the western seaboard. The place had an atmosphere of dedicated reverence and it was easy to imagine the days, over a thousand years before, when the Romanized Briton had returned from wandering in France and Italy and set up his own haven of worship.

With a heart overflowing with gratitude Margaret knelt beside James and thanked God for his goodness.

After three weeks of meandering travel that was a replica of the days they had spent in Dunnottar, except that James did not seek her bed, they came to Stirling and climbing the steep hill to the grey castle went to their rooms and called at once for a sight of the baby James.

Delighted with his progress they both held him and admired the well-shaped head and the brightness of his eyes.

James left when the nurses came to take the child to his cradle and the women who had not accompanied her crowded in to talk about her journey and the events of the past month. She was pleased to be among them again and ready to take up the duties she had laid down during her pregnancy; they found her more animated than all the time of her marriage.

"Where did you go, your Grace?" Agnes Hepburn asked.

"Through Paisley to Ayr and Wigtown and many other places I do not remember clearly."

"You did not stay at Cassillis?"

Elizabeth Barley moved quickly to throw a log upon the fire and most of the women held their sewing needles for a second before plunging them again into their tapestries.

"I do not think so," Margaret replied, "but as I said, I do not recall all the Abbeys where we rested. Why do you ask?"

"For no particular reason — it is a place I have heard spoken of," Agnes replied smoothly.

"If you stayed at Ayr it is unlikely you went to Cassillis for they are too close," said Lady Hamilton. "Are you going to remain here for your supper or will you join the King?"

Margaret dined with the Court and retired early, tired after the travelling.

Archibald attended her to her chamber door.

"Archibald," she enquired curiously, "what is there at Castle Cassillis that should merit my attention?" There had been something in the way Agnes had asked about the place that had rivetted her attention to the matter and it had been on the tip of her tongue to ask James to tell her of it during the meal. She could not say why she had not been able to broach the subject.

Archibald regarded her with a puzzled frown.

"Cassillis, my lady? I cannot think of any reason why you should be particular interested — there is nothing of antiquity to warrant your regard as there is at St. Ninian's."

"Well, who lives there, Archibald?"

"Lord John Kennedy, I believe."

"Thank you," she said quietly while the palms of her hands were suddenly moist with sweat and her mouth was parched. As she undressed a dull, cold ache of pain began to trouble her breast while her brain repeated, "Kennedy — Kennedy!"

Surely Agnes was not trying to tell her that James had visited Janet Kennedy during the time of his pilgrimage on her behalf?

For days after their return she tormented herself with the thought of James making love to his old mistress while she lay and waited for him on a bed of sickness. At length she could no longer restrain herself. They were sitting together in a window seat in the Queen's parlour, but she still could not bring herself to ask James in a direct way.

"The little lady Lady Drummond seems to be making good progress with her sewing and the alphabet," she said as casually as she was able.

"I am glad to hear that," James said, regarding her quickly.

"Have you good news of" — it was begun now and she had to continue — "of James Stewart?"

"He does well with his tutors in St. Andrews. I hope when he returns he will be able to take his place among those who help me govern."

James stopped and took Margaret's hand.

"Why do you want to know?"

Margaret shrugged and bowed her head unable to speak. She did not want to hear any more; James had answered her question, for it was certainly from Janet Kennedy he would have had news of the bastard son she had borne him.

The pain that had been gathering in her breast over the last days tightened its hold of her, threatening to choke her and she stood up abruptly so that her embroidery fell to the floor. Without waiting to take it from James who retrieved it for her she rushed out of the room and threw herself on her bed in a storm of weeping.

From that moment her love for James underwent a change and week by week deepened into a near hate that refused him entrance to her bedchamber and made her depressed and lonely. She was hurt beyond endurance that while she gave so willingly of her affection James thought so little of her devotion that at the first temptation he returned to his former mistress. In frustrated hours of self pity she had difficulty in preventing herself praying for the death of Janet Kennedy. For the first time for over two years she longed to return to England to her father and brother and sister.

8

THE following eighteen months were to be the most painful of Margaret's young life. For almost a year she nursed the grudge of James's infidelity, growing daily like a nauseous tumour within her very soul. When he discovered, as it was obvious he would, in a very short time, the reason for her displeasure, James made every effort to recompense her for his fall from grace; but he laboured in vain for Margaret had put up an impenetrable barrier which even his accomplished charm could not penetrate.

It was as if the love, so slow in its awakening, went out as a fire that has a pail of water thrown upon its heart while the embers smoked and hissed in a dismal echo of the warmth that had once been.

Margaret would have found life easier if she had become indifferent to James. Hate him she might, as she told herself several times a day, yet she could not ignore him. Every smile he bestowed upon her waiting women, wives of visiting nobles or even servant girls was regarded by Margaret with suspicion until James confessed to Bothwell that his patience was sorely tried. When he later sought the beds of his mistresses with increasing frequency this petty tyranny was excuse enough without the refusal of the Queen to accept his advances.

Bothwell, plagued with aches in his back and legs and beginning to feel his age grew exasperated with both his royal master and mistress; romance seemed a very small part of the business of life that really mattered while pride was a sin that needed rebuke. He, with many others at Court, were at their wits' end to find a solution to the impasse that daily became more impossible, when fate took a cruel hand in the proceedings.

The heir to the throne was the only subject on which James and Margaret could converse with any amity and the daily visit they made to the nurseries was often the sole occasion on which they spoke civilly together. The little James, happily unaware of his parent's feud, developed from a red-faced caricature of an old man to a fat, chuckling baby who lay and kicked his feet in contentment. His smile alone appeared to ease the burning resentment within his mother's breast and his progress formed the tenuous bridge between her and James.

So it was a bitter blow when the child suddenly sickened with some unknown fever and died after two days of hopeless anxiety in the royal household. Margaret was prostrated with bewildered grief and shut herself away in her chambers while James went about the routine of government with a set, white face.

On the evening of the pathetic funeral James came to Margaret's apartments and motioned for her attendants to leave them. For some time it did not appear as if the Queen realized they were alone; she sat and gazed, sightlessly, into the fire apparently deaf to the overtures he made. In despair he filled two goblets with wine and brought them to the hearth; Margaret shook her head when he proffered her the drink and James drank both in quick succession. He paced the floor, his shoulders hunched in dejection until once more he returned to the fireside. He looked down at Margaret and saw tears coursing down her cheeks unchecked; pity accompanied his own frustrated sense of loss and he threw himself on his knees before her, burying his face in her lap and sobbing unashamedly. Shocked to hear him cry Margaret involuntarily put her arms about him to afford him some comfort and in a second he tightened his hold of her and cheek against wet cheek they clung together.

Some time later she allowed him to lift her to her bed where she suffered him to help her undress and get between the covers. He left her long enough to dismiss her attendants for the night and returned to her bedside to take off his own clothes and gather her into his embrace. She was asleep almost immediately and at length he found his limbs relaxing and a blissful forgetfulness overcoming him.

During the following week he spent a great deal of his time with her; delegating his considerable state duties and endeavouring to arouse her interest in the heavy burden of living without their child. If she was slow to respond at least the hate which had suffocated their relationship over the past year was gone and James was grateful for this small chink in the gloom.

He endeavoured to widen this glimmer by interesting Margaret in the improvements he was making in the castle at Stirling and the considerable extensions just begun on the Church of the Holy Rude outside the battlements. But, although she accompanied him to watch the footings being dug for the foundations of the new choir and helped him choose some designs for the ceiling in his audience chamber, he had to prompt her suggestions and constantly bring her attention to the matter under discussion. It was the same with Robert Spittal, the tailor of Stirling who made much of the beautiful clothing they both liked to wear; even when Robert held up silks that glowed with jewel-like brilliance Margaret made only a half-hearted attempt at interest.

At the month's mind to commemorate the child's death one of the Barton brothers, who were good friends of James as well as captains and builders of his ships, came up to him after the poignant little service in the castle chapel and asked him to bring the Queen to Airth where *The Margaret* — named for her — was undergoing a refit.

"The poor we lassie looks as if a breath of good salt air would help to blow away the miseries; wrap her up well and bring her down tomorrow." John Barton said with the ease of long standing friendship and respect that existed between the King and his family.

"I'll try," James answered, "but I'll not hold out much hope of success; when new dresses fail to lift the spirits one wonders what will have the power to help her."

He did not have to wonder any longer than the following day for Margaret accepted his invitation to accompany him to the harbour with an almost childish eagerness. He remembered then her affection for the sea and hastened to send for horses and a litter to carry them to Airth. Margaret waved away the conveyance and chose to ride at James's side; wisely he made no comment on the ashen face or the overwrought set of her brows and himself helped her mount the mare he sent for.

A sharp easterly wind blew down the Firth and James was glad he had insisted upon Margaret wearing a fur-lined, hooded cloak; but she made no comment on the cold and spoke hardly at all until they passed the few, turf roofed houses that lined the only road down to the berths where the ship lay.

On board, John and his brothers Andrew and Robert had obviously made some provision against the King coming to visit them and while they entertained James and Margaret with their choicest claret, despatched servants for cold fowl and oatcakes. The small cabin, which was almost filled with a desk where papers and plans were scattered in profusion, was warm and friendly and while the men talked Margaret looked round at the surprisingly rich furnishings and silver vessels hanging on hooks from the bulkheads.

"When will you be ready to sail?"

James asked Andrew who commanded *The Margaret*.

"Early next month and the sooner the better I shall be pleased! I can't wait to get my hands on these pillaging Portuguese pirates and their Flemish counterparts as well."

"Surely you can hardly call the Portuguese pirates!" James said laughingly. "Just because I have given you my backing to redress any wrong they perpetrated against your father it doesn't necessarily follow they are all plunderers!"

"That's as may be," Andrew growled, "but to my way of thinking once plunderers — always plunderers! Don't fret yourself, my lord, I'll not involve you in any trouble if I can avoid it."

"I'm glad to hear it, I have enough on my hands without a full scale war against the Portuguese." James was immediately reminded of the reason for their visit and glanced at Margaret to see if she had overheard his unthinking remark but she was engrossed in looking at some charts that Robert had spread out upon the desk.

"When will you be coming to inspect

the progress on *The Michael*?" This from John who was particularly involved in the building of the largest ship Scotland, and probably the rest of Europe, had ever laid down.

"I hope to go to Edinburgh in the near future and I shall not rest until I have been down to Newhaven to see what progress you are making. It is never far from my mind that one day I shall send a fleet to banish the Turks from the Holy places and start a modern crusade."

"My grandmother writes to tell me she would gladly go, even in the humble capacity of a washer woman, if it would mean the eventual restoration of Christianity to the lands overrun by the infidel," Margaret said, joining in the general conversation.

"Your grandmother seems a lady of remarkable courage, my lady," Robert said kindly.

"I confess I have not thought much of that, but it would seem she is brave enough if she would face the dangers of following an army to fight the Turks. But, James, you do not intend going yourself to the Holy Land?"

Whatever James might privately have hoped he now shook his head; he was searching for a truthful way of telling his wife he might lead a force at some future date when he was mercifully relieved by a steward coming to announce the meal was served in the larger mess cabin amidships.

Under the fatherly eyes of the Bartons Margaret ate more than she had done for a long time and when they climbed on to the deck to make their farewells she smiled to see the pale Spring sunshine lighting the foam-flecked water.

Returned to Stirling James was closeted with Elphinstone and he was not able to go to Margaret until late in the evening. He found her making a design for a cushion seat based on a drawing of *The Margaret* that Andrew had insisted she kept as a memento of her visit to the ship.

Admiring her handiwork he asked her quietly if he might return to her bedchamber after she had retired for the night. She was so long giving a reply that James thought she had not heard him and was about to repeat his request when she whispered he might come if he so desired.

In the brocade-curtained bed he made no move to make love to her and folded her against him like a child; he thought she slept and was beginning to feel drowsy himself when she startled him into complete wakefulness.

"James, do you love me?"

"Of course, you know I do!"

An overwhelming tenderness for the uncertainty that made her ask the question caught at James's throat and he tightened his arm about her; she sighed and relaxed in his embrace. Once more she was quiet and then when she spoke it was not of themselves but about her grandmother and namesake.

"Did you ever hear ought of romance concerning my father's mother?"

James, somewhat bewildered by this abrupt change of subject, smiled in the darkness.

"I don't believe I knew very much about her until your father came to the throne and then her fame as a very wise woman began to filter through even to the Scots; did I, perhaps, hear that she

179

had married your grandfather because of a dream she had had?"

"Yes, she told me that story herself but it wasn't about anything to do with her marriage that I am curious; it was rather to do with something she said to me when she was talking to me about coming north to wed you — "

"Did she tell you to prepare yourself to marry an ogre?"

"No; to the contrary she spoke of you with great kindness and when I said I would not come because — " she broke off and moved restlessly away from him.

"Did you say that?" James questioned gently.

"Yes." The voice was husky and defiant.

"Why?"

"Because she told me of the Lady Margaret Drummond and Mistress Kennedy."

When she blurted out the difficult words James had a sudden insight into much that perplexed him in his wife's attitude towards him and he pulled her against him, overcoming her resistance.

"Her wisdom was certainly no legend if she tried to make your task easier! Did you not realize that from the very beginning I was trying to tell you that I would make every effort to give you happiness?"

"Yes, perhaps I did." The admission was wrung from her.

"You must have realized that I could not have reached the age of thirty without having given my heart to somebody during that time and when Margaret Drummond died I was prepared to shower you with affection. Did I fail?"

"There is still Janet Kennedy," she said very low, against his chest.

Janet Kennedy! Witch of a woman that she was, James knew he was a fool where she was concerned and the hours he snatched to bed with her when he had made pilgrimage to St. Ninian's had been transports of sensual pleasure that had lingered for days after he had parted from her. Pleasure that had been further titillated, he ruefully admitted, by the knowledge that old Bell-the-Cat was still anxiously trying to marry the girl. James could not face the prospect of lying to his wife and he said very quietly: "You denied me your bed, what would you have me do?"

He was prepared for an instant withdrawal from his embrace but instead Margaret took his hand in her own and cradled it against her cheek.

"Forgive me."

"Very gladly — but for what?" This girl would never cease to surprise him.

"I am a fool to grasp for these things beyond my reach when I have so much within my compass already. If I remember that was the advice my lady grandmother gave me and I have been slow to take advantage of her counsel."

She turned her face towards James and he kissed her, very tenderly, on the mouth. Once more he thought she was asleep when she said, drowsily, "I wish I knew what it was she was trying to tell me about the man she loved and could not marry."

"You'll have to ask Hal when you see him!"

"Do you think I ever shall?"

"Perhaps; who knows."

Why Hal? she thought vaguely as she

182

drifted to sleep. Of course it would be because her grandmother was now very old and her father would not make the long journey north to visit her in her husband's kingdom and only Hal was young and capable of coming one day in some unknown future. That meant, her tired brain registered, that she would probably never see either the Lady Margaret or her father again; but then, she had always known that and now, suddenly, within the safe keeping of James's tender embrace, it no longer mattered as much as it did.

After four years of marriage she was beginning to grow up.

9

IN later life when she tried to recall the tenor of her relationship with James during the years that led up to the disaster on the field of Flodden, Margaret found it was impossible to remember her exact feelings when so much was taking place, both in their personal lives and in the affairs of Scotland, England and France. She could only surmise that in the face of family tragedies and the crumbling of the very alliance her marriage had sealed, their erstwhile disjointed propinquity developed into a mutual understanding.

During 1508 James was the most feted monarch in Europe, taking over from Henry VII who grew more avaricious as his health failed and the years took their toll. Louis of France, playing on James's interest in the sending of a crusade to the Holy Land, sent ambassadors to Scotland to enlist his support in a revival of the 'auld alliance' and the occasion was marked with pageants and jousting in which James himself took a leading part.

Margaret was expecting a child once more and she sat in a splendidly hung box and watched as her husband entered the lists and acquitted himself with considerable skill against his French visitors. Margaret was certain James saw himself as a Christian Champion not unlike the noble Arthur from whom the Tudors claimed descent and she willingly agreed to call the expected child by the name which had also been given to her much loved older brother.

Some weeks before the child was due Margaret went with James to Lochmaben to wait in its peaceful surroundings for the birth; but unfortunately the baby was a girl who died almost immediately. Now the Queen was beset not only with the ills that seemed inevitable with her confinements but the despair that she would ever bear a living healthy child.

Death seemed an integral part of the pattern of Margaret's existence when in the following April her father died and her grandmother two months later.

Margaret could hardly believe that the boy with whom she had shared her childhood was now King of England; her grief for the loss of both the people who had made up the substance of her young life would have been greater than it was if it had not been for the knowledge that she had again conceived and had hopes of bearing the only heir to both kingdoms.

The unreal quality of her life at this time was enhanced by the marriage of Hal to Arthur's widow, Katherine of Aragon. During all the time she had lived in Scotland there had been a seething mass of unconfirmed rumours concerning the future of the Princess of Wales; it had even been mooted that Henry VII intended to take her for a wife but Margaret had been unable to reconcile this preposterous plan with the image of her father and mother's life together.

She had closely questioned Dr. West, her father's emissary, when he had come to Scotland to explain his master's detention of the Earl of Arran and Sir Patrick Hamilton as they had tried to pass through England without a safe conduct on their way to the Court of King Louis. Dr. West, more worried by James's refusal to give him an interview than by the matrimonial state of Henry or Katherine of Aragon, could only tell Margaret that her father certainly had no plans for remarriage at the moment and that Katherine of Aragon was comfortably housed close to wherever the English Court was in residence.

"There is still talk of her marrying with Hal?" she asked the envoy.

"Papal dispensation has been sought but yet the marriage has not taken place; I do not know for what reason."

"Could it be because Hal is not prepared to wed with his brother's widow?"

Dr. West had looked away, unable to decide if it was his place to discuss the academic question of whether Arthur's and Katherine's marriage had been consummated with the sister of the bridegroom, and had made some banal and noncommittal reply.

"I believe there was some talk that the Lady Margaret, Countess of Richmond and Derby was opposed to the idea," he had murmured later as the thought occurred to him.

"Was there?" Margaret had asked more sharply than seemed necessary.

Now, in 1509, both Hal's marriage to Katherine and his coronation were accomplished deeds. The treaty of peace between Scotland and England which had seemed in some jeopardy when Henry VII had detained the two Scots on their way to France was reaffirmed with brotherly letters passing between James and Margaret's brother.

In truth James was too taken up with his plans to lead a campaign against the Infidel to have any animosity towards or armaments of any kind at hand to spare for use against England. He was pushing on with schemes to enlarge his navy and was tearing down huge tracts of forests in Fife and elsewhere to build his ships.

Nor were his dreams for the future his only concern. The Bartons, true to their promise of ridding the seas around Scotland of pirates and sending James from time to time barrels of the heads of their victims as proof of their boast, had fallen foul of the Portuguese by taking one of their ships and commandeering the cargo which happened to be owned in part by an Englishman, a Fleming and a Frenchman. James heard this disturbing news as he waited at Holyrood for Margaret to give birth to their child. At any other time he would have been infuriated by the foolish action of his trusted friends but Margaret's coming ordeal and the hope of an heir pushed the piracy almost from his mind.

To the great joy of James, Margaret and the kingdom the baby was a healthy boy. In jubilation he was christened Arthur. When she recovered from the birth, which she did with more speed than ever before, Margaret wrote to Hal telling him about the child and asking her brother what had become of the legacy left her by Arthur and intended for her on her father's death. Hal wrote her an affectionate letter congratulating her on the birth of an heir and making promises for the despatching of the valuables she mentioned. Once or twice she had spoken of the matter to James and he had smiled indulgently and told her she had baubles enough and surely need not press her brother for more. She was inclined to agree but had told him she wanted the jewels more for sentiment than for anything else and decided not to worry him further if she should again write to Hal on the subject.

James now felt free to renew his overtures to the Pope about mounting an army for the Crusade but had to display the most diplomatic prowess when Louis wrote to him asking that the army he had ready to fight the Turks should be lent to Louis to fight his enemies in Europe. This James might have done willingly if it had not been for the fact that Louis was using his army to fight the Pope. James saw the wisdom of retracting his offer and devoted more of his energy to keeping law and order within his own borders; with a son to cherish and rear for the throne nothing else was of such importance.

But once again the fates were inveighed against James and Margaret and the little boy died when scarcely a year old. Their grief was pathetic, touching even the hearts of the most sophisticated courtier; nor was the absence of their intimate friends felt more keenly than at this time. The loyal and trusted Bothwell had died in 1508, while Elizabeth Barley had married and Alice had been stricken with some disease which crippled her joints and made it impossible for her to serve her mistress. Young Angus had also left court to marry and his grandfather and father no longer appeared either socially or at Council meetings since old Bell-the-Cat had raided the Kennedy castle and carried off Janet to make her his wife.

This wedding probably marked the turning point in Margaret's own marriage for from this time on she felt almost certain that James was faithful to her. She could not be sure if this were because no other woman interested him as Janet had done or if it were a severe fit of conscience that struck him down. The year had been marked with strange and wonderful happenings in the heavens during which time a comet of remarkable brilliant had trailed a sweeping train of light across the night sky for weeks on end. The superstitious read all manner of evil portent into the omen and when the heir to the throne died it seemed as if their frightened prophesies were coming true.

On the advice of the Queen's physician who was afraid for the unhinging of Margaret's mind if she were allowed to brood on the death of yet another of her children James took her with him to the shrine of St. Duthois. Here they both prayed for forgiveness of past misdeeds which had led to the punishment of the death of their babies and another chance to produce an heir.

Their prayers were answered and their grief slightly allayed by the discovery that Margaret had conceived once more and should be brought to bed in the Spring of the following year.

They came back from the pilgrimage in time to receive ambassadors from Hal who came north to explain to James the naval engagement which had taken place shortly before in which the English had given chase to a Scottish vessel which they suspected of piracy. During this brief battle Hal's Admirals, the Howard brothers, had succeeded in destroying one of the Bartons' ships and killing Andrew, who was the captain.

James, despite the death of his heir at about the same time, had been deeply angered by what he could only think of as an outrage against his shipping and had written a strong protest to his brother-in-law. By the Treaty he had signed with England he knew (whatever his captains had been about) that he was in a position to have the Howards tried before the next meeting of the Warden Court that presided over differences of this kind.

Although James hid what happened next from Margaret he was completely surprised by Hal's decision to free the crew who had been taken prisoner by the Howards as a result of the engagement and the letter which Hal wrote to him rebuking him querying his right to denounce the Bartons' men as pirates.

"Insolent young puppy!" James said indignantly when the ambassadors brought him the news. Insolence which was not made any easier to bear when James discovered that the Howards were clamouring for Hal to declare war on Scotland as a reprisal for the Bartons' acts of piracy.

193

Quite suddenly, without warning, the peace which had for so long prevailed between Scotland and England was threatened; James heard with disquiet that Henry of England was sending armed men to garrison the border fortress. Indignant and also very worried James increased his pressure upon his ship-builders and armourers and sent a messenger to the Pope saying that as King Henry of England had violated the peace treaty existing between them by killing his subjects and imprisoning others he, James, was no longer bound to adhere to the terms of the treaty.

James kept his preparations from Margaret but he could not hide his anxiety from her and when she pressed him to tell his troubles begged the question by asserting that the Bartons had been causing him some trouble with their action against Portuguese ships. Margaret seemed satisfied with his explanation and James gave commands for players and minstrels to come to Holyrood and entertain his wife.

Dunbar wrote a play for the household to give before the King and Queen and

Margaret was much taken with the performance of the young Sir David Lindsay, who, dressed in blue and yellow taffeta, took one of the leading parts. She sent for the youthful actor after the performance and congratulated him upon his fine singing voice and the polish of his character acting. David Lindsay accepted the praise with refreshing grace and an absence of conceit which impressed Margaret. He stayed talking with her for some time and later, on many occasions, came with Dunbar to sing or read to her.

James was glad enough to find her made happy by their company as he wrestled with the problem of the quarrel which threatened to break off his country's relations with England. He was genuinely troubled to fall out with Margaret's brother yet felt he could not allow this young man, so much his junior, to insult him by killing his admiral and imprisoning good Scots.

In April, 1512 Margaret gave birth to a child who was baptized James. Unlike her other children this one was fair and plump and suckled well from the outset; unlike the others also he slept contentedly and Margaret kept his cradle constantly at her side, going a hundred times a day to peep into the fleecy blankets where he lay in rosy sleep. With James's permission she appointed David Lindsay to be his usher and the young man proved utterly trustworthy; when the Court moved to Stirling in the May after the birth it was David who superintended the immense amount of work involved and Margaret confessed to James that all had gone more smoothly than she could ever remember. James was only too delighted for her to be happy and encouraged her to rely on Lindsay for support.

She had been at Stirling for a few days when Dr. West, now an envoy of her brother's, came to offer his master's congratulations on the safe delivery of Scotland's heir. Margaret was pleased to have this opportunity of finding out how her brother and sister in England were faring. After they had eaten dinner in the Great Hall of the castle she sent for Dr. West to come to her in her parlour.

Margaret had wine poured for them and

then dismissed the page who served them; she eagerly questioned the ambassador about Hal and Katherine and Mary who was now growing up but she sensed somehow that West was not as forthcoming as she remembered and a slight constraint fell between them.

The man offered his own congratulations upon the birth of the Prince and asked, rather stiffly, if he might be permitted to see the baby on the following day. Margaret agreed willingly and once more the conversation faltered; she now embarked upon the tedious matter of the legacy which she still had not received from Hal and which she believed to be the second reason for Dr. West's visit.

"May I ask if you have brought my brother's bequest to me, Dr. West?" she said pleasantly.

"No, my lady, and shall not if the King of Scots breaks his promise to honour the treaty of peace between our two countries." Dr. West's face was suddenly suffused with purple and he was breathing hard as he sat back in his chair. Margaret regarded him stupidly, as if her ears misheard.

"I do not understand you, sir!"

"My meaning is plain, Madam; if the King of Scots persists in war, the King of England, my master, will not only keep the legacy but will take from him the best towns he has in Scotland!"

Margaret was stunned; her pulses began to race and in order to cover her confusion she stood up hurriedly and moved towards the window. As she did so the curtain over the door was pushed aside and James came into the room with Elphinstone and the Earl of Arran. As if nothing untoward had happened West stood and making his excuses withdrew.

It was late before Margaret could ask James what the man meant by his rudeness to her; she had been in bed some time before he came to her and when he put out his arms to embrace her she held herself aloof.

"What is it, my dear?" James asked anxiously, "you are not feeling unwell?"

"I am quite well," she said huskily, "but I am so worried!"

"About what? Surely not our little James? he looks bonnier by the hour I am sure."

"No, not that James — it is about my legacy."

"Oh, surely, not that all over again! I thought you had agreed to drop the matter."

"It doesn't concern the actual jewels but it is what Dr. West said to me — "

"What did he say to you?" James voice was sharp in the darkened room.

"He said . . . " Margaret hesitated; the enormity of what the man had actually said overwhelming her.

"What did he say?" James asked with quiet urgency.

"He said I should never have my legacy while you intend making war upon England — oh, James, what can he mean? Surely you would never dream of going to war with Hal! Tell me it isn't true!"

"I wish I could, little sweeting, but there are times when a country's honour is at stake — and this is one of those occasions." He sounded tired and distant.

Margaret sat up in bed and agitatedly fumbled for the curtains to draw them back and let in the light of the oil lamps burning over against the wall. She looked down at James in the pale glow.

"Tell me I am dreaming," she beseeched him. "Don't tell me that after all these years my marriage to you has been in vain! Oh James!" The throaty voice was blurred with the tears that began to seep down her cheeks.

"Nothing has been in vain; you and I are happy together and have a son and heir. For his sake I must keep Scotland strong. What inheritance will there be for him if I allow anyone to trample upon us?"

"Hal would never do that to you!"

"I cannot be sure what he will do; Lord Dacre who came with Dr. West tells me that your brother is intending to claim the pension from King Louis that France has owed to England since Eleanor of Aquitaine brought her dowry to Henry II."

"However ridiculous that might seem to you, it cannot possibly have any significance to Scotland!"

"But it has."

"Why has it?" Margaret demanded, suddenly very afraid.

"Because I have recently renewed my age old alliance with the King of France and his enemies are mine."

"I don't believe you — I can't believe you! What are you saying? What have you done?"

In that moment as he heard his wife cry out against him James wondered — not for the first time — what he *had* done; his anger against Hal for the murder of Andrew Barton had cooled slightly and the enthusiasm with which he had sent his allegiance to Louis did not burn as brightly as it had done at the time but he knew that if he did not assert himself now Scotland was lost as a power in Europe.

The charm with which he had engaged the affections of the women who had loved him during the thirty-nine years of his life came to his rescue.

"Dearest Margaret, all I have done is safeguarded the future of our son; you would not have him brought up in constant danger of losing his inheritance, would you?" As he spoke he turned towards her, stroking her back as he would have gentled one of his hawks, and was rewarded with hearing her sigh as she nestled against him.

"Don't go to war with Hal, James, I cannot bear to think of you taking up arms against my brother. You have brought so much prosperity to Scotland that you cannot be thinking of throwing it all away on such a foolish pretext as a pension that was first granted hundreds of years ago!"

"Well, it isn't only the pension," James said sleepily and a little crabbily, "there is the question of the withholding of your inheritance."

"I don't care a jot for that if it means going to war to obtain it."

"You are right, dearest, but I will not be threatened by young Hal — or anybody else for that matter — and, if it is any comfort to you I haven't yet signed the final draft of the treaty with Louis."

"Oh, I am so glad; now I can sleep in peace."

Yet she was never to know complete peace of mind again for while Dr. West lingered in Scotland and attempted to force James to give up the projected

French alliance and James kept him in suspense, Margaret was also a prey to doubt and fears for the future.

She heard with sorrow that Hal was indeed preparing to invade France and made enquiries that convinced her that James was pressing forward with his own warlike activities. Her only consolation was the thriving child who grew daily and eased her anxieties with the comfort of his sturdy body as he jumped and crowed on her lap.

On her twenty-third birthday in a gale that blew the shutters from outside the windows into the moat beneath the castle walls a French ship dropped anchor off Leith. It brought the ambassador of France with his monarch's treaty for James to sign. Louis realized that someone had to force the moment of decision upon the King of the Scots and he meant that man to be himself.

As Margaret watched the vast store of gifts the French King had sent with the ambassador being displayed for James and her to see she could not restrain the shiver that went through her. Elphinstone, who stood at her elbow, noticed her huddle into her cloak and put his arm out for her to lean upon.

"Your Grace, I too, am against the path which the King intends to follow and I shall do my utmost to prevent him setting out."

But she could not rid herself of the presentiment of evil that gradually became part of her daily life and by the beginning of the New Year was sick in body and soul. Plague was rampant in the boroughs and at the same time as James sent out notices calling his men to practice their archery and swordplay he made a proclamation promising death by hanging to anyone who was unwell and tried to come among other people in the towns.

The French ambassadors returned to Louis in February; they had no sooner left the Forth than Dr. West rode into the city of Edinburgh with letters from Hal begging James to settle their differences.

James received West courteously and sent him home with brotherly letters to the King of England. Margaret, slowly recovering from her illness, could only hope her husband intended to abide by the sentiments he expressed but was very much afraid she hoped in vain.

10

THE Palace of Linlithgow was in a turmoil of excitement; Scotland was preparing for war.

The unsettled peace which had struggled to survive throughout the spring and summer of 1513 had finally collapsed when James had taken the decision to despatch his fleet to the aid of his ally, France. All had known there was no other course open to him once Henry of England had sailed against Louis and was laying siege to French towns while his army pushed daily into the interior of his enemy's country.

Margaret, the wise Bishop Elphinstone and, strangely enough, Old Bell-the-Cat, who had recently taken to coming to Court again, were the only people to oppose James in his plans to aid Louis. The younger nobles were as eager as their King to set forth and attack England from the rear while she was engaged in a war with France. This was the classic moment at which to launch such a campaign and James's call to arms was enthusiastically taken up by his commanders.

Throughout the time of suspense which had existed, letters had been sent to and received from Hal. Margaret's brother had written to James in the most affectionate terms and James had answered with cordial sentiments that were only faintly overlaid with criticism that Henry should harbour thoughts of war against Louis and cling to the jewels that were really due to his sister. James had sent the most sincere sympathy to the ageing, but still valiant Surrey on the death of his son, Sir Edward Howard, in the first raid the English had made on the French.

Margaret had seen this magnanimous gesture as a sign of her husband's intention to call off the animosity between Hal and himself, for it was Howard who had been responsible for the death of Andrew Barton. But she was to be bitterly disappointed for James meant to do no such thing and even when Henry wrote saying if James would retreat from his purpose he, Henry, would declare the baby James, Duke of York and heir to the throne of England, James refused to budge from his stubborn path to war.

In vain did Margaret plead with him to think again of the consequences of his action, calling his attention to what would become of Scotland if he should lose any attack he mounted against the English.

"Lose?" James had echoed incredulously, "I have no thought of such a thing! I shall be able to call upon about a hundred thousand men and we have the Navy and all the armaments that we have been preparing over the years in the arsenal at Edinburgh. Besides you are forgetting that Henry (the intimate pet name of Hal had been dropped) has taken vast forces with him to France."

"You do not think he will leave behind him a strong army to protect the country?"

"Of course he will do that! But it is bound to be a weaker force than the one he will employ in France and the men I shall take against him are well trained in the Border warfare in which we shall challenge them. Stop worrying yourself about what is man's business and go and play with Jamie."

It was easy enough to accept him at his word and go through the pleasantly furnished rooms in the new Palace to the nursery above her own bower and sit on the floor to watch the beautiful babe her son had become; yet it was not so easy to push from her mind the thought of what this hateful war involved. It was bad enough for a man to set forth to try and conquer his brother-in-law's country but to call out half the adult male population to wage that war was both foolhardy and extremely dangerous. The plague which had been rife for over a year had taken a heavy toll of life and it was inevitable that however the fighting ended many more men would lie dead on the fields of battle. This seemed, to Margaret's womanly mind, an utter waste and she could not bear thinking about the fatherless bairns and the lonely widows who would remain.

On the evening before James left to issue the final summonses for his army to attend him on the Boroughmoor outside Edinburgh in about ten days time Margaret and he walked in the long twilight beside the loch. This kind of intimacy had become more and more rare as James pushed ahead with his martial plans and Margaret had been more than a little surprised when he had agreed to accompany her. She had heard from David Lindsay that the day's session of the Council had been a particularly stormy one and she had thought it possible James would leave for Edinburgh as soon as they had eaten dinner. She was, therefore, very happy to have succeeded in persuading him to spare her at least an hour of his company.

The sun was sinking behind the Palace as they set out on the walk around the loch and it threw the battlements and high towers into dark relief.

"It may be that Linlithgow is not as romantic and isolated as Dunnottar but it has a great charm of its own, don't you think, James?"

James gave her the first look in weeks that really saw her as a person and he smiled with genuine pleasure.

"I suppose Linlithgow is my favourite

home but now that you recall the pleasures of Dunnottar to me I am persuaded that there, above anywhere else, I have been most happy."

"Do you really mean that?" she asked tremulously.

"Yes, I do and if it pleases you when I have made this mission into England I shall come and fetch you from here and we shall go to Dunnottar before the winter begins."

James put his arm about her waist and with a return to the ease of their earlier relationship Margaret rested her head on his shoulder and listened while he pointed out the birds nesting in the reeds at the water's edge and the fish leaping after the myriad of flies that swarmed over the darkening surface of the loch.

He climbed the turnpike to her chambers sending a page to inform his attendants that he would ride to Edinburgh with the den and at her door sent her ladies away.

"This night I shall put my wife to bed," he told her lightly, and turned to the hearth where a small fire crackled with pleasant warmth, "Come and sit down while I play to you."

James poured wine from the silver ewer on the table against the wall and kneeling proffered it to Margaret who sipped it while she sat back, staring into the flames. When he took the lute from the corner of the room and began to play a musical version of one of the poems Dunbar had composed especially for her she looked at him with a deep, penetrating gaze that he found strangely disturbing. The tune finished he dropped the lute and lifting Margaret in his arms carried her to her bedchamber. He made love to her with great tenderness, possessed by some emotion he had never before experienced and when she slept lay awake staring into the magnificent, starlit sky. She woke shortly afterwards with tears streaming down her face and clutched him to her breast in an agony of fear.

"James, James, don't leave me — don't leave me! I have had the most horrible dream where I saw you plunge over the cliffs at Dunnottar and lie mangled and horribly mutilated on the rocks beneath.

Oh James, hold me close, I am sure this is a sign you should not undertake this hateful contest with my brother's kingdom!"

He comforted her, assuring her dreams were only projections of fear engendered by the thoughts of the day, but she was a long time in relaxing and she had only just fallen asleep again when he had to steal away to ride to Edinburgh.

When she awoke, recalling with misery the fantasies of the night, she propped herself against the pillows and tried to think of some way in which she might persuade James to remain at home and not embark on the senseless war to which he was committed. Margaret felt exceedingly guilty that the matter of her legacy had been so enlarged that it now formed a part of James's quarrel with Hal and she now knew a hopeless urgency to discover some method of making reparation. If she had been more religious she would have made a retreat for a week of prayer as James did during Lent when he lived with the monks in Stirling but — Suddenly as she wallowed in torturous self-disgust she was presented with a bold idea that just might dissuade James from setting out to do battle. Leaping from her bed she rang her silver handbell for her attendants and began pulling on the clothes which James had unceremoniously thrown over a stool.

Impatiently she waited for her hair to be arranged under the pearl-adorned velvet cap and when it was completed she sent for David Lindsay and stood at the window of her parlour preparing what she was going to say to him. David came in, tall, loose-limbed; his face beneath the intelligent forehead pleasant featured and open. He bowed to Margaret and she motioned him to sit with her at the window.

"David," she began a little breathlessly, "Would you say my lord, the King, is more given to belief in the supernatural than most men?"

The young man regarded her with his head on one side while he weighed up the significance of her question.

"I believe it would be correct to say His Grace puts some store on omens and signs — perhaps in excess of what the average person might do. Why do you ask, my lady?"

"Before I answer you, Sir, I must tell you that I am greatly troubled in my mind about the King's intention to make war on my brother's kingdom. While I have made more fuss than was probably necessary about my legacy it was due rather to the sentiment behind the matter than the value of the jewels and now that my husband adds this to the list of his grievances I am caught up in the whole preposterous business. We are guilty before God of a crime akin to that of Cain's murder of his brother if we embark against the English and I would do anything to prevent the army setting forth!"

"What have you in mind, your Grace?"

"I want you to tell me who you think is the best actor among the lesser known players who take part in your mimes and charades; not someone who acts the great characters but one whom you consider to excel in a minor role. Is there a man of that calibre?"

Margaret's expressive eyes were haunted with fear and, not for the first time, Lindsay was moved with compassion for her; she had suffered much in the ten years she had been Queen, with her health far from good, to say nothing of her husband's faithlessness and the loss of three of their children. Lindsay saw also that Margaret had become an attractive woman as she matured, losing the plumpness which had marred the contours of her face and figure. He had hoped as Jamie thrived and the King gave up his liaison with Janet Kennedy that the Queen might have a real chance of happiness but James had chosen this moment to begin his preparations for war; this was probably inevitable as the kingdom was enjoying a peaceful prosperity hardly known within the country since the time of the first James and the King was bound to look beyond his borders for wider scope to his ambitions. It seemed a great misfortune that James should choose his brother-in-law as an enemy rather than pursue his ambition to rid the Holy Land of the infidel. David, well schooled and a scholar of St. Andrew's University, could see no logic in the King's action when it was widely known about the Court that

Henry VIII had promised to make the wee Jamie Duke of York and heir to the English throne if his marriage to Katherine of Aragon remained childless. What unseen demons pushed the King of Scots in his unworthy pursuit of glory-by-conquest? This vexed issue brought David back to the matter the Queen had broached and as he replied he admitted to himself that whatever she had in mind intrigued him.

"There is young Archibald Angus, returned to Court now that his wife died in childbed — "

"I was indeed sorry to hear of that," Margaret interrupted, "but both of them so young it was perhaps hardly surprising; had not Bell-the-Cat heirs enough that he must push his grandson into marriage before he is out of skirts?"

"Perhaps with Gavin in the Church the house of Douglas is concerned for the future with only two males to carry on the line!"

"They are sufficiently proud to feel Scotland would suffer if they were not present to do their share of government — but I digress from the subject. Young

217

Angus is too well-known for the task I have conceived; tell me of someone else."

"There is a groom who tends the horses I ride, a born mimic who can hold his fellow servants spellbound with his storytelling," David said slowly.

"He sounds the very man!" Margaret exclaimed. "What age is he?"

"About fifty, I would think, slim built and balding."

"Excellent! Listen and I shall tell you of the plan I have in mind and then you may go and fetch the fellow that we may rehearse him."

James returned to Linlithgow to make his farewells to his wife and child before setting out for the Boroughmoor and Ellem in Berwickshire where the entire Scottish army was to muster. He arrived in the early morning and announced he was to leave after a service of intercession in St. Michael's Kirk the same evening.

He gave up the day to Margaret and Jamie, walking with them on the sloping lawns outside the Palace and when the babe had been put to bed talking with Margaret in her apartments.

Although Margaret sent for food for them to eat together she found she could swallow nothing and contented herself with a few mouthfuls of wine. James grew quieter as the time to leave for the service drew nearer.

"Come with me to my bedchamber," he asked her, "I have something I wish to show you."

In the chamber James pushed aside the rushes from the floor in one corner and revealed a large trap door; much mystified Margaret followed him down the steep stairs to a stone walled chamber. Here, piled from floor to ceiling were boxes bound in iron; choosing one at random James took a key that hung from a chain about his waist and beckoned her to look. Margaret saw a gleaming hoard of coins and caught her breath at the vast amount of money that must be contained in the chest.

"This is my treasure house," James told her quietly, "I am confiding in you in case I should not return from this fight against the English borders — "

"Don't say that!" she cried. "I would rather you stayed here and hid from me for ever the storehouse of your wealth."

"It is as well you should be acquainted with my secrets for I have also made my Will and appointed you Regent of Scotland, so that you, as the best person, may take care of Jamie and bring him up as we both would wish. Don't cry," he said softly as she began to whimper helplessly, "you are a woman now and well able to fend for both the child and yourself. Here in this box I have placed the last instalment of the subsidy Louis has been sending me and more should come when La Motte returns next Spring. Elphinstone knows what I have done and I have appointed you and him to be guardians of Jamie until he is old enough to reign by himself. There is only one thing I would beg of you, my dear, and I am at a loss to put it to you properly, but I would beg you, if I should die, for Scotland's sake, do not marry again!"

"Please, please," she begged him, sobbing aloud. "Do not speak of not returning to me; it is only for your sake I am able to carry on."

"Nonsense!" James said briskly, "there

is Jamie to consider and his future is all important. Come, my sweet, where is that proud Tudor blood, that dared face all opponents? I do not want to go away from you with the memory of a tear-stained face; come, this should cheer you a little."

He stooped to open a coffer stowed on a ledge in the wall and Margaret, going reluctantly to his side, was overawed despite her real grief by the sight of the precious jewels and priceless plate displayed within. No wonder James had chided her for her obsession with her unpaid legacy when he had so much put away in his treasure house. Making an effort she dried her tears and in a muffled voice thanked him for taking her into his confidence. Subdued she returned to the bedchamber and accompanied him to the panelled oratory where they both knelt and prayed. Finishing her prayers before James, Margaret watched him covertly through her opened fingers. Her heart misgave her as she looked on the shining, well-brushed hair, untouched with grey and the sturdy set of the shoulders on which she had so often leaned; unable to bear the pain the sight of him invoked she turned her gaze to the ceiling and concentrated on the designs carved in stone on the elaborate roof. The little unicorn resting beneath a tree was an especial favourite of hers as was the maiden holding a beast's head on her lap; but never before had the simple motto meant as much as it did at this moment. 'Jamais alleurs' she read while the tears began to flow again. 'Always present and never away'. What irony!

James kissed her before leading her from their apartments to the church but wisely did not prolong the good-byes. St. Michael's was crowded with a large congregation and James took her to stand with the immediate household in St. Katherine's Chapel. Margaret avoided looking towards David Lindsay who stood not far away and knelt at the wooden desk to pray.

Vespers were almost concluded when there was a commotion at the door of the church and a murmur went through the people. Alternately hot and cold Margaret stayed with her head bent until she heard a voice demanding "The

King!" Steeling herself to be brave she managed to raise her head sufficiently to see a man, dressed in a blue robe, with yellow locks falling from a bald pate, grovel before James and speak low to him. Straining to hear Margaret caught only a few words.

"Sir King, my mother has sent me to thee, charging thee not to go where thou art purposed; which, if thou do, thou shalt not fare well, nor none that is with thee!"

As swiftly as he had appeared the man disappeared even while James, in perplexity tried to reply.

"Follow him!" he cried to Lindsay and others of the household.

"But which way did he go?" Lindsay asked under cover of the choir singing. Those about began pointing in all directions and Lindsay and two others set off to follow. Lindsay, passing the lepers who were watching the proceedings from the peephole outside the church, ran towards the Palace when they told him they had seen a blue-robed figure running for the outer gateway. Once inside the courtyard he stood long enough to get his breath and by the time he came back to report to James who was already mounted in preparation to ride to Edinburgh he was able to say, quite truthfully, that he had not seen anyone within the Palace precincts.

It was impossible to tell from the expression on James's face if he were moved by the occurrence in the church and as he had made no change in his intention of leaving at once it was obvious the Queen's ruse had not succeeded. A swift glance at Margaret told Lindsay that she was bearing her disappointment with queenly dignity and when James took the stirrup cup which she proffered and wished him Godspeed there was no tremor of emotion in the husky voice.

The King's cavalcade clattered down the cobbled steep hill to the town and when they were lost to view Margaret turned towards the Palace; she crossed the yard and climbed the turnpike of her own apartments until she reached the small open windowed room at the top. As she went through the doorway she saw the look-out above her solemnly staring out towards the east. Breathing heavily and giving her eyes time to clear after the exertion of climbing the hundred and forty steps which had brought her to this vantage point she looked in the same direction and saw a small cloud of dust on the road that led to Edinburgh. She watched until there was no vestige left of the cavalcade as it disappeared away from her and with a last lingering look at the distant Grampians went slowly down to her lonely apartments.

In the endless days of waiting which were to follow, when rumour and counter-rumour went through the Palace like wind in ripe oats, she could not shed tears or occupy herself with womanly duties. She shunned the company of her musicians and poets, preferring to walk by the loch and take an occasional ride on the most docile mare the stable could find. James had only departed a few days when she realized she might be pregnant again and she wrote to him begging him to take care for the sake of her unborn child.

At first he sent messengers to her every day but as his army advanced towards the English border news became scanty and not very dependable. Margaret heard with something approaching despair that Surrey was in command of Henry's forces and that Katherine of Aragon had announced her intention of accompanying him in her husband's absence in France.

"I must write to His Grace and beg permission to go south to speak with my sister-in-law; perhaps my voice will bear some weight in putting an end to this foolhardiness," she said desperately to Lindsay and Angus when they crossed the sward after attending evensong in the kirk.

"I do not think you will obtain permission," Lindsay said sadly. "In Edinburgh all who were sufficiently courageous tried to dissuade the King's Grace from embarking on this expedition but he set his face against the weal of the common man. Others sought to put him off the war by employing supernatural aids, even as we did, but the King was not made afraid by visions at the Mercat Cross or anywhere else. We can only hope that he is right in what he believes and that he will bring home to Scotland the honour he seeks."

"Our experiment was not crowned with success, I know, but I must admit that I was horribly frightened myself when that awe-inspiring apparition appeared so unheralded within the Kirk. Probably my fears were engendered by the panic that overcame me at the thought of the King discovering who had mounted the scene but the man disappeared with such skill that he almost had me convinced I was witnessing a genuine augury of doom."

Angus looked curiously at the Queen as she spoke but he made no comment; it was widely believed that the wild-locked man who had variously been put as a reincarnation of St. James, St. Andrew or even St. Peter had been the brainchild of someone (even perhaps an English spy) who wanted desperately to dissuade the King from setting out to do battle but he had not thought the Queen might be behind the plan. Truth to tell Angus was in the process of falling in love and this overwhelming fact held him in thrall and allowed him no time for pondering on any other subject; the Lady Jane Stewart, a descendant of the Black Knight of Lorne who had married Jane

Beaufort, widowed Queen of James I, was a comely young woman with red-gold hair whose favours were eagerly sought by the young men who served the King in his household. She had recently come to act as one of Margaret's ladies of the bedchamber and had a ready wit as well as an enchanting smile; Angus found himself among the many who hung about the antechambers of the Queen's Hall in the hope of receiving a share of her attentions.

Now he found himself interested in the Queen's concern for her husband and later talked deep into the night with Lindsay about the relationship existing between the royal pair. He confessed he had been so taken up with his ill-starred marriage and his devotion to Jane Stewart that he had given little thought to the Queen whose page he had been in the distant days of Dunnottar.

In the weeks that were to come his regard was sharpened by the enormity of events that shaped not only the future of Scotland but his own as well.

11

ALEXANDER GORDON, third Earl of Huntly rode slowly from Edinburgh to Linlithgow; he was mortally tired and utterly dejected. Before his eyes, which were heavy lidded and veined with weariness, visions of what he had witnessed on the field of Flodden shut out the gentle vistas of rolling countryside. Many times during the week which was past he had wished he might have been among the thirteen nobles of the age-old houses of Scotland who had perished in the mud and slimy stench of the battlefield; it would have been easier to die than face living with the memory of what he had seen.

There was, also, the prospect of confronting the Queen with the news of which he was the baleful bearer; never a lover of the English he hated them now with a passion that ate into his soul.

He, Angus Bell-the-Cat and Home were the only surviving senior lords in the

Scots Kingdom; they, apart from Arran who commanded the fleet, now held sway over a band of striplings and babies. Gordon's mind shied away from the events culminating in the confrontations of the two armies but he could obtain no peace from the despair that perpetuated his misery.

At last, unheeding of the sunshine that turned the hills into tawny splendour, he tried to bring some order into the sequence of horror imprinted on his brain.

He admitted that much of his reluctance to face the facts was engendered by the enormous sense of guilt inculpating him in the debacle; how many times had he since chided himself for not listening to Elphinstone and Bell-the-Cat! It had been easy within the safety of the Council chamber to override the gentle churchman when he had cautioned the Scottish nobles against their hotheaded pride and it had been a simple matter to accuse Angus of being against the King for very personal reasons. But it had been unforgivable not to give ear to Angus when, on the very eve of the battle, he had begged James to return to Scotland giving Surrey only the satisfaction of knowing he had intimidated the King of the Scots with the great army he had summoned against him.

Alexander Gordon could see James now as he stood, eyes ablaze with enthusiasm, and rebuked old Angus for timidity in the face of the enemy. Despite his forty years James had retained the youthful lines of his face and the colour of his hair and those who witnessed the scene contrasted his vigour with the dour, heavy strength of his rival in love. Angus had said little except that he was too old for the type of warfare which Surrey had inflicted upon them but to prove he was no coward he would leave his sons to bear the honour of his name.

What must be his feelings now with both of them lying dead within the scooped out pits of Branxton churchyard?

Alexander had seen enough in Edinburgh as he rode through the deserted streets to know that it was not only those of high birth who suffered. All the weary way from the battle field he had been accompanied by the silent remnants of the proud army that had set out from the Borough Moor; pity had welled in his breast for the maimed who dragged limbs and the sightless who leant upon their haggard companions. He would have given much to be possessed of magical powers that might reverse the agonies of the reunions and bereavements about to take place.

Within the city there was no trading and the Burgh Council had issued instructions that no one should go abroad in the streets unless it were to pray in the Kirk. The feeling of doom was almost tangible, underlined by the white banners hung from doorways to proclaim the existence of plague in the house. Overall the bells tolled without ceasing, mourning the flower of the manhood that had perished in useless warfare beyond the Border; the dolorous noise proclaimed to heaven the despair and misery of the widows and fatherless who clung together behind their closed shutters.

Alexander made an attempt to encourage those who travelled with him but his forced words of cheer were received in dour and grim silence. It was perhaps as well that James had perished with so many of his countrymen for he had genuinely loved his people and wanted their prosperity.

What devil had incited him to this foolhardy war with the English? Why could he not have been content with harnessing his energy to improving the lot of his countrymen? What further promises of glory could he have craved when once his brother-in-law had given him his word that if he and Katherine should not have an heir the little Jamie should sit upon the twin thrones of England and Scotland? What renown could he hope to earn that he was prepared to sacrifice his people's welfare to obtain it?

And yet, as James's kinsman, he had wanted much the same thing as the King — the overthrow of the English in battle followed by a tremendous drive deep down into the fat pastures of their habitual enemy. Perhaps this, with the lure of easy harvests and a rich future, had been bait enough.

At first, when the great army mustered

at Ellem and set out on the road for England, there had been an optimistic atmosphere of near-carnival. The pipes had played for singing and dancing and there had been much comparison of skill with the long spears and bows. The guns from Edinburgh castle excited awestruck interest and when they were hauled off by teams of creamy oxen the soldiers in their wake felt secure in their uncanny power.

The Scottish army crossed the Tweed and laid siege to Norham Castle; although the English commander was stubborn and it was six days before he surrendered the optimism still prevailed. Etal and Ford capitulated more easily, even if the Scots lost a good number of men, and there was open talk of King James leading a victorious army into York for Christmas.

What held James back from pushing the advantage he had gained remained the biggest mystery of the disaster to Alexander. He did not believe, as many of his fellow nobles had done, that James was smitten with desire for Lady Heron, the mistress of Ford Castle, and that he would not move until she had succumbed to his advances, but rather that the King had doubts for the first time about his success in the coming venture.

James had with him not only his entire nobility, apart from Arran, but also his bastard son, Alexander, brought home from studying with Erasmus in Italy. It might have been James was reminded, as he lost men in the storming of the English castles and by the plague which they had brought with them, of the apparitions that had foretold disaster. Whatever it was, sudden passion or fear, James hesitated; it was not only the King who doubted, for each day his commanders reported a dwindling of the number of men under their banners. It was impossible to retrieve these deserters who crept away under the shrouding of night and hid themselves in the folds of the Cheviots.

While he hesitated and debated his next move James heard that Surrey had set out to halt his advance. Now he was forced to take action and gave orders for the Scottish Army to take up positions ready to check the English who hourly came nearer.

Surrey, once the recipient of James's lavish hospitality, old now, but still capable of leading his huge forces, also had his sons, the Howards, as leaders under his command. He sent a Herald to James challenging him to do battle with him before the coming Sunday. James, hearing that the company numbered among them the Howards who had been instrumental in the death of Andrew Barton, replied strongly and immediately that he would accept the challenge.

Alexander remembered how he had seen men slip away in the rain and far from sending after them recognized that had he been in their position he might well have been tempted to do the same thing. Only the long-won honour of the Gordons prevented him from following their example and by this time he knew he was not alone among his fellow nobles. With Angus departed for his home there were many who had lost the fiery enthusiasm for the fight that had borne them along previously.

In the treeless wastes of the Cheviot hillsides the Scottish army took up battle stations and waited with growing discomfort. Hopes arose as another Herald came from Surrey but this turned to disappointment when the King of the Scots sent him away and remained in the impenetrable position he had taken up. Inactivity breeds its own troubles and when an unnatural quietness fell across the lands where the English were known to be encamped speculation grew in the Scottish ranks about a possible withdrawal by Surrey and his men. Once more this sanguinary hope was squashed as James discovered with dismayed horror striking into his bowels that Surrey had outmanœuvred him and crept northwards to cut off the Scots line of retreat.

Giving the order to strike camp immediately James moved the Scottish army to face the English; oxen slipped and slithered in the mud but the men, glad to be on the move, went into their prearranged positions with the King in the centre and Argyll on the right and Gordon himself on the left. To the consternation of his nobles James sent his horse away and decided to fight on foot; in vain Gordon begged him to reconsider this gallantry but the King was adamant. His men, Highlanders, men from the Isles and lowlanders from every clan, were obviously heartened by this gesture and Gordon comforted himself with the knowledge. The situation, which had become extremely hazardous with Surrey's unchivalrous but masterly strategy, needed good generalship and who was he to question James's methods.

The King appeared tense but perfectly controlled as he superintended the drawing up of his troops into the formations that had always been the recognized positions in warfare. As soon as they were ready he gave the word for the advance and in complete silence the enormous mass of grey-clad Scotsmen moved forward at the same time as the guns in the rear opened fire with a great roar and belches of smoke that hung in the drenched air.

Surrey and his sons were not slow to appreciate the tactics of the King of the Scots and they ordered the immediate throwing in of their army. The English pushed forward to meet with the Scots as the Scottish shots went harmlessly overhead and landed a long way behind them.

At first the Scots seemed to be having an easy victory but as the English gunners found their range they ploughed through the squares of Scottish reserves and the hillsides rang with the screams of the injured and dying. Surrey, seeing the success of the Scots on his left, rallied his centre and right and in moments the two sides were locked in bloody and mortal hand-to-hand fighting. The Scots were hampered by the overlong spears which proved too unwieldy to use and their hand-sewn shoes which slipped on the wet earth; with difficulty they threw down the spears and took off their boots to defend themselves in hose only. Those about the King, who had the best armour, found this was a drawback rather than any protection for in the appalling conditions under which they were engaged in fighting for their lives the weight tended to hold them down and prevent the free swing of their arms.

As the dark began to fall the two sides hacked away at their opponents in desperate, angered quiet and James fought as valiantly as the Scotsmen standing at his side. More than once those who could spare a fleeting second to look about saw James wielding his sword and flattening those who dared approach. But Gordon, bringing in his mounted troops in a counter attack, saw the arrow which plunged barb-deep into the King's chest and witnessed the royal standard disappear in the confusion of the fighting.

With the death of their King all heart went out of the Scots and the men who were able to do so turned and ran leaving a few to fight hopelessly against an implacable enemy that was buoyed with the smell of victory. In moments the English broke through the remaining Highlanders who were now the only Scottish troops offering resistance and Gordon watched with fascinated terror as the great, sturdy men of the north scattered and fell. Digging his heels into the flanks of his horse Gordon shouted to the small handful of mounted soldiers that were within earshot to come with him into the attack but they gave him no answer and sped away into the cover of the hills. With the stench of sweat and blood oozing from the ground all about him Gordon knew the day was lost and giving the command for retreat galloped after the bedraggled remnants of the mounted troops.

The night which followed was the worst of his life; together with a handful of men he had found a cave in the hillside beyond the castle of Ford. With him the men made clumsy attempts to wash off the mire and congealed blood in the brown water of a little waterfall and took it in turns to keep watch and drink from the flasks of spirits some of the more fortunate had retained. His ears rang with the noise of the clashing of arms and the screams of wounded horses and his brain was overburdened with the suffering he had been forced to witness. Only by planning for the morrow could he keep himself from sinking into a hopeless rage.

With the first glimmer of morning light he sent scouts to find out if there were any survivors hiding nearby and bring them to him to organize a return to the scene of the fighting. There was, perhaps, the faintest chance that there might be some of the wounded with sufficient life in them to recover if they were rescued and almost as important, there were the expensive guns which had been James's pride and which they had abandoned in their flight.

To Gordon's surprise his scouts brought in nearly a thousand men and he formed them into some sort of order and retrieving loose horses managed to mount most of them. Ahead of the troop he rode towards the ill-fated field of Flodden and averting his eyes from the indescribable carnage which littered the earth saw the guns in the distance. He stood in the stirrups and waved excitedly for the Scots to follow him but halted them hastily as he took in that there was a party of men already preparing to drag away the artillery. He was about to form the troops into a semicircle to ride down onto the gun positions when a shot landed heavily behind him and was followed immediately by another and another. Gordon realized somebody had quickly taken the initiative and the Scots behind him would be wiped out if he carried on with his intentions of saving the guns. Turning towards them he pointed to the north and shouted for them to save themselves and go home. Very eagerly the men complied and Gordon dug in his spurs and followed.

This had all happened days before and he was now approaching the hill leading up to the Palace of Linlithgow. Here he had to face the unhappy duty of telling the Queen she was a widow and the mother, instead of the wife, of the King of the Scots.

As his small party clattered up the cobbled slope curious cottagers came to stand in the low doorways but he kept his face towards the massive building in front of him and left the telling of the disastrous news to the servants who followed behind. It was enough to encounter Margaret.

Alexander climbed the winding stairway to her chambers and found her anteroom filled with the officers of the day. He sent a page for Elphinstone who was living in the Bishop's apartments and as he accepted a cup of wine told the men and women who clustered around him about the disaster at Flodden; they received the news in stunned incredulity and then broke into an excited babble of questions. Alexander answered as well as he was able and broke off when he saw Elphinstone and David Lindsay come through the low doorway.

"My lord Bishop," he said, falling on one knee and kissing the ring held out to him, "may I speak privately with you — and with you, Sir David."

"You have the look of one who bears ill tidings," Elphinstone said as they came into the Presence Chamber.

"That I do, my lord, and my tongue is hesitant to impart the dire heaviness of the news I bring."

"The King?" Elphinstone asked quietly.

Alexander shook his head as one who cannot believe his own words, "The King is dead!"

"Do not say so!"

"I cannot do other than tell you what is the truth."

Lindsay brought stools to a table and

the three men sat down.

"There has been a disaster on the field of Flodden of greater magnitude than anything that has struck Scotland before; we are a nation stripped of King and nobility. In a brief but bloody engagement with the English we have lost both our sovereign and the heads of all the Houses except my own. Angus warned the King on the eve of the battle that he had little hope of victory and he went home, leaving his sons to carry the honour of his name — and they both perished."

"How shall we tell this to the Queen?"

"I have asked for your support in the matter for I do not feel able to break the news alone."

"So the wee Jamie is King of the Scots," Lindsay said slowly. "What a burden for a bairn not yet two years of age!"

"We are forgetting that," Elphinstone said grimly and put his hand angrily to his cheek to wipe away the tears filling his eyes. "Come, we had best go quickly to the Lady before she has wind of the tragedy through the bletherings of her ladies."

They went through the antechamber, brushing aside those who sought to detain them and went unannounced into the Queen's parlour. Margaret, who was sitting with several of her women, rose at once and hurried towards them.

"You have news, my lord Huntly — tell me!"

Alexander glanced at the women and Margaret, interpreting the look, signalled for them to leave; they went slowly, unwilling to miss what Alexander had to tell.

When the door closed behind the last velvet skirt Elphinstone moved nearer to the Queen and Alexander and David knelt before her with heads bowed.

"Put your trust in God," Elphinstone said quietly.

"Tell me your news," Margaret said firmly.

"Our Lord the King is dead; killed with his nobles and thousands of his loyal subjects on the field of Flodden."

"I was so afraid of this very thing!" Margaret cried and clasped her hands to her breast. "Oh, poor James how he would hate himself for bringing such calamity to his country! Tell me he did not suffer!"

Lindsay handed her some wine and she drank almost without realizing she had put the cup to her lips.

"The end came quickly," Alexander assured her while his memory conjured up the sight of the King's body arrowed and then cut with sword thrusts almost beyond recognition.

"So Scotland is vanquished?" Her voice was level but choked with unshed tears.

"Yes, my lady."

"And my son is the King of the Scots."

"Sovereign lord of a band of striplings and bairns. Only Arran, Angus, Home and I remain to serve him."

"Angus? Old Bell-the-Cat did not fight then, after all?"

"No; to the last day before the battle he maintained the King would stand no chance of victory and he withdrew leaving the Master of Douglas and one other son to lead their men. His heart will be heavy when he knows both sons and two hundred of the clan died with their King; is young Angus in the Palace?

We had better send him to console the old warrior."

"Angus is not here; he begged permission to ride off after the army to persuade his grandfather to allow him to join in the fighting and I said he might go for I was certain Bell-the-Cat would not listen. But my lord, tell me what you can and then we must make resolve how we are to face the desolate future."

Alexander, despite the solemnity of the moment, could only admire Margaret for the control with which she met personal and national disaster; never a man to stay long at Court he had not had much opportunity of judging the character of the Queen and was inclined to think of her as always prostrate upon a bed of sickness or childbirth. She surprised him now with her unconscious dignity. When she had heard as much of the sorry story of Flodden he could bring himself to tell her, she begged to be excused to pray in her Oratory.

On her return, her eyes heavy and rimmed with red Margaret announced that she would leave on the following day for Perth.

"The King must be crowned — and as quickly as possible! You, my lords, will be the first to know his Grace . . . " she faltered. "My husband, left this Will in which he names me Regent of Scotland during my son's minority. While you read the document and set about the ordering of what must be done, I will go down with Gavin Douglas to pay my respects to the corpse of my lord."

Alexander gasped.

"My lord Huntly?"

"Your Grace," Alexander stammered, "I have not brought the King's body with me."

"Not brought it?" The icy control floundered in the emotions which caused a physical pain in her breast. "Not with you? Where does he lie?"

"I do not know, your Grace," Alexander muttered helplessly. "We returned to the site of the battle after the night had passed but were unable to come close enough to pick up our dead and wounded because the English opened fire upon us with our own guns. All I could discover was that the dead had been buried in graves within the yard of

Branxton Church." He could not bring himself to say that vast pits had been dug and horses and men bundled in together.

"I see; well, there is nothing for me but to wait until my brother's commanders send me word of where they have buried the King until we should be able to give him honourable burial."

"Leave the matter to me, my lady and I shall set in motion the necessary mechanics of recovering the body." Elphinstone spoke quietly and Margaret looked at him gratefully before taking her leave.

"Do not be too optimistic, my lord," Alexander said ruefully as the door closed behind her, "when I last saw the battlefield the corpses were all stripped naked and it would have been difficult to tell noble from peasant."

"The King always wore the chain at his waist, let us hope the ravagers showed respect for that, if for nothing else. Will you come with me to the chapel to pray? I think Scotland and all of us are going to need the help of the Almighty."

12

IN the months and years that were to
follow Flodden more could have been
accomplished if the tolerant teachings
of the Almighty had been remembered
with as much fervour as His aid was
sought by Elphinstone and his clergy.

Margaret, sitting one July day in 1514,
at her tall desk in the window of her
apartments within the Blackfriars Priory
of Perth laid down her quill unable to
give her complete attention to the papers
before her; for the thousandth time since
she had been widowed she went over the
sequence of events that had followed on
the ill news Huntly had carried.

Buoyed by some strange energy that
might have been engendered by the new
life she carried she had made immediate
plans for her son to be taken to Perth
while she gathered the household at
Linlithgow together and prepared, with
all haste, to follow. Immediately she had
gained the sanctuary of the priory she

had set in motion the proceedings for the coronation of the infant King at Scone and amid scenes of obvious sadness the baby had been crowned.

This vital task completed Margaret returned to Stirling and sent out summons for her first Parliament.

December twenty-first, 1513, had been the date set for this historic meeting and before the remnants of the great houses came together the Queen did not waste her time. From Perth she had already written to her brother, now returned from France, and resident at Richmond, imploring him to cease making war on Scotland if for no other reason than to spare misery to his sister who had taken up the burden of kingship against such odds.

Henry had been sympathetic — war with Scotland had not been his wish when all was said and done and having gained his ends in France his immediate desire was for peace. He had commiserated with Margaret in her predicament, sent sympathy for the state of her health, told her that King Louis had agreed to pay the pension for which he had gone to war and promised her that the body of her husband was safe in Richmond.

During all the months since James's death Margaret had striven to recover her husband's body, sending Heralds to London as soon as she had learnt Lord Dacre had removed the royal corpse there, and had obtained no satisfaction whatsoever. At length she was forced to accept that the English had no intention of giving back the body and shut her mind when information reached her of Henry's fear of committing it to the earth when James had been excommunicated by the Pope for disobeying the papal command not to invade England.

The day of the meeting of Parliament arrived in a swirl of icy rain and lowering skies and Margaret could still remember the dismay with which she had looked round the chamber and counted the men who had come to her support. Besides some of the lesser Lords which included Drummond there were only the Lord Chancellor, James Beton, the Earls of Arran, Huntly, and Home, (returned to Court under the somewhat dubious aegis of having been absent after Flodden while he looked to the interests of his followers; interests, Huntly told Margaret bluntly, that included the pillaging of the dead on the Field) the young Angus, who came in the place of his grieving grandfather and who was now his heir, Elphinstone and the rest of the clergy.

It had not been an easy session, for when Beton read the Will of the late King, appointing Margaret as his Regent during the baby King's childhood, there had been murmurs against this divergence from the normal practice of investing power in the nearest male kin. Elphinstone, who was a pale shadow of the great priest he had been, had suggested Heralds should be sent to France to invite John Stewart, Duke of Albany, James's first cousin, to return to Scotland and take up some part of the government of the realm. To Margaret's relief the others had quashed this suggestion and stated they had every confidence in the last wishes of their late King and would honour his will and support his widow. However, it was stated and generally agreed by all present that if the Queen should remarry she should forfeit her right to hold this high office. This had seemed an easy enough condition with which to comply and her obvious pregnancy had underlined the fact; Margaret had been granted the Castle of Stirling to remain as her own residence for herself, her son and the yet unborn child.

Sitting back, easing her aching body and longing to be released to relax in her own bower, Margaret had been rivetted to attention when Beton raised the subject of the King's treasure and stated the royal coffers had never been lower. The Queen kept her mouth closed in a thin line, soothing her conscience by telling herself that the gold and plate she had taken from the secret storage place in Linlithgow and hidden once more in Stirling was her own as she had not yet received in full the amount the Scottish government had agreed to pay her on her marriage. Heated argument broke out.

"I say again," Elphinstone said, looking up from where he stooped over the council table, "we should send to France for the Duke of Albany. Coffers that need replenishing want the strong hand of a man to extort money from the people."

"Surely, if our late beloved King felt confident in his Queen's ability to raise the necessary sums for the continuing of government we should abide by his decision?" asked a clear young voice from the furtherest end of the chamber. Margaret glanced gratefully in the speaker's direction and saw it was Angus who spoke. She smiled and across the dim room their gaze met and held for a moment while the point was discussed and later determined in her favour.

At length the business was finished and Margaret was escorted from the place to the care of her ladies; she was pleased with the outcome of this, her first session, and sat down to write a long letter to her brother telling him of its success.

In April she had been brought to bed of a fine son; it was the easiest confinement she had ever experienced and she had chafed against the drawn curtains and the shuttered windows where she was forced to remain for the appointed time laid down by the Ordinances of her grandmother. Perhaps it was the fine Spring weather outside calling her to escape and be young again or had it been another more dangerous excitement stirring her blood?

When had she first known she was falling in love with Angus? Was it when he had saved her from the censor of her peers or had it been at Christmas time when he had gallantly sung for her while the rest of the Court had made the most of a bleak festival by following their own pursuits? Or again had it been when she had heard old Bell-the-Cat had died and left Angus his vast estates and fortunes? She shied away from this mercenary streak running through her nature like fool's gold in a piece of rock but admitted any man looked more handsome when his pockets were well filled.

Whatever it had been that aroused her interest in the young man she was now utterly and completely enthralled by him. His face obtruded between her papers and her pen; his voice dominated the birdsong or the piping chatter of the little King. She wanted Angus as she had never wanted James and the physical pain of her need was worse than childbirth.

With an iron determination she had

controlled her sudden-sprung passion, sending the young man who daily seemed to grow more handsome, on journeys to the Marches and to Perth.

In his absence she applied herself with diligence to matters of State until her depleted nobles were all won round to the wisdom of keeping her as Regent. She knew she had a fine grasp of the country's needs that was part of the training James had given her and she applied his statecraft with pleasure.

When an offer of marriage came from Louis of France who was widowed on the death of Anne of Brittany she was as flattered as her Parliament were delighted. They did not press her to accept immediately but Margaret knew she could not consider the possibility; and she did not have to look far for the reason. She had made one marriage for the sake of a kingdom and she now felt life must grant her a choice of her own. This self-revelation brought her up with a jolt causing her a malaise that kept her within her own rooms for almost a week. Marriage with Angus was out of the question! She was Regent of Scotland.

But there were other means of gratifying passion.

The only stumbling block to making Angus her lover seemed to be the restraint of Angus himself; always polite and attentive, ready at any moment to do her will he made no attempt to dally with her for intimate talk when his work was completed. Margaret forced herself to accept his cool approach to her as a sign of the necessity for her to preserve a level head and when he returned from attending a Border meeting at Jedburgh sent him again to Perth with documents for Beton.

He was absent on this mission as she sat at her writing desk and in a sudden longing for his company Margaret threw down her quill and hurried to the privy garden where her sons would be taking an airing under the watchful eye of David Lindsay and their nurses. Jamie tottered towards her as she came through the gateway and she caught him up in her arms and covered his face with kisses. The woman who was cradling the infant Alexander against her breast drew back the fine wool shawl to show his mother how he progressed and putting down Jamie, who clung to her skirts, Margaret took the babe and crooned softly to restore its sleep.

She stayed as long as she could but at last knew she must go back to her papers in the loneliness of her chamber. With a sigh she restored the babe and bent to embrace Jamie and throw some wooden balls at the skittles David had set up. The child's face puckered into a plaintive cry as she kissed him farewell but David was instantly beside him taking up the game where Margaret had left off. Margaret gave him a look of gratitude before walking quickly from the homely environment. If only David Lindsay had the power to heal her inward tears as he did those of her son!

Elizabeth Barley, widowed at Flodden, was the only lady-in-waiting on duty in her room when Margaret came through the door and she rose from the window seat putting aside her piece of embroidery.

"The Earl of Angus is returned from Perth, Your Grace, and seeks an audience."

"Did he so?" Margaret replied as quietly as she was able while the blood pounded in her ears. "Go and tell him I wish to speak with him."

As Elizabeth went to do her bidding Margaret resumed her seat at the desk and with great will power focused on the columns of figures written on the parchment. She was almost mastering the meaning of one particularly difficult account when her lady came back with Angus. Margaret nodded her recognition of his presence and coolly continued her work before pressing her hands to her aching eyes and dismissing Elizabeth.

"You are tired, my lady?" Angus asked as he proffered his hand to help Margaret alight from the high stool.

"A little — it is these wearisome papers that tire me. But you have news for me from Perth? What thinks our trusty Beton of my preferment of your uncle Gavin?"

"Truth to tell, my lady," Angus answered ruefully, "he did not seem overjoyed at the idea of advancing Gavin to the see of Dunkeld!"

"What possible objection can the man

have to the appointment?" Margaret cried.

"I think if he were pressed Archbishop Beton would say my uncle spends too much time at his verses and too little at his vespers."

"Fie on his narrow-mindedness! Surely a poet is as the psalmists of old — we must bring Beton round to my way of thinking. But tell, you are well?"

Angus regarded her quickly.

"I am in excellent health, your Grace; the sun was shining and the air like wine as my grandfather and I rode from Perth."

"Your grandfather came with you?"

"Yes, he brings news to you of the progress he has made in settling the dispute of Mistress MacClellane of Galston. He begs me to ask you to grant him audience later this day."

"Of course, he may come as soon as you depart."

Angus bowed and moved towards the door; he stopped with his hand on the latch when Margaret said his name.

"My lady?" the handsome, open face was anxious to please her every whim.

Margaret, filled with a longing that forced her to sink on to a window seat, replied the matter could wait and turning to stare out of the small casement dismissed him.

Lord Drummond was announced not long afterwards and when the topic of Mistress MacClellane had been discussed Margaret could not help speaking of Angus; Drummond who had already lost three daughters in the cause of love was not slow to realize the Queen's infatuation with his good looking grandson. He was sorry for her widowed plight and ready for any advancement the popularity of Angus might bring the families of Douglas and Drummond.

"Why do you not give a hunting party followed by a supper?" he asked.

"That would be an excellent idea! But I forget, my days of mourning are not yet completed and I would not err in my husband's memory." The voice, eager at first, became husky with disappointment.

"If you keep the company small and intimate there can be no man at Court would quibble."

So it was that a few days later a small band set out for the neighbouring wooded hills; the weather continued warm with blue skies studded with soft white clouds. The sport was as good as the weather and when the horses clattered home over the cobbled courtyard in the early evening the thick stone walls echoed the unusual laughter and light-hearted banter of the riders.

Later, when an amethyst twilight brought in a starry night of perfect tranquillity, the Queen presided at an informal voide of cold meats and raspberries drenched in cream. It was with difficulty she kept away from Angus, talking with great animation to Lord Drummond and David Lindsay of any subject that came into her head. The fresh air had brought colour into her cheeks and before the supper she had had her hair washed and brushed until it shone in a golden mantle down to her waist. Her excitement had a tinge of near-hysteria that suddenly changed into an icy determination when she overheard Elizabeth speaking to David and caught the name of Angus.

Striving to answer Drummond coherently she strained to catch what Elizabeth was saying.

"I think you are right," David's calm voice was agreeing. "She is a most bedworthy young woman."

"So Angus is not alone in thinking that way! I wish you no harm, Sir David, but you have your royal charge to guard and Jane Stewart would make Angus an ideal match." Elizabeth laughed pleasantly and she moved off with Lindsay to replenish their goblets from a silver ewer on a side table.

Margaret gave her attention to Lord Drummond as their voices died away but she glanced covertly round the chamber until her unwilling eyes saw Angus deep in conversation with one of her ladies. Margaret knew, with a pang of despair, the shapely back and red-gold hair belonged to Jane Stewart and realized at the same instant she could not live if Angus should make the girl his wife. As she played out the rest of the evening, courteously speaking with all her guests, she laid plans to keep Angus with her when the others went to their chambers.

It was quite usual for her to work late on papers received during the day and she sent a page to bring the roll pertaining to the case of Gavin Douglas and bade him put them on the desk in her parlour. This completed she found herself able to spend the unending hours until her guests departed in a state of detachment. She had no difficulty in telling Angus she had a matter on which she needed his advice and asked him to return to her later when the last of the men and women had said their good nights.

The new-born determination stood her in good stead as she dismissed her women and told them she would prepare herself for bed when she had completed the work piled on her desk.

"I shall stay outside the door and you can call me when you are ready," Jane Stewart said in kindly tone, "you look tired, your Grace and I do not mind waiting for you."

"That is very thoughtful of you," Margaret answered controlling her voice to keep out the unwarranted annoyance the girl's courtesy evoked, "but I have no idea how long the matter will take and wish you to retire immediately."

"Very well, my lady," Jane answered quietly and with Elizabeth and the others curtsied and went out.

Once the door closed behind them Margaret went into her bedchamber and took off her velvet coif and the heavy overdress of brocade that covered her delicate robe of gauze. She had drunk more than her usual quantity of wine during the evening and was utterly calm as she went about the preparations for receiving Angus.

In the parlour the fire she liked to see burning at all seasons of the year was newly replenished and she brought cushions and a table with wine and beakers close to the hearth. She had just drawn back the heavy drapery at the unglazed window when she heard a discreet knock on the door. In a clear voice she gave permission to enter; at the same moment the Watch below called midnight and the moon disentangled itself from a ribbon of milky cloud.

Any man — older and less susceptible than Angus — would have been stirred by the sight of the Queen standing at the casement bathed in light which glittered on the gold threads of her filmy dress and unbound hair. With the sense that is especially perceptive to a romantic invitation he knew he had not been summoned to work on dry documents and after he had greeted Margaret went, without her bidding, to bring them wine. Returned to the casement they stood facing one another sipping and talking of the peaceful quiet of the city and the happiness of the day they had spent.

"You enjoyed the hunt?" Margaret asked huskily.

"All men enjoy the chase, my lady."

"When the roe deer is your particular quarry?"

"There are other objects I would rather hunt — "

"And if the prey prove willing?"

Margaret turned away from him, putting her goblet down on the stone sill; the cold-blooded execution of her scheme deserting her as her body and mind trembled to hear his answer.

"I should count myself especially fortunate."

Radiant as the unveiled moon above her she turned back to Angus and he took her in his arms, his strong grasp crushing her against him. His mouth sought hers and they kissed, eagerly, with small cries of delight. Margaret was transported into a dizzy world she had not believed existed. At last she disengaged herself and led him to the cushions beside the hearth.

"Let me look at you — properly, as I have desired this many a long day. Oh, Angus, I have pined for you these months past! Thank God we are together at last. Now that we belong together nothing shall part us and I shall set about the arrangements for our marriage."

"Marriage, my lady?" Angus sat up swiftly, taking his head from her bosom, his face registering shocked dismay, "there can be no talk of marriage between you and me!"

"But of course there can! I have my lords and clergy eating out of my hand and they will be able to gainsay · me nothing when I tell them it is my indomitable intention to have you and nobody else for my husband — "

"But, my lady — "

"My name is Margaret — call me so."

"But Margaret, in the King's Will he stated quite clearly that if you remarried you would be deposed from the Regency!"

"That is so," Margaret answered calmly, "but my lord husband was not to know on whom I should bestow my favour; he could have no possible objection to one of your distinguished house as my consort."

Even as he murmured unintelligible words of agreement Angus was only too forcibly reminded that the astute James had probably made the condition of his widow remaining unmarried to prevent just such a match as she was now proposing. James had had many more years than his wife in which to learn of the feuds and power-seeking ways of the hot-headed clansmen over which he had ruled and he had had no illusions about their greedy self-interests.

But he was young, the woman beside him was highly desirable, willingly receptive and a Queen Regent; he drew her down beside him and kissed her mouth and tantalizingly revealed her bosom. There was time tomorrow to consider the irksome advisedness of becoming her husband or not.

13

THEY were married on the sixth August, 1514 at the church of Kinnoul near Perth by Walter Drummond, dean of Dunblane and a nephew of Lord Drummond.

This worldly and wily old gentleman had quickly seen the advantages for his family if one of its members could be wedded to the Queen Regent. The Drummonds and the Douglas's stood to gain an enormous amount by the union; Angus had been stupefied when he went with his problem to his grandfather and Drummond had roared with laughter in his face.

"Don't come to me with that miserable countenance! Go to the kirk and fall on your knees to the Almighty and thank Him for the wonderful opportunities He is holding out to you! Think, boy, you might be father of a future King of Scotland and England!"

"How can that be?" Bewildered, Angus

could think of nothing but Drummond's eagerness for him to accept a marriage that had seemed to his innocence to be utterly out of the question.

"The expectation of life of the offspring of James and Margaret Tudor can be counted in days rather than years, as you know quite well; who is to say that your lusty seed might not produce heirs to flourish like mountain heather? Where's your spirit, lad? Go out and bind the Queen to you with cords of iron."

"But there is Jane Stewart — she and I had some kind of understanding we might wed in the New Year."

"Don't tell me you would rather have a pretty face than a kingdom? With your country in the state of flux it has enjoyed since Flodden you might think a man of your great family would have more to dwell upon than bedding with a milk-sop maiden! Get to your wooing and let me hear no more of such childish mewling."

To tell the truth Angus did not have much difficulty in allowing himself to be persuaded to encourage the Queen in her ideas of matrimony. Drummond had convinced him the nobles would accept him as the Queen's consort once the deed was accomplished much as Margaret had persuaded and it was pleasant enough to dally with her.

From that first evening when she had declared her love Margaret had sought every opportunity of being alone with Angus and enjoying the mutual passion existing between them. The warm, scarcely dark nights, were cover for their meetings and this love making became a necessary part of their life, although Margaret steadfastly refused to give herself completely to him. This, as she had known it would, forced him to agree to the marriage.

Despite his grandfather's complaisance and his own eagerness to wed with a Queen Angus still had misgivings.

"Even if all the French-inclined nobles in your realm don't rush to call John Stewart to come from France to take away your Regency what will your brother have to say about our wedding?" He asked Margaret as she lay cradled against his breast.

"As long as you incline towards the

English as your family has always done Henry will find no fault."

"But has he not written to you suggesting a union with Maximilian the Emperor or Louis of France?"

Henry — or Wolsey who now conducted most of his correspondence — had suggested very strongly she should consider marriage with either of these powerful men but she was not prepared to give ear to their requests. She was a sovereign in her own right and she intended to govern Scotland as she thought fit!

"There has been some talk; but let sister Mary marry one of them — she is a virgin and her maidenhead can be spared in the interests of England this time. Don't let us waste our time in the useless discussion of where I should grant my matrimonial favours — I am determined you shall be my lord and I'll hear no more of the matter! Kiss me and make me forget the tedious matters of state."

"But supposing my fellow nobles do not agree with your choice and my life is endangered?"

"I shall not suffer you to be hurt on my

behalf! Do not tell me that magnificent body hides a craven's heart?"

"That it does not! But I cannot help thinking it would be wiser for us to become lovers and not run the risk of losing so much."

"Do you imagine I am a light-of-love to enter into a clandestine affair with you?"

This was the first flash of real temper Angus had encountered since he had first held her in his embrace and he hastened to turn away the discomfort of the moment with soft words and not such tender caresses.

By the time he left her chamber an hour later, warm with love and wine, he had agreed to a wedding to take place three days later. In his present frame of mind he would have found it difficult to deny Margaret anything; she had never looked more beautiful and her high rank made him dizzy with hopes for the future.

Before the simple and extremely secret wedding to which only the women of the bedchamber were accomplices the Queen called a meeting of the Drummond family, and Gavin Douglas, now the only poet who sang her praises, for since Flodden William Dunbar had not been seen at Court. In the face of all opposition Margaret had created Gavin Bishop of Dunkeld and as Drummond and Angus were announced she sealed a letter she intended despatching to the Pope asking for the See of St. Andrews to be granted to Elphinstone whom she knew perfectly well was too frail to accept. This would suit her plans for the future when Gavin could be advanced to this important position in the Church and afford her strong support.

Margaret rose to greet the Douglases and Lord Drummond, calling for wine and bidding them to be seated.

The ageing Drummond knelt to the Queen and kissed her hand. "Madame, I am honoured that you have chosen my grandson for your new husband; Scotland will have occasion to bless the day you made this decision!"

"Well spoken, Sir!" Margaret replied.

"In the years to come Angus will be a bulwark against those in our kingdom who lean towards the French influence and who long to have John Stewart come here. What can they be wanting that they cry to have a stranger rule over them when we have good men of our own and England behind us!" Lord Drummond knew this was what Margaret wanted to hear and she turned gratefully towards him, her eyes ablaze with passion.

"Exactly, Lord Drummond, you are well aware that I hated the idea of going to war against my brother's realm and if my advice had been taken Scotland would not be in the sorry plight it enjoys now."

"You have received the blessing of King Henry for your marriage?" Drummond asked guardedly.

"There has not yet been time for His Grace to reply to my letter but I know he will be happy the inclinations of my heart coincide with union to the House of Douglas who have ever been held in respect by my brother." If, in the long hours of the night when her need of Angus kept her restlessly awake, she had misgivings about Henry's reception of her momentous news, now was not the moment to disclose them. She smiled brightly and announced Gavin's promotion which was well received by her captive audience and then went on to talk about her wishes that her marriage should remain a closely guarded secret until she thought the moment ripe to make it known. She had no difficulty in binding the men to honour her behest and when the final arrangements had been made for the wedding asked Angus to summon her Steward to serve them supper in her parlour.

The day of the wedding was heavy with thunder-charged clouds massing in the eastern sky and on the return journey from the service at the Altar of the Church in Kinnoul great drops of rain splattered Margaret and Angus and those who accompanied them. As the handful of people climbed the stone stairway to her chambers to eat the nuptial feast lightning tore the premature darkness and thunder pealed across the hills.

The company was forced into a brittle gaiety prompted by the fear for the omens that might be read into this spectacular weather and Margaret's parlour was soon awash in high pitched laughter and over-loud voices. The waiting women, except for Jane Stewart who had begged to be allowed to return to her home at Traquir as soon as she realized her hopes for marriage with Angus were doomed, clustered round the few men who were present and made much of bringing them food and drink. It was not long before most of those present were inebriated and willing hands carried Margaret to her bedchamber and helped her prepare for her bridegroom.

She sat up in the damask hung bed, with her golden hair spread across her naked shoulders and waited for Angus to be brought to her; she had drunk sufficient wine to be oblivious of the pointed remarks of her women and had time to think, very briefly, of the difference between this and her first marriage night before a noisy rapping upon the door announced her husband.

With dignity she dismissed her giggling attendants and watched as Angus sent away his servant and secured the door with a bolt in the latch. It was late evening now, with the sky cleared after the storm and a fresh, rain-washed breeze coming through the open casement. Angus snuffed the candles burning in silver sconces on the table against the wall and asked if she would like to keep the one by the bedside alight. She nodded and he came and sat beside her on the silken coverlet, his bedrobe open to the waist. Margaret put her hands to his shoulders and kneeling pulled his head against her breasts; he buried his face against her soft warmth and together they sought the yielding embrace of the feather mattress and abandoned themselves to the pent up passions of the last weeks. Their lovemaking was of animal splendour, entirely without subtlety and yet pleasurable and stimulating. They laughed together enjoying their bodies' perfect mating and when the final libido released their overwrought emotions Margaret cried for joy against his strong chest.

Yet, strangely enough, when she awoke on the following morning she discovered within her consciousness a sense of disappointment and loss. She could not define her feelings but knew James had taught her a more gentle approach to the art of bedsport which Angus had not touched upon. She was aware she had given him no time for delicacy for her need for him had become a hungry craving and she had been over ready for his advances and she knew too he was young and inexperienced where James had been well schooled in the art of love.

Pushing aside her surprising sense of inquietude she woke him by kissing his mouth and demanding his attention; he was instantly awake and in the next hour she completely forgot her slight unease in the young vigour of Angus's passion.

Strengthened by her marital happiness Margaret resolutely carried out the offices of government. Her mind seemed clearer than she could remember and she was happier than she had been since before James told her he intended making war on her brother's kingdom. True enough, she could not bear Angus to be out of her sight for any length of time and sent pages scurrying to bring him to her for the least excuse. He came willingly enough, delighted to be of service to this radiant being who was both his Queen and his ardent bedfellow. The secrecy of their marriage heightened its warmth and it was pleasant to stand behind Margaret while she bent over papers and discussed rents and dues with Archbishop Beton and imagine her pliant body utterly responsive to his in their great private bed. They would chuckle over this double life when the day's work was finished and the door of their chamber shut against the inquisitive world outside. Angus mimicked the sonorous voice of Beton for her delight and he would tell her of the restraint he practised when she had given him an intimate sidelong look when the prelate was begging her approval of some dreary document and he had longed to pitch parchment and priest from the room and tumble her on the floor of the parlour.

His lovemaking was innocent and single minded, inclined to be rough; but it brought her physical contentment and if at times her innermost heart craved a slightly more ingenious technique she was old enough to count her blessings and open her arms to receive his homage.

Yet, if she was mature enough to accept this small deficiency she was too young in her hopes their marriage would remain forever secret. She prayed as she had never before prayed to the rather vague Godhead of her imaginings that they might be allowed to remain in this glorious state of isolated eroticism until the end of their lives and for a time it appeared as if her wishes would be granted. Buoyed by this seeming benevolence Margaret allowed Angus to sit beside her on the dais in the Refectory and kept him at her side when she took her Court to winter in Stirling.

Here, within the confines of her own castle she gave orders for Angus to have apartments close to her own and despite the warnings of Elizabeth Barley that all those about her might not regard her actions as leniently as did her own women she continued to show her favours to her husband in a manner that began to arouse the suspicions of the most unobservant.

If Angus pressed her to be careful she would comfort him with the undeniable fact that she was Regent of Scotland and held in high esteem. He was more than ready to be reassured and when she turned her back on him and told him to unlace her dress and carry her to bed he was lost to the powers of reason.

His grandfather, on the frequent occasions when they met, told Angus he would soon have nothing to fear and it would be possible, probably before Christmas to announce the fact of their wedding. Angus, in his quieter moments, wished he had the same optimistic approach as Drummond but accepted the older man knew more of the ways of the Court and was therefore wiser in his beliefs.

What happened to burst the bubble of their complacency none of them was ever to discover; but by November the well-guarded secret was common property and Margaret's name with that of Angus was being bandied from one end of Scotland to the other.

14

PERHAPS it was Jane Stewart, frustrated in her virginal couch at Traquir, who first voiced the whisper that was to become in a remarkably short time a roar of angry protest against Margaret and Angus; nobody could be certain. But when the Queen promoted Gavin, Angus's uncle to be Primate of Scotland on the death of the unhappy Elphinstone she brought glaring attention to her attachment with the Douglas family.

For the French biased members of the Council this was sufficient to demand an immediate meeting to consider what should be the next step of the Queen's Ministers.

Margaret was at Stirling with Angus, her sons and Lord Drummond when this assembly took place and was unaware of its portent; she was enjoying the return to domestic life and having received congratulations on her marriage from

Henry in England was lulled into believing she had also won over all the peers of Scotland to support her in her new marriage.

It was a very rude awakening, therefore, when sitting one morning in November with Angus and Drummond by the fire in her parlour, to be brought to her feet by Lord Lyon, King of Arms who burst into the room without courtesy and demanded she should hand over the royal children and Angus. In the shocked disbelief of the moment Drummond, in blind panic and rage, thrust out to prevent the herald proceeding further towards the Queen and struck the man a glancing blow across the face and chest.

Stunned, Sir William Comyn halted and then while he fought for breath and composure, his face contorted with hatred he tried to speak and turned away, stalking indignantly from the room.

When the Queen and the others had recovered from the surprise of the extraordinary incident Margaret clapped her hands for pages and was escorted to the children's nursery to see for herself that the Herald had not molested the little King and his brother. Satisfied they were unharmed she returned to speak with Angus and Drummond who had hastened to the gateway to discover if Comyn had departed or had brought sufficient followers to begin an affray. They came into the parlour together.

"So they do not accept our marriage as I had hoped!" Her voice was low pitched, a mixture of anger and disbelief. "How can they grudge me a little personal happiness when I am prepared to give Scotland my entire energies to produce a stable government?"

"They do not see the situation in quite the same way as you do, Madame," drily commented Drummond, "we must face the unwelcome fact that the Council is largely composed of men who fear the grasp of the Douglas clan more than anything else in the world."

"If they will only give me time I shall prove to them they have nothing to fear, for my husband and I shall work together for Scotland's weal!"

"Well said, my love," said Angus who came to her side and placed his arm about her waist.

"Our first concern must be to see if we can prevent Beton and his minions from sending to France for John Stewart," said Drummond as a knock was heard on the door of the chamber. Drummond went to see who came and ushered in Adam Wilkinson, Margaret's secretary, who bowed over her hand, and asked incredulously, "Is what I hear true, your Grace?"

"What do you hear, Master Wilkinson?"

"That Lyon Herald has been here demanding the King and his brother."

"You have heard only too well," Margaret told him throatily. "We have discovered our ministers have no respect for their Regent's privacy or rule; what's to be done?"

"It would be best, your Grace, if there is to be any question of taking sides if you had the Great Seal of the Realm in your possession."

"Sound advice, Master Wilkinson; will you bring it to me, Angus?"

Margaret unconsciously drew herself very tall and turned an imploring, anxious face to her husband. It would have been difficult to refuse her and although Angus heard her supplication with an inward dread he stoutly protested his support. "I'll set out as soon as I have gathered together a suitable band of men."

But before he had accomplished this, other disquieting news came from St. Andrews where the newly-elected Primate was besieged by Hepburn who had been the Council's choice to follow Elphinstone. With Hepburn was an army summoned by Beton. Angus left Stirling with the double purpose of depriving Beton of his badge of office and relieving his uncle in the sea-bound castle on the east coast.

When he had departed Margaret gave strict orders for the reinforcing of the guards about the castle and sat down to write to Henry. Now was the moment to enlist the support of her brother's mighty realm to aid her against those who rebelled in opposition to her rule. Not for the first time since James had been killed she wished she had the guidance of the man who had, for so long, known and loved Scotland. Margaret began to appreciate how much wiser and stronger he had been than she realized; in his slight, wiry frame had existed a power of compelling leadership which had welded his quarrel-prone nobility into a wholesome, almost single-minded instrument of government. It was only old Bell-the-Cat, with his personal axe to grind, who had stood out against James and Margaret experienced a pang of doubt as she thought of her husband's warrior like grandfather — was it only jealousy over the Kennedy woman that stirred the animosity between the two men or did it go deeper than that? Was there, perhaps, something in Drummond's laconic statement about the Douglas family which had its roots in truth?

Shrugging off her misgivings Margaret drew her quill and parchment towards her and began a long and explanatory letter to Henry. As she wrote, in her angular script, she hoped Wolsey and her brother would read the contents together and see more than she was able to put down. Her quill remained poised while she sought for phrases to express her fears for the future of her sons and herself.

"'My adversaries continue in their

malice, usurping the King's authority as if I had no authority. I beseech you make haste with your army on land and sea for the counter-party have laid siege to the castle of St. Andrews whither I have this day sent my husband to break it. All the hope that my enemies have is in the Duke of Albany's coming, which I beseech you to hinder in any way; for if he happens to come before your help I am sure some of my party will incline to him for dread of the future. There are some lords of my party who dread the loss of their lands but I tell them their goods and acres shall not be scaithed. The king, my son, and his little brother prosper well, thank God, but I am feared the lord-adversaries will besiege us here at Stirling. Give heed to Adam Wilkinson who brings this letter, for he gives me good service and is entirely trustworthy. I beg you to note that if I sign my letters Margaret R. they are only state papers and forced upon me for signature. I shall always put, your loving sister when I write to you my true mind. Brother, all the welfare of me and my children rests in your hands, which I pray Jesu to help and keep eternally to his pleasure. Your loving sister, Margaret R.'"

Almost as soon as Adam had left with this letter for Richmond Margaret found her fears of being entrapped in Stirling were correct and with all haste she left secretly for Perth. Great scudding clouds filled the skies as her party, unheralded and dressed in the plain dress of merchants and their wives and families, rode out of the castle and took to the sodden heath roads. She knew no peace of mind until the gates of the Blackfriars had been bolted behind her. Angus, unsuccessful in his attempts to relieve Gavin and obtain the Great Seal joined her and as the slow days went by watched their world crumble about them.

The Council deprived Margaret of her Regency and sent Lyon Herald to France requesting John Stewart to come to Scotland with all urgency to take up the government of the realm until the little King should be old enough to rule for himself.

Impotent, Margaret raged in the cell-like apartments of the Blackfriars against the obdurate determination of the Council. She would not admit, even to herself, her own share in her undoing, and forced herself to believe James would have approved of her remarriage to the beguiling young Angus.

When the Council withheld payment of her dower rents she began to feel the real pinch of her helplessness. The treasure James had bequeathed her melted in the payment of her servants and in the buying of the food and necessities of her household. Once or twice she came to the point of asking Angus to give back to her some of the costly jewels she had bestowed on him in the first passionate infatuation of her marriage but her Tudor pride forbade this grovelling and she could not bring herself to broach the subject. Angus was either too blind to recognize her need or unwilling to part with the silver cups and ornaments that were now part of his new life.

In the early spring Margaret knew she was expecting Angus's child and began to give heed to the suggestion of Henry and Wolsey that she should bring her sons to England for protection. She realized she was powerless against the odds piling up against her and her only strength lay in her possession of the persons of the baby king and his brother. In England with Scotland's sovereign and Henry at her side she would be practically invincible.

She and Angus were almost asleep, lying in the old-fashioned tester bed in their chamber, when she brought up the matter with him.

"What think you of escaping to England at the earliest opportunity?"

"Going to England?" Angus was pleasantly drowsy, "I had not thought of it Meg."

"Do you think it would be a good idea?" Margaret persisted.

"I'll need time to think it over; surely we shall do well enough in Scotland when John Stewart comes here to uphold your position."

This was a novel approach to an arrival Margaret could only think of as a complete usurpation of her dwindling powers. "How can this be?" she demanded sharply. Angus had some unexpected facets to his character and there were occasions when she suspected he was too easy going on her behalf. Angus rolled reluctantly on his back.

"I hear he is a likeable enough fellow, honest dealing with a fair mind; he would not be one to sit by and see his cousin's widow and children ill-treated."

"But how can you know this? His father was an enemy of James's father and for that very reason was banished into France. You cannot want me to believe his son is of a different metal?"

"Perhaps John Stewart's mother, Anne de la Tour d'Auvergne, had a softening effect on him for by all accounts he is not of the usual run of fratricidal Stewarts and you might do well to view the future with a little more optimism. Come, here, old lady, and go to sleep; forget all about the realm and its complications. Have you forgotten you are soon to bear a lusty Douglas son who will gladden your motherly heart and fill your days with pleasure?"

Margaret allowed herself to be persuaded and told Henry's messengers when they next came to her that she appreciated her brother's concern for her safety and bore his advice constantly in her mind.

With her advancing pregnancy she began to have less need of Angus's physical possession of her body and she began to find also she was happier when he was not always about her. He seemed to develop habits which she had not previously noted and which now caused her minor irritation. On one or two occasions she found his overbearing treatment of their servants unnecessary and slightly pompous.

But where John Stewart was concerned it appeared his judgement had been shrewd for Albany was most reluctant to take up the office of Regent of Scotland. From the beginning the Council's supplication met with trouble; the ship carrying the Lyon Herald was wrecked and the crew and passengers only rescued with difficulty and when they were finally brought into Albany's lodgings at the Court of the new King of France, he flatly refused to return to Scotland with them. He would only give his promise to think over the matter.

The Scottish deputation, under stringent instructions from Beton found themselves quarters and prepared to lay siege to

John Stewart's obduracy. It was a long, patience consuming wait but eventually the dark-eyed, graceful Albany gave in to their pleas and agreed to follow them to Edinburgh at the beginning of May. Highly delighted with the success of their mission the Scots returned home.

Margaret received the news with an emotion she was surprised to describe as relief; her fate had been decided one way or another. She had never felt more isolated; only Drummond and Angus, who seemed to spend a great deal of his time hunting or fishing, were able to give her meagre comfort and counsel while Home and the other heads of the clans kept rigidly away from her.

More to give herself something to do than anything else she removed herself and her family to the stronghold of Edinburgh Castle and prepared to wait. Robert Spittal, her tailor from Stirling came to take her usual Springtime orders for new clothes but she told him sadly she had no money for robes and mantles. The little man, a great benefactor of his home town, was moved to compassion for one he had known at the height of her beauty and power, and offered to alter some of her favourite dresses to suit her changing figure. She accepted his kindness a little diffidently remembering James's warning of not allowing herself to be indebted to tradesmen as his great-grandfather James I had done and who had subsequently paid with his life for the indiscretion. But Robert Spittal was too kindly and sympathetic to harbour thoughts of vengeance and so it was when she set forth to meet Albany she was confident she looked attractive and comely.

She had not intended to move so much as an inch to greet her unwelcome successor but she had been prompted to make the effort when she heard, with some amusement of Albany's cool reception of Lord Home who had ridden to greet him with high hopes of being prominently placed in Albany's government. John Stewart had been distant and extremely unfriendly, treating with reservation the ambitious borderer whose conduct at Flodden had been highly questionable and Margaret's informant told her Home had ridden off to his domains in high dudgeon. This easy defeat of one of her most outspoken critics and enemies warmed Margaret's heart towards the new Regent while it made her even more curious to see James's cousin and assess the man for herself.

They met in Holyrood Palace where John was to reside and Margaret was ushered into his chamber to find him writing at a costly inlaid table James had had imported from Italy when he was furnishing the place for his bride. John Stewart rose to greet her, coming across the room with a lithe, easy stride, his hands held out towards her. He overcame the awkwardness of this, their first encounter, by bowing and saluting her on the cheek. His well-tended beard grazed her face and she was swept up in the manly essence of his body and clothing, her antipathy melting as she knew a ridiculous longing to throw herself upon his mercy and beg him to join forces with her and rule Scotland as her late husband had ordained.

As she recovered her composure John led her to a high-backed chair and poured wine for them both. She took the goblet, glad to have some stabilizing object with which to occupy her hands. While they talked pleasantries she gained equanimity to study the man who stood, leaning against the fireplace looking down upon her.

He was uncannily like James but darker, stronger built and possessed of eyes that were fathomless in their blue-black depths; his voice was pleasant, musical, with a heavy French accent adding to its sensuous quality. Margaret found herself listening for the sheer joy of allowing his words to pour over her like balm.

" — do you not think?"

"I am so sorry," she stammered, "I am afraid I have lost the gist of what you were saying — "

"It is of no importance, my lady; I am sure my presence here is sufficient to set your thoughts on other tracts than my conversation and I apologize. Will you do me the honour of accepting my sincere good wishes for your welfare?" He was smiling, a gentle kindly smile and Margaret nodded without speaking.

Albany went on to talk of her children and her life as the wife of the King of the Scots. He was interested also in her father, mother and grandmother.

"Even in France we have heard of this fearless woman who did so much to help her son to the throne of England; could it be, cousin, you have inherited her genius?"

Margaret shook her head, feeling inadequate and exposed in her lack. She sought protection in attack.

"My lady grandmother was perhaps never left friendless, to care alone for my father," she parried, a little wildly.

"But you are not alone, surely," Albany said suavely. "You have a husband, which was more than could be said for The Lady Margaret Beaufort when the Earl of Richmond died before your father's birth!"

Margaret felt herself blushing in a frustrating embarrassment causing the palms of her hands to become damp and chill at the same moment. She glanced up at John Stewart and to her great relief found he was regarding her with a tempered amusement.

"I do not mean to anger you, my lady, or tease; forgive me. I trust we shall meet soon again."

The interview seemed to be at an end and Margaret rose from her chair and made her farewells. Albany accompanied her to the door.

"When is your child expected?"

She spun round at the sudden question.

"In the autumn, September — October."

Did he miss nothing? Yet the words he said as he kissed her hands were stranger still.

"It is a thousand pities, Madame, that the babe within your womb is not mine, for then who knows what the future might have held for us both?"

She thought much of their import over the ensuing weeks as the Council summoned Lord Drummond to answer for his conduct in striking Lyon Herald in the previous autumn and Gavin Douglas was imprisoned.

Try as she would Margaret could not see this as a token of Albany's friendship towards herself and her interests; it was only too obvious the new Regent was being guided by the Council to further their own ends without giving a fair hearing to her supporters.

When she heard of Drummond's imprisonment in Blackness Castle on the Forth she once more put on the becoming robe Spittall had altered for her and with the remaining precious drops of scent, brought for her from France by the French Ambassadors before Flodden, at her throat and wrists set out again for Holyrood. She had herself carried in a screened litter and was glad to be shut away from the curious eyes of the populace of the city. She who had once entered the place with such hopes for the future now felt afraid to venture out in the narrow, thronged streets. No longer did the people of Scotland regard her with respect and admiration.

As before Albany received her alone, with great courtesy and before he could stop her she threw herself (not easily) on her knees and poured out an impassioned plea for the release of Drummond and Gavin Douglas. John Stewart stopped the torrent of words and helped her to her feet. Was it by accident or design his cheek touched her bare throat as she came close to him? Whichever it was she was confused and lost the thread of her pleading. She looked at him imploringly and saw again the amusement of the previous encounter but now mingled with it an emotion she could not define.

"I am assured — "

"By whom? Those who are my professed enemies?"

He continued as if he had not heard her.

"I am assured Scotland is safer with Lord Drummond and Bishop Douglas in places where I am certain of their movements."

"But they are my only friends!" she blurted out.

"Are they? I would not rate your powers of compelling willing friendship so low — and are you not forgetting Angus — once more?"

She was forced to leave without receiving any assurance of his intentions and for days was restless and ill at ease. Several times she almost made up her mind to seek another interview but was restrained not by reasons of politics but by the more primitive patterns of their man and woman relationship. Then, unbelieving, she heard Drummond had been released to a restricted confinement in his own home of Hawthornden. Her heart leapt with pleasure and she sought out Angus to tell him the good news.

"As I said, Meg, yon Stewart is a fair dealing man. Is it not as I told you?"

"Perhaps you are right," she agreed slowly, "but it is early days yet." She would have preferred it if Angus showed some misgivings at the way the Council was manipulating their lives through Albany.

"Cheer yourself, Meg! Your glooms are tied with the carrying of the babe. I am sure the future is not as bleak as you would have me believe. Does not this act of Albany's convince you he means you and the bairns no harm?"

She agreed with him because this was what she wanted but this time Angus was too sanguine in his hopes for the future. Before the month was out the Council, with the Regent as its spokesman, gave orders for Margaret to give up the care of her sons to an appointed board of eight guardians. Margaret was dismayed and the almost sensual bond forged between her and John Stewart disappeared in a terrified fear gripping at her very entrails.

She was shocked out of her terror by Adam Wilkinson who came running to tell of a deputation already marching up the long slope of the Castle Hill.

"They are followed by the entire population of the City and they intend to deprive you of the little King and his brother."

Margaret discovered a courage she had not known she possessed.

"Call together my household with the children and their nurses."

"You do not intend to hand them over, my lady?" Adam asked incredulously.

"I most certainly do not! I intend to show them I am a Queen and the King is my son and we do not submit to their insolence."

She assembled her puny force of servants and children with Angus and stood waiting for the approaching delegation as it mounted, with the crowd roaring behind, the cobbled rise to the gates of the castle. She stood just within the

307

huge, stone gatehouse in the centre of a half moon of frightened men and women, holding Jamie's hand. Strangely now she knew no fear, although the noise of the men and women advancing towards her household had a menacing, animal quality she had never heard before. With difficulty she held herself erect and smiled.

The crowd saw her, waiting fearlessly, and their mood changed abruptly. They were, after all, only there to witness the clash between the deposed Regent and the emissaries of Albany and they were as ready to take sides with Margaret as with the four lords sent to bring away the little King. Someone cheered and a neighbour took up the cheer and in a few moments the loud acclamation made the Council delegation exchange glances of obvious discomfort.

It was Margaret who silenced the cheerful noise. She advanced towards the people, still holding her small son's hand.

"Tell me the cause of your coming, Sirs, before you draw nearer to your sovereigns!"

"We are come to demand and receive the infant King and his brother as ordered by Parliament." The spokesman said in a voice which gathered strength as he proceeded.

As Margaret heard the words she had so long dreaded she gave a sign to the doorkeepers to lower the portcullis and the great iron gate fell down into place. The crowd applauded this show of spirit and were not quiet until Margaret once more called for silence.

In a loud clear voice she told the assembled people the Castle was her own enfeoffment made so by their own beloved James of sacred memory and no one could encroach upon her property.

"I need six days, my good people, to think over the demands of Parliament. My charge is infinitely important and, alas, my councillors be few. Good day to you all!"

With more aplomb than she felt she turned on her heel and led her party back into the castle, heartened a trifle by the sight of several women brushing tears away with the corners of their aprons. She had won a respite for a few days but would her luck hold? Exhausted with the strain of the encounter she leant heavily on Angus's arm and suffered him to lead her back to her parlour. After staying to pour wine for her he left her, saying he wished to see to the positioning of the reinforced guards on the outer wall.

She was sitting back in her chair with her eyes closed when Adam came into the room telling her he had a messenger who came from Lord Home with a parchment he was to deliver only to the Queen.

"Lord Home?" Even in her exhaustion she was surprised. She took the roll from the man, bidding him sit in a corner of the chamber, while she read. At first she had difficulty in focusing on the strange writing but eventually deciphered her one-time enemy was pledging his support should she need it to counter the enmity of Albany and the Council. She could hardly believe she was being offered the first friendship she had had since her marriage to Angus.

"Tell your master I am happy indeed to receive his letter and would ask him to come to me with as much secrecy and urgency as he employ."

The rough fellow, clad in leather breeches and sheepskin jacket bowed and went off with Adam. As the door closed behind them Margaret wondered how deep must Albany have wounded Home's pride that now the man was proffering her his aid. She gave thanks for the well chosen moment of his support. In the six days she had begged she had much to accomplish.

15

"I COME not with you to Stirling!" Angus spoke the words with petulant stubbornness and Margaret regarded him with despair.

"But I am your wife and am great with your child — how can you abandon me now in this hour of my great peril? If I do not flee and protect myself and my sons Albany will take us and all will be lost for me even as it was when my uncles were torn from grandmother Elizabeth Wydeville and thrown into the Tower, never to reappear! Angus, I beseech you, if you care at all for me, help me now to escape to England where I shall be safe!"

"I have never agreed with your mad plans of going to England; once there your brother will keep hold on the little Jamie and force him to become his liege — "

"That is cruel and unjust — Henry has given his word that James shall be his heir if Katherine has no children!" Margaret was stung into anger and the sight of Angus standing like a petulant, sulky boy while she needed the help and comfort of a real man, proved more than she could bear. "Get you gone from my sight and look to your own interests; I was a fool to ever think there was more to you than a handsome face and body."

"Be reasonable Meg! If I go with you to Stirling, or anywhere else for that matter, Albany will confiscate my estates and the Douglas inheritance will blow away like smoke from the heather fires."

"The Douglas inheritance!" Her voice was throaty and heavy with sarcasm. "What is that beside the future of Scotland? You are only a petty chieftain after all, Angus, and I should be deceiving myself to think otherwise. Get you gone before I call the guards to have you thrown out! Thank God there are other men more willing to assist me than my mewling husband."

"Other men?" Angus asked, stayed in his hasty exit towards the door, both by what she said and the sudden realization that when she raged as she did now she was almost breathtaking in her beauty. He was fascinated by the new light shining in her eyes and the swift rise and fall of her bosom. He hesitated and would have remained but she turned away from him, picking up a silver bell to send for Robert Barton, Comptroller of her Household. When the man came she entered into a quick discussion on what could be speedily prepared for a hasty departure. Angus, with a final look at his wife, went quietly from the room.

Before setting out for Stirling Margaret sent Adam to Home with messages asking him to defer his visit to her until she had finally decided upon the best course of action.

It was now the fifth day of those six she had begged from the Parliamentary delegation who had come to her at the castle and with no real hope of the Council accepting her offer she wrote them a letter telling them she would submit her children to the custody of the Earl Marshal, Lord Home, Sir Robert Lawder and Angus if the Council would grant her the right to care for them herself and support them from her dowry.

Almost as soon as the Herald had departed with the missive she gave orders for the withdrawal to Stirling; her fears were becoming an almost physical phenomena that were omnipresent wherever she moved about the chill rooms of the castle.

The journey to Stirling was uneventful and the sun shone on the splendour of the purple heather and glinted splinters of quartz from the tumbled boulders through which they picked their way. It would have been a perfect day for the hunt and she thought with a pang how James would have loved to have ridden out beside her with his hawk at his wrist. Did John Stewart care for the chase as James had done?

Did he particularly care for hunting when she was his quarry? Margaret shuddered, but it was not only because she was afraid for what might happen in the future but also for the growing attraction the Regent had for her personally. Many times during the day she told herself not to be a fool and to think what she should do once she arrived in her dower house but in her mind she could see only the fathomless eyes of Albany as he had looked down upon her with gentle irony.

Within Stirling, with the portcullis down and a doubled guard on duty, she slept dreamlessly and deep. She awoke full of renewed vigour and hope and was breakfasting on ale and bread when Robert Barton came to tell her her spies in Edinburgh reported Albany was leaving the city at the head of a large force of men and coming towards Stirling.

Her tranquillity shattered she turned her energies to her immediate plans to meet the challenge of the Regent. She was alone now, defenceless without Angus or Drummond, and with no army to meet the soldiers coming to lay siege to Stirling. But women were given other weapons with which to fight more deadly than spears or broadswords and guile came high on the list.

She sent Elizabeth Barley for parchment and a quill and sat down and wrote to Home telling him to keep himself in readiness to come to her aid when she despatched a certain messenger to Blackatter Castle giving him the rendezvous. This accomplished she dressed with infinite care and sent word to the royal nurseries for her sons to be put into their finest clothes and brought to wait upon her in her parlour.

The day was the longest she had ever known and the sun was blazing vermilion in the western sky before the lookouts reported a sight of Albany's army. Margaret sent a Herald to meet the advancing Regent and carrying Alexander and leading James by the hand she went slowly down the very steep courtyard and into the bailey. Here she came to the main gateway and entered the thickwalled lodge house. In a firm and low voice she asked the sergeant-at-arms for the keys to the castle; holding them against the body of her infant son who sat on her arm, she took up a position looking down the hill to the town.

Albany led his troops up towards the castle and the first thing he saw as he prepared to position his men was the Queen, standing quite alone with Jamie clutched at her skirts and the babe nestled against her throat. He reined in and jumped down turning towards them.

"Madame, I am delighted to have met up with your Herald and received your communication."

Margaret did not speak; she could not if she had wished for her throat was dry and closed against speech while her heart beat with a tremendous hammering in her breast. Silently she bent and handed Jamie the bunch of keys, indicating the child should hand them over to the man who stood before them. Jamie looked up at her and then as she nodded her approval gravely presented the massive bunch to Albany who now knelt on the paved earth.

Taking the keys John gathered the flaxen haired boy into his arms and held the small face against his own while he looked at Margaret. For a moment she allowed herself to gaze at him then closed her eyes to shut out the sight of him who stirred her so strangely and so deeply.

"Come into my dower house — " she began.

"Said the spider to the fly?" he asked with the trace of mockery never far distant from his speech.

"If you will," she replied casually and led him back through the courtyard to the dwelling house beyond.

That night the Regent and she presided at a feast where she met for the first time for many months those lords who had withheld their support from her cause. They and she viewed each other warily as the meal progressed.

"Lord Home does not honour us?" John asked Margaret when the platters were emptied and the guests laughed and quarrelled noisily throughout the long hall.

"Does he not?" she said, glancing down the tables apparently unconcerned.

"I cannot see him; but we shall not worry ourselves about Lord Home, he is probably too busy running off with neighbours' sheep to be interested in affairs of state." But she knew he was only too well aware of where Home stood in this matter and she was not comforted by the knowledge. She turned the conversation by asking him to speak to her of France where she might well have gone as a bride of the now dead

Louis. His face took on a new animation as he told her of the country of his birth and she realized with dismay he would much rather be in France than here, governing a strife-torn kingdom. Probing her own hurt she asked him about his wife and was slightly mollified by his noncommittal replies.

"Wives are well enough when they bring vast stretches of land and strings of handsome children."

"And yours brought you both?"

"Anne was an heiress in her own right so her dot was large and rewarding."

"And children?" she persisted.

He did not answer at once but took her hand which lay beside his on the polished board and picked up a goblet which he raised to her lips. She drank while her pulses raced and then stared into the depth of his eyes as he finished the wine at a gulp.

"I have no children, Tudor enchantress, and I told you at our first meeting the Angus brat you bear should have been mine."

His hand tightened on hers until her bones felt the pain of his grip.

"If I were not so superstitious I would curse the babe and wish we might go from here and make that child this night. You wish it also, don't you, Margaret?" She gasped and tried to take away her hand but he held it closer and imprisoned it against the silk stuff of his open necked shirt.

"Answer me!" It was a command and she obeyed.

"Yes." It was only a whisper and as she said it she knew she betrayed her cause and her sons.

"Go then and get on with business of having the child while I seek out the lodestar of our destinies."

His directive towards the birth of her child so suited her purposes Margaret was surprised into a smile of real pleasure and she saw at once John had misinterpreted the cause.

"Why do you not laugh and smile more often?" he asked her, "for it becomes you well."

"Do you think I have had so much to make me happy?"

"You have had two loving husbands and are Queen of Scotland — surely that is sufficient for any woman?" His hand caressed her fingers and she was content to allow the tenderness for it soothed the ache of her disappointment in Angus and helped her forget the desperate schemes she was hatching for the escape of her sons and herself into England. As she enjoyed the proximity of this man who had the power to move her as no other had ever done she found herself wishing she could trust both him and the Council; but she knew she would never be easy for the safety of Jamie and Alexander while she was at the mercy of these men who cared nothing for her since she had broken her word to James. Only in England could she hope to influence her brother to back her cause and help her keep her children as her own until Jamie was of an age to rule for himself.

"Or perhaps it is not?"

"Not?" she queried, mesmerized into a trance-like state where the guttering sconces on the stone wall no longer existed and she was cosy and safe in the pleasant house her father had built at Richmond.

"You do not need to answer, for your hand lying in mine so trustingly when we are sworn enemies is proof enough life has not given you what you crave — don't snatch it away, we have few enough occasions of real happiness to reject them when they are offered. May I escort you to your room for we must make the arrangements for our return to Edinburgh tomorrow."

Albany rose and bowed to her and she took his proffered arm and went with him to her apartments. This was the first she had known of her impending return to the capital and it strengthened her determination not to weaken in her resolve to flee. If she was to be ordered in such a manner what further privations might be in store for her children and herself?

"Send away your women," Albany told her as they climbed the narrow stairway together, "there is much I would know about you and James and I do not feel in the mood this night for carousing with a lot of uncouth Scottish chieftains."

"Fie on you, the Scots have Universities almost as old as England and France! Do not underestimate our learning and our search for knowledge!"

"You have spirit, Margaret Tudor, I'll say that for you and I'll confess I tease you a little because when I am in France I am all Scots and now that I am here, in this mist-bound wilderness my praises are all for France."

They had come to the door of her room and going in together Margaret dismissed Elizabeth and one other woman who stood up sleepily to await her bidding. If they gave the Regent and Margaret curious glances as they went away neither of them noticed.

Margaret poured wine from the silver jug into the horn cups while John walked about the parlour and the small bedchamber; he found the lute James had played so often for her and brought it to the fireside where he drew his fingers across the strings sending gentle melodies drifting like an autumn haar around them both. She sat very still shutting her mind to everything but the unexpected delight of being alone with John; after a few minutes he put down the lute and came and sat beside her on the floor, against her chair, taking her hand and holding it against his cheek.

"Tell me of James."

The watch had called the midnight hour and only the owl's hoot filled the unbroken silence of the night when at last he said he must be going from her. She was desolate at the thought of the empty time until it was day but stopped herself from stooping to ask him to remain with her; she must keep a small remnant of her pride for she sensed that with the morrow they might never again be given the charmed intimacy of the evening just gone.

She was in his arms before she was aware of how it came about and his mouth was on hers hard and fierce before she had time to avert her head. She struggled against him for a moment but then with a little moan gave way to the wanton delight of his embrace. At last they stood apart and he kissed the hollow of her throat where the pulse beat rapidly against the delicate skin before raising her hand to his lips.

"I would stay with thee until the crow of the cock but that could only mean I should bed thee and perhaps endanger your life; it is better we part now and wait for what the fates have in store for us. Good night, Tudor Rose, and remember whatever happens I mean thee no ill."

She was carried to Edinburgh and was lost in a haze of remembrances that outweighed her anxieties for her sons; she could think only of the crescendo of emotion marking her affinity with John Stewart. Time and time again she chided herself for her weakness and only came to terms with herself when she made up her mind to forget the brief hours of their shared passion as soon as she arrived within the confines of the castle on the pinnacled rock.

This was more easily thought of than accomplished but by the latter half of the month she was able to send a secret letter to Lord Dacres in his capacity as Warden of the Marches telling him she was retiring to Linlithgow for the Ceremony of the Lying In as prescribed by her grandmother.

At the same time she wrote to Home and informed him she intended using this period as a cover for her escape to England and begged him to meet her at a prearranged place a few miles from Linlithgow.

Margaret marvelled at the way Albany permitted her to make her arrangements but realized he was well aware of the mystique and ceremony attached to such times in a woman's life while at the same time she was acutely conscious her children were being guarded day and night. Whenever she visited them in the nursery she was forced to answer to several strange sentinels before she gained their rooms and once inside other people beside Sir David Lindsay were always present.

At Linlithgow it was exactly the same; no impediment was put in the way of her going to her gracious palace beside the loch but Albany's men made up the accompanying troop of soldiers and she was allowed only a handful of women.

Albany came to wish her a safe journey and an easy and successful confinement and only the strong grasp of his hands on her own spoke of the extraordinary bond between them; his words were formal and polite. Resolutely she shut her mind to her need of him and concentrated on the vital business of extricating herself and her family from the grip of the Council and their unknown designs on their freedom.

Once inside the palace she set in motion the intricate mechanism of the Ordinances; forbidding men to come into her apartments and ordering the sealing of all the windows and casements. When this was accomplished she went to her Oratory and confessed before receiving the sacrament; now began the most testing time of the ordeal in front of her.

During the next night she awoke Elizabeth and complained of pain and a desperate awareness of approaching death. Greatly alarmed Elizabeth sent messengers to Tantallon where the spineless Angus had hidden himself to escape the confrontation between the Regent and his wife.

Angus came on the evening of the following day but before he arrived she had received messengers from Lord Dacre who brought letters from Henry begging her to escape into England before Scotland had become completely under the influence of the French and a note from Dacre himself applauding her decision to take to her chamber for her lying-in. She was grateful for this acknowledgement of her missive to him for it meant he would be making preparation to receive her and her sons once they had made good their escape from Linlithgow.

Angus came into her room, sheepish and aggressive. He flew at once into the attack.

"What is this I hear about you and John Stewart?"

"What do you hear?"

"That he and you are overfond and keep company until late hours of the night; does he make a better bedfellow than I?"

"Don't be ridiculous, my lord! Have you such a short memory you have forgotten I am with child?"

"Lust knows no barrier when it seeks satisfaction."

"You disgust me! Pray account to me for your conduct since we parted last!"

"I have been at home, minding

my affairs. You should count yourself fortunate I did not answer the Regent's command to join him when he rode against you at Stirling!"

"What prompted such gallantry? Surely it could not be affection for your wife? But come, Angus, we are not children to stand here quarrelling; there is work to be done and you must help me set about my going from this place tonight."

"I came because I was told you were ill unto death; I did not intend to give support to your wild schemes for escaping." He looked at her properly for the first time. "You look better than I have seen you for some months — was your illness but a pretext to make me come to you?"

"Yes," she nodded impatiently, "and now that it has served its ends we must plan for tonight with great care; we cannot afford for anything to go amiss."

"Are we alone in this?"

"Not quite; Home has so fallen foul of the Regent he will back my cause with all his forces. He and I are to meet at Newton and we shall rest at Tantallon before pushing on to the border."

"I like this not at all," Angus told her uneasily, "you are so near your time and we shall be unable to move quickly. What will befall if John Stewart should have wind of our schemes and apprehend us?"

"We shall just have to hope he remains ignorant of everything; he accepted my retirement here with alacrity because he knows the ritual attached to a confinement and will not dream for a moment of me having any other thought but for the coming child."

"I am glad you are so easily satisfied; for my part I shall not know a moment of peace until you are safely over the border."

With ill grace he sat down and listened while she outlined what she purposed and by the time they had supped he was ready to do what she asked.

Margaret dismissed her women, telling them she was fatigued and wanted no one to keep her company but Angus when he had returned from the chapel where he had gone to be shriven. The ladies took a while to convince she was well enough to be left alone and then, a little reluctantly, went away to their own chambers. Once they had departed Margaret waited in a mounting state of tension for Angus to come for her; she filled in the long minutes with gathering together a hasty bundle of the barest necessities and had just tied them in a tartan shawl when her husband came in and told her the men he had chosen to accompany them were ready to leave.

"And the children?" she asked breathlessly.

"They are being fetched at this moment."

Very quietly she and Angus stole out from her parlour to the head of the turnpike and crept down hardly daring to breathe. Angus led her out into the inner close and keeping under the shadow of the wall glided passed the kitchens to the gatehouse. Here she had a hurried glimpse of the porter's lodge, where two guards lay trussed on the floor, before a pair of strong arms lifted her unceremoniously and carried her to a waiting litter. She was no sooner lying among the cushions than she felt the conveyance move off across the drawbridge.

Margaret parted the curtains and leant out to ask if the children were safely away.

"They are quite all right, Meg, just lie back and leave this to us." Angus's voice was full of authority and she was glad to take him at his word and relax among the pillows.

"Perhaps it would be better if I had the little Alexander in here with me," she said sitting up again and calling through the curtains.

"Don't fuss, my dear," Angus told her sharply, "we have enough to do to get well away before the guards call up the whole Palace."

She resigned herself then to holding her peace but her head began to ache with the jolting movement of the litter and the strain of not knowing where she was and what was happening. She was grateful at least for the peace of the night and the muffled noise of the horse's hooves as they picked their way through the scrub on the edge of the track linking Linlithgow with the Queensferry road.

It was about an hour later when she heard a quick challenge come from Angus and the litter stopped.

"It is I, Home," came a soft call from ahead.

"Well met!" Margaret answered, drawing back the curtains and asking the carriers to help her alight.

In the starlight she could make out a fairly large assembly of horses and men and Home dropped from his saddle to kiss her hand.

"All is well?" Home asked as Angus joined them.

Angus did not reply immediately and Margaret glanced quickly from him to the company of men who had come with them from Linlithgow. There were but four men beside those who had borne her litter and she was suddenly gripped with a sickening sense that something had miscarried.

"The children — I cannot see the children!" she cried.

"We were forced to leave without them — " Angus began.

Margaret turned on him in fierce anger and terrified disappointment. "We should not have left without them — you should have told me — I would never have given my consent to coming away without Jamie and Alexander! Oh, we must go back and find them! What will become of them?" She began to cry, great, helpless gasps of despair.

Angus was moved with pity for her distress.

"I am sorry, my dear, I waited as long as I dared and when David Lindsay had not come at the time we arranged there was no help for it but to leave without them."

"We must go back!"

Home began to speak quietly to her, comforting her with rough kindliness. "Don't fret, your Grace, I'll do my best to bring the bairns to Blackatter; when once you are safe in Tantallon I'll send out a band of my ruffians to set fire to one of John Stewart's garrisons and while he is dealing with that I'll rescue your sons."

"Do you think you will be able to do that?"

"You can rely upon me to do my very best. Come now, my lady, we'll help you up beside Angus and he can carry you across his saddle 'till we reach his home."

"I would rather we returned for the babies," she said in a thick, tearful voice.

"But it is not possible; if the Regent takes you now, no one will be able to save you. Come, I'll mount and you can sleep in my arms and forget your troubles," Angus told her forcing cheerfulness into his words.

Unwillingly Margaret allowed Home and one of his men to put her up in front of Angus; beside her headache she now felt sick and spiritless. She wished most fervently she had stayed in Stirling or Edinburgh and given herself over to the Regent's protection to do as he wanted with her and her children. What did it matter if France did split Scotland away from England? She was tired and weary of the whole business and as the cavalcade moved off eastwards, where already a thin, pale light was showing, she would gladly have thrown off the panoply of royalty and retired to live in seclusion.

Despite the discomfort she slept off and on until they came to Tantallon, Angus's home built on the edge of high cliffs overlooking the Firth and the North sea. It was now broad daylight and the larks sang overhead with a joyous song that mocked Margaret's misery.

When she was helped to dismount she swayed on her feet, hardly able to stand and gladly allowed herself to be led to a hastily prepared bedchamber.

Her last words to Angus, who came to see she had everything she wanted, before she fell asleep were to implore him to make haste to rescue her children.

"You sleep, Meg, and by the time you wake you will be reunited with the boys. Try not to worry and leave it to Home and me."

She smiled at him wanly and almost before the door closed behind him, slept the mindless sleep of utter exhaustion.

16

ONCE more she was seated painfully before Angus, as they rode towards the borders of England and Scotland. Not only had Home failed in his attempt to bring her children to her but he had set the forces of the Regent against them all for the havoc he had wreaked on the garrisons of the Scottish Army.

Margaret had been ill most of the days they had waited at Tantallon; an illness of mind and body. Neither had she been helped by the complete lack of news from her brother in England; each day she had hoped for messengers who would bring her the formal invitation she needed to cross the frontiers of the two countries and come safely into England. As night fell on every hopeless day she had become listless and apathetic, caring for nothing but the messenger who would release her from the Scotland that had become completely abhorrent to her. Her mind refused to dwell on the fate of her children or upon John Stewart and she could recall nothing of the bright passion flaming between them only a short time before. She could not eat and her sleep was disturbed with dreams where she was perpetually fleeing from many-headed monsters who leered and grimaced at her. She was alone for much of the long daylight hours while Angus went about the business of defending the castle against sudden attack.

Margaret was sunk in hopeless despair when Home had ridden in through the surrounding enemy troops and begged her to be gone with all speed. So precipitate had been her flight she had been miles on the road to England before she realized she had come without her jewels and the one good dress she was keeping to put on when her child was born and she regained her figure. So deep was her anxiety and despair she could not even bring herself to tell Angus of her loss and concentrated on watching the road ahead of them for a sight of the Englishman bringing her news from Henry.

Just before they came to Coldstream

Nunnery Margaret was seized with pains in her back and stomach. She implored Angus to take her into the place where the Prioress was an aunt of Robert Barton.

"We should press on, Meg, every moment we delay puts you in more danger."

"I am wearied unto death and will not go a step further without the permission of my brother."

Angus reluctantly consented to allow her to remain within the nunnery for the night and gratefully handed her over to the Prioress and her nuns who clustered round her, clucking their sympathy.

Here they waited, Angus fuming and Margaret gaining a little strength under the kindly care of the ministering women.

They were visited by Lord Home's mother who brought Margaret some baby clothes she had sewn and who sat with her and helped her pass the hours with womanly talk of their babies and household affairs. Margaret was incensed to learn her good natured visitor had been apprehended on her return journey to her son's home by an over-zealous French commander of the Regent's army who had plucked her from the broad back of her pony and ridden off with her to Dunbar where he had caused her to be shut up in a bleak cell with a diet of bread and water.

"You can see with what forces of cruelty we are dealing," Angus told Margaret as he made his daily plea for her to leave Coldstream on the following day, "If you remain here your peril grows by the hour."

She was weary of his importuning to be gone and when she thought of it was somewhat surprised he showed such eagerness to go to the England of which he knew so little.

"You know I do not intend to leave this place until I receive Henry's invitation. Once I cross the border I am entirely at his mercy and without money or jewels I shall be utterly dependant upon him for the very food I eat."

"While you remain here you are in danger of the Regent's discipline and if what he has meted out to old Lady Home is any example of his punishment I do not hold much hope for your chances."

"John Stewart would not allow Lady Home to be treated so churlishly! I am sure he does not know how his commander has behaved."

"So you are still his champion and would take his part against those who befriend you in your dire peril!" Angus could not hide the sneer and his pleasant, handsome face registered his impatience with her. It became obvious as each tedious day superseded the other the forbearance James had always shown her in her pregnancies was not to be found in Angus.

"I am not his champion," she told him wearily, "I am only a woman, sick with worry, and trying to see good where so little seems to exist."

At last she had word from Lord Dacre to say he had received letters from Henry and was sending an escort to bring her to his home at Morpeth Castle where his wife awaited her with every comfort, including a train-load of necessaries for her confinement provided by Katherine of Aragon. Margaret was happier than she had been since she left her children and set out for Morpeth in high hopes of seeing an end to her troubles.

The imminence of her delivery forced upon her the compulsion to travel by litter and this made their journey slow and tortuous. They were within striking distance of Hardbattle Castle, one of Dacre's garrison outposts within the English border when she realized her labour had begun and it would be impossible for her to continue. Angus took one look at her face and frightened beyond measure gave the convoy leader to understand they could go no further.

Lord Dacre was within the castle when violent rattling of the Scot's swords upon their shields brought the lookouts to the ramparts. He came personally to the portcullis and refused to permit anyone inside but the suffering Queen.

Margaret was past caring and allowed two gatekeepers to lift her from the litter and carry her inside without protest. Angus and Home watched with dismay as the great gate thundered back in position and left them, looking slightly ridiculous outside.

"This is carrying things too far!" Home exploded.

"I hope there are women within to help her," Angus said, his conscience disturbing him when he remembered the pain gripping his wife.

Margaret was all too soon to discover she was the only female within the grim fortress. When she begged for Lord Dacre to bring his wife the Warden of the Marches admitted she was not with him but at Morpeth awaiting the coming of the Queen.

"Is there no one here who can help me at this time?" she gasped as a sword-sharp stab of pain caused her to draw up her knees.

"Your Grace, I much regret, we are but a border garrison and we are nothing but a company of rough soldiery; the best I can offer you is our apothecary who tends our wounded."

A few minutes later a wiry, small man, clad in a brown robe came into the barren room into which she had been carried. He brought with him a burly, red haired man who came quickly to the wooden bed and grasped her hands in his.

"I'm the father of eight, your Grace,

four of them living, and there's not much I do not know about childbirth. Hold on to me and shout your lungs out if you feel the need — no one can hear you and it'll relieve your feelings. That way, master surgeon here can get on with helping the babe into the world and I'll soothe you the best way I may."

Margaret looked up into the kindly, weather-beaten face through a haze of pain and saw him come and go away from her as waves of agony shot through her. Her labours had never been easy and this one, coming as it did after days and weeks of physical strain, was the worst she had ever known. At the end of hours of torturous effort she gave birth to a baby girl.

Across her prostrate, inert body the little surgeon and the borderer looked at one another from red-rimmed eyes and crossed themselves in the knowledge her life was held by the most slender of threads. But very much to their surprise she rallied and by the second day was able to call for a priest to christen the child. On the day following she asked the borderer to obtain parchment and writing equipment from Lord Dacre so that she might send word to Albany of the birth of her child and her wish to return to Edinburgh and the little boys from whom she had been separated.

Quite suddenly her brain was cleared and she knew this was what she wanted most in all the world; if Albany was also in Scotland this was not, at this moment, of any import.

It proved easier for Dacre to despatch this letter, dictated by the Queen, to the Regent than to get word to Morpeth and thence to Henry in Richmond. This was brought about by the Scottish soldiery who were daily creeping nearer to Hardbattle and laying siege to the comfortless place while they successfully prevented the arrival of anyone from Morpeth who might have alleviated the distress of Margaret. Dacre knew also from the spies who were occasionally able to slip through this cordon that a large army under Albany himself was making its way towards the fortress.

Dacre afterwards confided to his wife the anxiety he suffered while the Queen was in his care through three long weeks.

Not only was he without the assistance of one woman but he had no clothes in which to dress the infant and very little delicate food to give a nursing mother in exceedingly hazardous health. The Queen also was demanding to be allowed to return to Scotland and begging him to find means of bringing this about. At last, in despair, he told his wife he could think of no other course but to permit Angus and his friends to come within the castle and hold discourse with Margaret. When Lady Dacre asked him if he had taken all precautions to see the suffering Queen was not worried by the troop of rebel lords who came to visit her he confessed he had not given any thought to their upsetting her.

This, indeed, was only too true and once Angus had come to his wife to look upon their new-born daughter a conference had taken place about her very bed. At first she had taken part in the discussion, eagerly setting out her claim that by returning to Scotland she would bring peace to Scotland and help her son to his future place as King of the Scots. She was flattered to see Arran — who had returned to his homeland with Albany — was also present with Angus and Home and she hoped he would persuade the others to let her have her way. When she saw they were all bitterly opposed to her placing herself under the domination of the Regent her head began to throb with a hammering that forced her to lie back among the chaff-filled pillows and close her eyes in an attempt to shut out their voices and ardent gestures and declamations. After an hour of heated talk they agreed they would do all in their power to rescue the little Jamie and his brother and would not stop waging war against John Stewart until he had surrendered and consented to Margaret being reinstated in his place. Too tired to think she nodded when they asked her if she were with them in their plans and was almost fainting by the time they had found parchment and signed their names to the deed. From the wooden chest in which the infant lay a series of hungry howls announced the new Lady Margaret Douglas required feeding and Angus, grinning a trifle, hooked up the swaddled babe and handed it to Margaret to nurse. Weakly, she made a motion with her hands to be left alone and as the baby took suck the bare, windowless room became blissfully quiet. When the apothecary-come-midwife looked in a few minutes later he found both mother and child asleep.

Margaret was still confined to bed when Dacre permitted an envoy from the Regent to bring letters for her from John Stewart and the Council. He was so anxious for the continuing health of his royal patient that he would have welcomed any crumb of comfort that could have been brought to her through the enemy lines posted outside the castle. Every morning the apothecary gave his reports of the Queen's health and Dacre admitted he was an extremely worried man; if Margaret died what would he do with a newborn infant, alone in a beleaguered garrison?

Margaret dismissed the herald who brought the rolls of parchment and asked for more tapers to light her dim chamber. She read the missive from the Council first and was perplexed by the reasonable tone of its contents.

'Madame, we commend our humble service to your Grace . . . ' it began and continued by assuring her they intended her no harm and would restore to her all her benefices, the guardianship of her children and the release of the still imprisoned Gavin Douglas if she would return to Scotland and carry out her duty to her country.

After she had finished reading Margaret delayed the breaking of the seal on Albany's letter but at last, with shaking hands, she slipped her finger through the wax and slowly unwound the roll. It was a letter of great compassion, ignoring her own foolishness in what had befallen and regretting his part in the series of misadventures which had brought her to her present unhappy and dangerous situation. It was also a letter of love and great intimacy for it touched upon things known only to them both and stirred Margaret to a new awareness of her dilemma. She read again and again the stylized French he had used and knew her first desire was to return over the dangerous road she had just travelled and find solace in the arms of the man who was her avowed enemy. She recognized, also, her great mistake in marrying Angus and bringing her realm and herself into a strife-torn disorder. If only she had possessed the wisdom and foresight to curb her passion and keep it for one who was worthy of what she had to bestow!

Margaret began to pray for Albany to take Hardbattle and end, once and for all, the conflicting disturbance within herself. Even as she voiced the difficult words she had little hope of their being answered for she was religious more by custom than conviction and her Tudor powers of reasoning would not allow that God should grant her requests when she paid so little heed to His word at any other time. Yet still she prayed, desperately and often, for a clash of arms that could only mean the Regent was pitting his forces against the English garrison.

She was to be disappointed; unknown to her Albany had raided the stronghold of the Homes and had taken the small, pugnacious head of the clan into custody.

While the Regent pressed on towards Hardbattle he left Home in the charge of Arran who had been easily persuaded to release Home and join forces with him and Angus. It was this turncoat action which had brought the feeble Arran to Margaret's bedside with the others and occasioned the Regent to change his plans to come to Hardbattle and wheel towards Arran's territory where he confiscated all that untrustworthy noble's lands. While John accomplished this Margaret was able to rise from her bed of sickness and Dacre sent word to those waiting at Morpeth to come with all speed and secrecy to relieve him of her presence.

On a dull, windless November morning exactly matching Margaret's own mood of disappointed apathy she was taken from Hardbattle and conveyed to Dacre's other castle.

No sooner had she been received into the tapestry-hung chambers where warmed beds and hot water awaited her and her daughter, she succumbed to an illness of the bowels and a feverishness of mind overwhelming in its severity. Her sorely won return to health was dissipated in two or three days of the flux and she lay in the unfamiliar, curtained bed unsure of where she was and what had befallen her. In her delirium she called upon James and John and raged against whose who had brought her to Morpeth.

When Angus was asked what might be done to help his wife he could think of nothing but the ministrations of her priest who had been left behind long ago in Linlithgow. Dacre sent secret messengers into Scotland and after a time they crept back to Morpeth bringing Dr. Magnus with them. It would have been almost better if they had failed in their efforts for the priest brought news which sent Margaret, showing some signs of recovery, almost into the arms of death.

Lady Dacre would not permit her patient should be told the ill tidings but Angus overrode her thoughtfulness and strode into Margaret's chamber where she still kept her bed and broke the news himself.

Margaret regarded him with a dazed disbelief.

"What are you trying to tell me?" Her

voice was pitifully weak, a ghost of the throaty sensuous sound that had first enthralled John Stewart.

"I am telling you your baby son, Alexander, is dead; poisoned more than likely by that foul fiend of an Albany! Why should he, the most healthy of your babes, suddenly sicken and die?"

"Angus — Angus! Do not tell me my baby is dead!"

She began to cry, tears of despair and weakness. Angus made clumsy attempts to console her but at last sent one of the women who hovered about in the room for Lady Dacre. The Chatelaine of the castle arrived with a goblet of diluted poppy juice and a very severe admonishment for the husband who had gone against her earnest plea for restraint.

For a month Margaret lay again between life and death, lying most of the time in a coma of blessed relief from anxiety and pain, only now and then moaning as a wounded animal. Towards the end of the first week in January she was brought letters from John Stewart but she was too weak to read their contents and they lay, their seals broken, on the pillow beside her. Angus took the precaution of reading them and instructed Dr. Magnus to reply to them civilly but coldly. He knew, only too well, the rapport existing between his wife and John and grasped eagerly this heaven-sent opportunity for stirring strife between them. On his bidding Magnus wrote also to Henry and Katherine beseeching them to write letters of kindly sympathy to Margaret begging her to lose no time in coming to the sanctuary of their court in London.

The crisis of Margaret's illness came one wild January night in the middle of the month; while the rain poured from clouds only just clearing the surrounding hills. Lady Dacre's physician kept watch beside the Queen's bed. All day Margaret had sweated and tossed, knowing no relief from the pain in her emaciated limbs; the doctor was certain if she showed no signs of improvement she would be dead by the morning. He had sent to Aberdeen university for the latest medicine in the treatment of her disorder and receiving a phial of some golden liquid with instructions for its dosage had forced a spoonful between Margaret's pale lips two or three times during the day.

Only Lady Dacre and the physician were present when Margaret stirred and asked for broth.

"I am hungry," she whispered, "and where is my babe?"

From then on she began to get well; slowly but with strength gained by the hour. Her first thought after her children was to read Albany's letters.

"Have you replied to these?" she asked Magnus.

"Most certainly, your Grace." Something in his voice caused her to look up at him sharply.

"With the gratitude and warmth they deserved, I hope? In case my lord thought me remiss I had best dictate a reply in my own words — have you parchment?"

So she told Dr. Magnus what to say to John and he took what she said and later, in his own chamber, rewrote the letters to suit Angus and the English faction.

Lady Dacre could not do enough for the sick woman and when Angus, sickened with the perpetual illness of his wife, rode off, as he said to meet up with Lord Home, she made light of his absence and said he would return when it was time to escort Margaret to the English court.

Margaret had agreed to go to stay with Henry and was now too weak and helpless to argue; here, in Morpeth, she was too far from Scotland for John to come to her and in truth she would rather he did not see her in her present hapless state.

It was April before a large number of men, well dressed and equipped, came to fetch her to Henry. Sir Thomas Parr, Katherine's own equerry, brought a beautiful white pony for Margaret to ride as well as new clothes and silverware. Angus had returned on the previous evening and on the morning of their departure she was seated in the comfortable saddle of the sturdy little horse waiting for him to fall in beside her when she sensed a feeling of restraint among her escort.

She stopped talking to Lady Dacre, who stood at her stirrup, and glanced round the gaily dressed company of men and women; as she looked about her everybody started talking at once and occupying themselves with lacing a point or tying a shoe. Quite suddenly she knew the reason for the embarrassment.

"Where is Angus?" she asked Lady Dacre sharply.

Not daring to face her, Lady Dacre, flustered and fine-drawn after four months of continuous anxiety, busied herself with buckling a girth.

"He has ridden off, your Grace, and I do not think he intends to ride with you for London."

"How can I endure his callous behaviour another day?" Margaret said on a sharp intake of breath, "I had better be shot of him for good."

"Don't upset yourself, my lady, he will probably think better for his conduct within the week and will overtake you on the road."

"I would rather he stayed behind and saved his own skin! He cares more for that than for anything else in the world."

17

SHE stayed until May 1517 at her brother's court, basking in the affection of Henry, Katherine and her sister Mary, who recently widowed by Louis of France had now married her girlhood sweetheart, Charles Brandon, Duke of Suffolk.

Under the care they all lavished upon her Margaret slowly regained her vitality and good looks; her emaciated figure was restored to a comely roundness and her long, golden hair shone again with health.

At first no one bothered her with affairs of state but cossetted her with every comfort and entertainment Henry's rich and extravagant household could provide. Margaret found it restful and delightful to sit with Katherine and compare progress of their two baby daughters. Katherine was almost pathetically pleased with the child she had managed to bear after a series of miscarriages; her one hope was that now she had borne a living child she might present Henry with a son.

Henry gave Margaret her own establishment in Scotland Yard, where since the early 1400s the Kings of Scots had lived while in London and with Wolsey's help she managed to garner sufficient money to conduct its life.

She found Henry's right hand man a fascinating character but it was not long before she discovered the round, smooth face concealed an implacable determination to make England the greatest power in Europe. Henry, hunting, playing tennis, womanizing and eating and drinking with gusto was quite prepared to lean upon this shrewd statesman who had been able to bring about a union with France in defiance of all long cherished diplomatic moves.

When once Margaret was sufficiently recovered to discuss the future of Scotland Wolsey sat with her for hours pointing out the great benefits her country would derive from union with England. Time and time again he impressed upon her the necessity for sending Albany back to France and relieving the Scots from the ignoble influence of France.

"They seek only to make you a vassal!" Wolsey told her.

"And England does not?" she murmured.

"How can this be when the crowns are united with the ties of blood?" he parried.

"I hear reports that under John Stewart Scotland is enjoying a certain peace," she said mildly.

"That is as may be, but the ultimate aim of Albany is to bring Scotland within the orbit of France and I must impress upon you the urgency of ridding your kingdom of this man and returning to claim the Regency for yourself."

It was sometime after this conversation took place Margaret heard John was proposing to come south to put his case to Henry in person. It appeared, she was told, he was tired of the misrepresentation he received at the English Court and wished to speak with Henry so that Margaret's brother could hear his personal assurance he meant no harm either to Margaret or her son.

When Margaret was told the news of his possible visit she felt awakening within herself a longing to see him again but was sadly disappointed when instead Albany begged the Council to allow him to leave Scotland for a short period to visit his wife who was seriously ill. If it was any comfort to her Henry and Wolsey were delighted at this turn of events and redoubled their efforts to ensure when she returned north she would only consider the English claim to aid Scotland.

In all the months she had been in England Margaret received no word from Angus and then almost as she began her journey home, she heard the first rumour of his living with Jane Stewart in Tantallon. Although she no longer loved him she was furiously, unwarrantably jealous and refused to listen when Henry begged her to be reasonable and forgiving.

"There are more important matters than hurt feelings, Meg," her golden-haired, magnificently built brother told her. "You and I have our kingdoms to think on and it is only right to preserve the sanctity of our marriage vows!"

The train of attendants who accompanied her was very much smaller than the grand entourage who had taken her north for her marriage with James fourteen years earlier but she stayed at the same hospices and castles where she had been welcomed before. Many times during the endless seeming miles she remembered the frightened child who had ridden with such pomp to marry a man she had never seen and the thoughts made her recall James and their life together through the ten years of her marriage. Looking back on it, despite all the miseries of her pregnancies and the loss of their children and James's infidelities, she had been quite happy until her husband had begun to have his grandiose schemes for his kingdom. What was there in the love of power that spoilt even the best and wisest of men?

At Morpeth she was reunited with Lady Dacre.

"How well you look! And let me see the babe!"

Margaret displayed the little girl who grew daily more attractive and then went into the castle where over a year before she had not cared if she lived or died. She and Lady Dacre sat together talking far into the night.

"Has my lord of Albany departed yet for France?" she asked casually. In truth she did not mind one way or the other for Wolsey and Henry had so impregnated her mind with their implacable hatred of the Regent she was at a loss to know how to think of him.

"I believe he sails on the day after tomorrow — my husband will be able to confirm that for you. Is it your policy to wait until he has quit the kingdom?"

Margaret nodded. "My brother made me give him my word I should not set foot in Scotland until John — the Duke — had departed." Changing the subject abruptly she went on to ask about Angus and if the rumours she had heard in London were correct. Lady Dacre knew it was useless to lie and told her forthrightly Angus was living openly with Jane at Tantallon.

"What a fool I was to be taken in by his good looks," Margaret said quietly. "Ah, well, I had best be seeking my bed for I must look my most prepossessing on re-entering my son's kingdom."

On June 7th she had word to say Albany had sailed for France and she advanced to Berwick where she was met by a sheepish Angus. Remembering Henry's admonishment to preserve the dignities of marriage she greeted him with as good a grace as she could muster and he told her he had come to escort her to Edinburgh.

They rode there preserving a sullen politeness that was not helped by the knowledge Angus had been almost ignored by the Englishmen who had escorted her to Berwick. Fortunately Angus seemed delighted with his daughter and several times he took her up to sit in his saddle with him.

"Is it true London is plagued with the sweating-sickness?" he asked Margaret.

"Yes, it has been rife there for several weeks; even the great Wolsey has been ill with it. Have you had it in Scotland?"

"Fortunately not, the comings and going between the two kingdoms is so small it gives little opportunity for disease to spread."

She was very soon to know how much

the Scottish Council dreaded she might have brought the sweating sickness with her. When she arrived in Edinburgh the first thing she did was to ask to be brought to see her son; to her distress permission was refused on the grounds she might be carrying the disease upon her person.

"Do you think they make excuses?" she asked Magnus. "Is it perhaps because the child is ill or suffering in the mind and they do not want me to come to him?"

"No, Madame, I think it is much more likely the Council fear you may abduct him and return instantly to England. Bide your time until tomorrow and they will most probably have relented."

With some difficulty she reconciled herself to taking his advice and when the next day she sent messengers to Craigmillar where Jamie was lodged they returned to tell her she might proceed to the place to see her son.

Jamie had grown so much in the months since she had last seen him she found him almost a boy; she longed to gather him into her arms but managed to restrain herself until he realized who she was and then gradually, little by little, she drew him to stand near her until eventually she was able to cradle him against her breast. He talked to her in a soft, childish babble, and tears filled her eyes and closed her throat while she hugged him without speaking.

"Will you come again soon?" Jamie asked her gravely as she was leaving.

She nodded. "As soon as possible."

She knew, as she went slowly back to Edinburgh she would not be able to leave Scotland while the child was still so young for the sight of him awoke the most tender maternal instincts.

Many times in the coming months and years she was to think of this ride back to Edinburgh and the decision she had taken then for her life was difficult from the very outset.

It was Angus who proved the chief stumbling block and she wrote impassioned letters to Henry telling him of his brother-in-law's disgraceful conduct during her absence; not only had he carried off Jane but he had fathered a daughter on her and confiscated Margaret's dower rents to finance his unlawful union. She was therefore, practically penniless and had to support a large household by selling all the gifts Henry and Wolsey had lavished upon her when she returned to Scotland. It would have been easier if Albany had left money for her in the exchequer but a painful search through these had soon proved he had been able but lavish. Margaret did not dwell on this, neither on the uncomfortable fact that John had left de la Bastie, his French commander as Warden of the Scottish Marches. The Regents he had elected to govern in his name, Huntly, Arran, Angus and Argyle with Beton seemed to accept a foreigner in charge of Scots troops and Margaret thought it better to keep the information to herself; Henry would hear about it soon enough but not through her.

When she saw all the nobility together as she did as they met to attend Parliament she was forcibly reminded of the other rebel lord, Home, who had helped her to escape from Linlithgow and who, along with his brother, had paid for his treason with his life. She did not have to be a great statesman to realize Albany had secured peace on the borders with Home's execution while at the same time he had ridded himself of a troublesome opponent.

During the coming months she made every effort to make Angus restore her lands and income to her but he was adamant and refused to give in to her; Margaret was especially chagrined when Gavin Douglas, who had been her friend and for whom she had battled to advance in the church, sided with Angus and told him to keep what was a husband's right.

Although she saw Angus intermittently and he tried to make amends to her she now began to think seriously of divorcing him and wrote to Henry to announce her intentions. Both Wolsey and Henry wrote back instantly telling her not to do anything so foolish but to bear with the young man and try to rule Scotland properly with his help and that of the rest of the Regency.

This was far easier said than done for Arran, Angus, Huntly and Argyle soon quarrelled among themselves and not long after Margaret's return Albany's

Warden of the Marches, de la Bastie was murdered by a Home to revenge his kinsman.

It was about this time that she began to long for Albany to come back to Scotland and bring the peace he had contrived during the years of his Regency.

Margaret had news of him in France, where his wife had recovered, and it was obvious he had not forgotten Scotland for he negotiated a Treaty whereby France stood by her old ally and he promoted good trade relations for those Scots merchants who brought their wares to France. He also obtained a promise from the new king of France, Francis, that his eldest daughter should become the wife of James.

When she heard this Margaret wondered what would be Henry's reactions to this countering of *his* plan to wed his daughter with her cousin!

As the months dragged into years and the quarrelling increased rather than diminished and Margaret was forced to grovel to her brother for sufficient money to make ends meet she was further provoked by the Council suddenly withdrawing her permission to visit her son.

Once more Henry was bombarded with words in a lengthy letter in which she set out her grievances, telling him that not only was James kept from her but she had been forced to dismiss all her servants and would be starving if it were not for the kindness of Robert Barton, her old comptroller, who bought her goods out of his own purse.

She did not add she had also written to Albany asking him to approach the Pope with a plea to grant her a divorce from Angus. Yet somehow, in a mysterious way she was not able to explain, Henry discovered what she had done and showed his hostility to her plan, and concern for her soul, in the dire course she wanted to take by sending some of his own priests to dissuade her.

She received them and listened politely to their admonishments but did not intend to depart from what she had tried to set in motion; while they spoke, quietly, at first, of her scandalous wish to set aside her marriage with Angus she pondered the question of what celibates might know of the wedded state but began to lose patience later when their tempers and voices rose at her continuing rejection of their arguments. Henry Chadsworth, a particularly stern friar who came from the Observantine Monastery at Greenwich, was convinced Margaret only wished for the divorce in order to marry another man.

"Put away these foolish ideas of finding gratification in bodily lust," he thundered in an eloquence his congregations must have found irresistible, adding obscurely, "and foreign persons have no especial virtues to commend them."

He returned to England without convincing Margaret she was a sinner although, as mildly as she was able, she tried to point out it was Angus who lived in Douglasdale with his paramour while she was blameless of breaking her marriage vows. Yet, in the loneliness of her increasingly miserable household, she knew she committed a sin each time she thought of John Stewart, Duke of Albany, and wished he would return to give her support and comfort. Henry and Cardinal Wolsey seemed more and more remote as the months and years went by and replied to her impassioned pleas for money and help with cold words of wisdom and little more.

It would have helped if she had one friend to whom she might confide her troubles. Even William Dunbar had still not returned to court since Flodden; most people thought he had accompanied James to that field of disaster and perished with him, but travellers to Rome came back with stories of a mendicant Scottish friar who walked the length and breadth of France and Italy helping the poor and singing in the great halls of the rich to earn enough for his daily food and those, like Margaret, who had been his friend hoped he would return one day to Scotland. Her women were mostly loyal and sympathetic but they were happily married or betrothed and had no conception of the very real difficulties she faced; if they had children they did not know what it meant to come to each new day wondering if permission would be withheld to visit a little son and, although she had the baby Margaret to fondle and croon over the child was, after all, Angus's offspring and was startlingly like her father.

There were, naturally enough, the sychophants who sought her amatory favours but she found their advances tepid and tasteless.

Even Dacre who had been with her through some of the most dangerous days of her life seemed more inclined to take Angus's part than give her an understanding ear. When Henry and Wolsey appeared deaf to her opportunings she wrote to Dacre putting her case as strongly as she was able.

'My Lord Dacre,

I stand in a sore case for I get no help from my brother, His Grace the King or from the lord Cardinal; such jewels as his Grace gave me, at my departing, I must put away for money. I have discharged all my servants, because I have nought to give them.

'His Grace promised me that Scotland should never have peace from England unless I were well done by; which is not done for I never was so evilly treated. I beg of you to intercede with my lord the King, for all my hope and comfort is in him. And, my lord, this realm stood never as it doth now, nor never like to have so much evil rule in it, for every lord prideth who may be the greatest party and have the most friends, and they think to get the King, my son, into their hands, and they then will rule all as they will, for there is many against the Chancellor and think to put him down from his authority; and thus I see no good for my son or me.'

Margaret wrote this from Stirling where she was still allowed to reside by favour rather than by right and receiving no satisfaction from Dacre's reply she wrote again this time telling him in no uncertain fashion her intentions for the future. She was goaded into taking the course her feminine intuition told her held out the most hope for both herself and the young King. Henry was never to know how bitterly disappointed she was in his failure to render her the help and sympathy she so desperately needed at this moment. It was all very well for him, wrapped in the splendour of his court life, to rage at her weaknesses but his brotherly love would have been more welcome than clement weather at lambing-tide in her tribulation.

'My Lord Dacre,

'I thank you for passing on, as you have done, my pleas to my brother and the lord Cardinal, especially in the matter of my son's safety and welfare.

'You are well aware that what I have done in the past has been at my brother's bidding for what I was made to believe was the best for this realm of Scotland. For this reason I have trusted the lords of this realm and I have kept the peace as I was bound but I am no better off than before for I have never been so evil answered or disobeyed — particularly where my own lands are concerned. All this I have often written to the King my brother, the lord Cardinal and you. Howbeit I have had no remedy and am now forced to seek aid from the Duke of Albany for I have none here that will help my complaint or do me justice.

'You have asked me many times if I have submitted myself to the King of France and I now inform you that I have, with the agreement of the Council, for the welfare of my son and myself, written to this said monarch requesting he return the Duke of Albany to Scotland.

'My lord, I pray you remember, that if you were in another realm, helpless as I am, you would do what you might to please all and so must I. I therefore implore you to put my case fairly to my brother and the lord Cardinal; in the last correspondence I had with the King he commanded me to do nothing of which the Lords might complain and this I trust I have done.

'And suppose it bring evil to me, it is dishonour to His Grace, my brother, as well as to me. The unkindness I find does me more harm than anything in the world and I come to expect no help but fair words.

'My lord, you must pardon, I write

so sharp but it touches me deeply; God keep you,

'Your friend, Margaret R.'

Once she had announced her intention of begging John Stewart to come back both to Scotland and herself Margaret knew a tranquillity of mind she had forgotten existed. Once again she was able to look beyond the present misery of her existence and look outwards to the beauty of a Scottish summer day when soft sunlight played on the new leaves of the larch and the burns ran ochre-brown with the dancing waters of the melted winter snows. She knew it might be weeks or months before she and Albany were reunited but she did not doubt, for one moment, he would come.

Helped by this knowledge she was able to withstand the resentment of Angus when he discovered what she had done; leaving his mistress in Tantallon he came at great speed to Edinburgh where she was lodged for the winter and complained of her churlish treatment of him, her wedded husband.

"You don't give me a chance, Meg! I may be young and hot-headed, but you loved me once and if you would be reasonable we might still manage a co-existence that would help Scotland to live well under our rule."

"You ask me to be reasonable! I wonder that you dare to come to me with such a request! Was it reasonable of you to desert me on the eve of our daughter's birth and taunt me ever since I returned to this benighted country with your illicit domesticity in Douglasdale?"

As always when she was angry she was magnificent, colour high in her usually pale cheeks and her eyes sparkling with indignation. Angus was tempted to carry her forcibly into her bedchamber and reawaken the passion of the early days of their marriage but he confessed he was daunted by her air of majesty and contempt for his betrayal.

"You and I are best apart, my lord; in that way our temperaments do not seek to destroy the other and we may yet make some contribution to the common weal."

When he was gone she knew a few

minutes of contrition for she was honest enough to admit she had seduced him into the marriage that had brought so much unhappiness to them both and had it not been for her he would have already been married to Jane Stewart and bringing up a family in honourable wedlock. Her forgiveness quickly faded as she remembered the Douglas ambition had had just as much to answer for as her own cupidity and with this reassurance she dismissed him from her mind.

In October, 1521, she had word to say Albany had left his wife's estates in France and was hoping to be in Scotland before Christmas. Margaret was overjoyed and in a whirl of excitement forgot all her troubles as she did her best to refurbish her lodgings in Linlithgow where she had now taken up residence. This accomplished she had her women bring out all her robes and headdresses from the oaken chests in which they had lain since she came back from London and chose those which still became her, giving away to the needy all the rest.

This was a moment of exuberance to share with the world and she opened her heart and her slim resources to others; in a most unusual mood of benignity she visited the sick in the small town of Linlithgow and spent hours every day in the little oratory overlooking the loch. Heaven must surely smile upon this, her last bid for personal happiness!

18

THE twenty-first day of November, 1521, broke windless and without sun beneath a canopy of grey skies; the loch at Linlithgow was lifeless like dull pewter and the ducks floated without breaking the surface. It was a day of anticipation as if the world held its breath ready to gulp in the wind that would soon blow with great strength from the surrounding hills.

Within the palace in the Queen's parlour a small fire burnt with difficulty; the wood was scanty and damp but Robert Barton had promised Margaret he would go out himself to the crofters who usually provided the house with turf and garner the fuel for her warmth. To his surprise the Queen did not seem to notice the bleak cold of her chamber and made no complaint when he told her no provision had been made to lay in a store of fuelling for the winter.

"Quite soon, Master Barton, we shall

be able to bask in the warmth and charity of the Duke himself and I assure you we shall want for nothing."

"Indeed I pray to the holy Saints you are right, your Grace, for not only are we short of creature comforts but our provisions are hardly adequate for a shepherd's hut let alone a royal palace."

"Fash not," Margaret told him lapsing into the broad Scots James had taught her, "for I ken well we have seen the worst of our discontent."

"Amen and amen," the harassed comptroller told her, "we have had more than our share of anxieties and deprivations since your return from England."

"With the coming of the duke all our troubles will be at an end," she assured him smiling, and looking at her Barton was aware if the thought of Albany's coming brought the contentment he saw in her face his presence would be food and warmth enough.

"Do you think he will bring a large train with him as he did last time, your Grace?"

"I do not really know, Master Barton; I

believe the Earl of Arran is accompanying him once more, but apart from that gentleman I have not heard of any other."

Arran had fled to France after a disgraceful affair in Edinburgh when the quarrel brewing between himself and Angus had culminated in a fray in which seventy people lost their lives. Ever since Margaret's return the Regents, who had been appointed by Albany, had tried to oust the others and rule Scotland alone; this selfishness was demonstrated by several clan battles between the Douglases and the Hamiltons but the bloody fight in the narrow wynds of the city had been the main reason behind Margaret's last letter to Dacre in which she had stated she intended to appeal to Albany for help in keeping the peace.

Margaret still shuddered when she recalled the horror of the bloodshed perpetrated in the name of government. Arran and his followers had had much the worst of the day and Sir Patrick, his brother, who had tried to act as mediator was run through with a sword which the Hamilton's were prepared to swear was wielded by Angus himself.

Arran had managed to extricate himself from the melee and covered by the shouting and swearing of those who still fought for their lives made good his escape to Leith where he took ship for France. His going left Angus in virtual supremacy.

"Does the duke bring his wife with him?" In anybody else the question would have been impertinent but Margaret, brought back from her hideous remembrances, knew Barton only asked in order to make ready should the Lady Anne accompany her husband.

"I do not know, but I understand she does not have very good health and the winter is hardly the time for travelling." Especially, she might have added, as my brother prolongs its danger by refusing to give safe conduct permits to Albany thus forcing him to come by the sea as far as Leith.

"Do you know which day my lord the duke will come?"

Margaret shook her head. "When he has been to Holyrood he will doubtless send Heralds to tell us of his arrival and we shall have time to made all preparations for his reception."

In the afternoon the lake was ruffled with long swirls of wavelets as the wind gathered strength and Margaret sent for a cloak and walked on the battlements alone. She would dearly have liked to order a pony to be saddled to go hunting but the day was already fading with the coming of night and she lacked the fitting companion for a swift ride out into the hills where the dead heather glowed against the grey sky and rock. In a corner sheltered from the wind, now blowing with intensity from the south-west she watched the road from the east and saw in the half light a troop of men on horseback coming towards the castle. Her heart gave a great leap for joy and she called out to the man-at-arms standing in the nearest embrasure to tell her if he could make out the banner borne by the leading herald; when he told her it was that of Albany, she sent him below to warn the gatekeeper to lower the drawbridge and raise the portcullis. She stayed watching the approaching cavalcade until the houses clustering at the palace gates hid it from her view and went slowly to her apartments to prepare herself for what she realized was the most momentous meeting of her life since the day she had been presented to James at Dalkeith.

She did not hurry over the changing of her robe and redressing of her hair and chose simple clothes that were old, outmoded but yet flattered the still unspoilt texture of her fair skin and the beauty of her hair. She was sitting at her dressing table, her mirror of polished silver in her hand when Robert Barton came to announce the arrival of the Regent who sought an audience with her.

Margaret asked the comptroller to prepare supper for John and herself with the best the house had to offer and said she would join her guest in a few moments. She dismissed her women, and to control her trembling, forced herself to kneel in the oratory for ten minutes while she regained her control.

Serene and head held high she walked to the oblong chamber that was her bower and found John standing in his favourite position close to the fire. Hearing her come in he came quickly to her and taking her hands raised them to his lips; to her dismay she found her eyes filling with tears and could do nothing to stop them spilling down her cheeks. This was not at all the approach she had planned and she made a movement to take away her hands to brush aside the revealing tears but John, glancing upwards, saw the reason for her distress and not releasing her, brushed her face with his fingers round her own.

"This is a glad moment, Margaret, and your tears tell me more than words; don't let us dwell upon the cause but delight, instead, in our reunion."

He handed her to a chair and brought her wine from a table against the wall.

"Wine?" she asked. "You must have carried it with you for I have almost forgotten how it tastes!"

"Coming from France I should have been more than remiss to bring you no wine; drink it while I look at you and see if you have changed or not during the five years we have been apart."

He brought a stool and sat opposite

her frankly searching her face; while he did so she studied him and discovered he had altered little. He was now forty and still retained the grace and vigour which had marked him out from his fellowmen. His voice stirred the dormant recesses of her senses as he talked of nothing in particular but made her acutely aware of herself and their relationship.

"It is so good to have you here again!" she said suddenly. "My life since you went away has not been pleasant."

"I have but to look into your face to know that," he said quietly, "but this night I want to hear nothing of what has befallen; there is time enough for that when we are surrounded with worthy Beton and Arran and the rest. Tonight remember only that you are a woman and I a man and that we have not seen one another for a long time. Have you missed me, Margaret? Although," he went on without waiting for her reply, "I do not need to ask for your blood leaps to mine as mine does to yours; would you deny it?"

"No," she answered faintly, "you are perhaps the only positive thing in my life and I have existed for so long in the twilight of a half-living that it would be foolish and untrue to say I have no need of you."

"Where is your child?"

"James?"

"No, I know he is with David Lindsay at Craigmillar — I meant the Angus offspring."

"She is with her father," Margaret replied dully; this had been the final blow in her enmity with Angus. When Angus had peremptorily removed his daughter to Tantallon and deprived Margaret of the child's company it had been a cruel and unnecessary affliction to a woman already suffering more than was her due.

"Perhaps it is for the best," John said softly, "for you and I stand alone against them and we travel better without encumbrances."

Barton knocked on the door at this moment to say the food he had prepared was ready. He brought it in accompanied by two or three of Albany's own servants who carried armsful of logs.

"I asked Master Barton how you fared

for warmth and when I heard your supplies were low I sent to the Carmelite house nearby and requested a load of their dryest logs; in the morning I shall set about the restocking of the cellars with turf but this night I am afraid you will have to make do with wood."

"That is no hardship," Margaret told him gratefully as flames roared up the wide chimney and lit the bare walls of the room with apricot light.

They ate the frugal supper in companionable informality; from time to time John made her drink from his own wine cup and she began to experience again the sheer sensual pleasure of being near this man who had for long occupied a unique place in her thoughts and sentiments.

"Ring for Barton to take away the dishes, for I want you to myself for the rest of the evening," he said when he had eaten his fill.

After Barton had gone Margaret paced the room beset with a sudden restlessness and loss of confidence in herself; after all, except for the fact that Albany was her husband's cousin what bond was there between them? She had already had abundant proof of the short-lived passion Angus had roused in her — what was so very different about the delight kindled by Albany?

As if to answer her unspoken question he came up behind her, putting his arms about her waist and burying his face beneath the hair at the nape of her neck. Margaret held herself rigid and away from him but in a sudden rush of longing to be safe within his embrace turned towards him, saying his name over and over, softly on a little moan. He kissed her eyes, her cheek and at last her parted mouth. Margaret was lost, carried away in an awakening of passion that was unlike anything she had ever before known. John Stewart's ardour was gentle but strong, demanding while it protected and she answered him with a complete surrender of herself.

"Come back to the fire," he said gently disengaging himself, "and I shall bring your bedrobe and help you to prepare for bed in the warm."

While he went into the cold, draughty bedchamber she knelt down, staring into the now hot embers of the fire. Her body knew a delightful sense of anticipation and she was content to do as he bid her, asking no questions and prepared to allow him to lead her where he chose. He came back with the robe and putting it to warm, knelt in front of her and removed the cheveron from her head and pulled out the pins from her hair; it fell about her shoulders like the golden robe she had worn at her crowning. With gentle hands he unfastened the lacing of her bodice and she knew no shame when he touched her breast and ran his fingers along her throat to lift her face for his kiss. A joy, fierce and winging heavenwards, made her catch her breath on a sob and John turned away from her to cover her nakedness with the robe. She was glad of the warm, silken brocade when he took her to her bed and wrapped her with the blankets and fur overlay; he came in beside her and drew the curtains, shutting out the damp chill of the room and the world outside.

For some time he cradled her in his arms, soothing her with whispered words and the touch of his mouth on her face.

"I cannot believe you and I are really here, alone, in this bed where I have so often thought of you and been so desolate and unhappy," she said softly. "Tell me I shall not wake soon and find it all a dream."

"This is no dream and I am prepared to swear it was predestined from the first time you and I met; do you not recall I wanted to carry you off then, but you were great with child by Angus?"

Margaret shivered.

"Forgive me I did not intend to speak of him. Come, kiss me and I shall make you forget you ever knew him!"

Her mouth beneath his she was lost again, drowning in the awakening delight of the passion he invoked in her; when he untied the sash of her bedrobe she made no demur. His body was strong, his flanks smooth with no sign of softness; timidly she touched his back, stroking his shoulders and his waist while his hands drew her into an ecstasy where they became no longer two people but one enraptured in the other's delight.

If this was passion she had never before experienced that emotion for she gave herself in utter, bewildering joy to this man who was almost a stranger but yet part of her very soul. He made love to her as if this was the only thing he had ever really wanted in his life and she understood and responded giving him freely of herself. Reaching the climax of their rapture he did not fall immediately into a self-satisfied sleep but talked to her, stroking her sides until she was drowsy as he and they both slept.

She awoke with a start to see the cool, pale light of day through the bed curtains and sat up alarmed, pulling the bedrobe about her; John's hand touched her hair and his voice bade her lie again beside him.

"I have been watching you asleep, Margaret, and I have longed to wake you but had not the heart when you looked so utterly at peace. I must be going to the chamber the thoughtful Barton prepared for me above yours." Her arms tightened about him. "Do not be afraid, I have no intention of going from this place until you and I go together — and if you will have me I want to stay while we forge the bonds that will hold us together."

"Must you leave me now?"

"Don't make it harder for me; I shall return to you to break our fast in your parlour and then we shall plan how we may spend our days here together."

He bent over her kissing her eyes and the hollow at her throat and was gone, taking the first humanity she had known since James's death. Before she had time to sigh she heard him ring the silver bell she used to summon her women and thanked him wordlessly for his thought for her.

She did not see him after they had eaten some bread and ale until they met, with her depleted household, in the Great Hall and Albany presented the handful of men who had accompanied him from Edinburgh. Most of them were unknown to her and Arran was not of their number; she was glad of this for the delicate and intimate relationship flowering between her and John was not yet sufficiently well established to bear the sidelong glances of nobles of her own court.

During the morning she had talked with Robert Barton who was overjoyed at the changes Albany had already made in the kitchen and storerooms.

"I wish you might have seen my lord," he told her, "he came into the kitchen and asked me to show him the food we had ready for the winter; when he saw the miserable few sides of deer and pig we had hanging in the rafters he took his hat from his head and threw it into the fire with rage. 'How can those dastardly rogues on the Council allow their Queen to be treated thus? And what means the King of England to permit his sister to live like the widow of a poor crofter?' You should be pleased, Madame, you have a champion at last!"

As before they supped in her parlour where an enormous fire made the room pleasantly warm and cosy; Margaret sent away her women and waited on Albany herself. So precious seemed their time together she could not bring herself to share an hour of it with anyone else and she enjoyed also the unusual pleasure of having the undivided attention of the man who brought with him into her apartments a new dimension in living. When they had finished their meats and a cheese made from pressed curd Margaret peeled for him one of the oranges he had given her from his baggage; she handed him the quarters and watched the juice run over his fingers as he bit into the fruit.

"May I not prepare an orange for you? They are, after all, a present for you and you sit and look on while I enjoy them!"

Margaret laughed and shook her head. "I have pleasure enough for the moment."

She threw the peel into the flames where it curved and dried instantly sending an aromatic perfume into the room.

"Come and sit here, beside me," John said as he wiped his hands on a napkin and leant back in his velvet covered chair. Obediently she settled herself against his knees and he put his arm about her shoulders and cradled her to him. They sat without speaking gazing into the fire, at peace. At last he stirred a little and spoke gently.

"Tell me now of what has befallen you since last we met."

It was difficult at first for there was so much she wanted to pour out and explain but gradually she was able to make a coherent story of her misfortunes and grievances. John listened patiently, now and again asking her to repeat something as a particular incident or detail was not quite clear. When she told told him of her confinement at Hardbattle Castle his fingers tightened on her shoulders and he questioned her sharply about the letters she had both written and received during her stay with Dacre.

"Is this Dr. Magnus still with you?" Margaret nodded. "I am greatly desirous of speaking with him for from what I can hear our correspondence has been tampered with. Are you certain when you wrote to me you told me you wanted nothing better than to return to Scotland?"

"I am quite sure; all that seemed to matter when once the child had been born was that I should come back and ask you to help me in the government of Scotland."

"Oh, God, if I had but received your letters — who knows what suffering might have been saved us all! Did you write the letters yourself? No, of course, I remember, you were too ill to do that and Magnus scribed them from your dictation; a most marvellous opportunity to twist what you had to say to suit the purpose of your brother."

"So that explains so much of what I could not understand at the time. Why has Henry turned against me?" Her voice was husky with perplexity.

"I would not imagine your brother has changed his real feelings towards you, it is more feasible to reason that Wolsey — now he has obtained his Cardinal's hat — so longer needs the support of Francis of France and can afford to vent his displeasure on the sister of his King when she turns to me for help. My dear, you are the victim of diplomatic intrigue and I intend to do all I can to alleviate the distress this brings to you as a woman. Can you bear to tell me about Angus?"

Margaret went on with her narrative, steeling herself to speak of her disappointment in her young husband and his desertion of her as she finally went into England. Albany made no comment and she was grateful for his reticence for she knew where Angus was concerned she had brought her own unhappiness upon herself.

It was easier to talk of her stay at Richmond and Greenwich and the disappointment she had known when she had believed Albany would come to her there but had gone instead to France to look after his sick wife. Margaret hastened over this reference to Anne and spoke instead of her meetings with Wolsey when he had done his utmost to persuade her to bend Scotland to England's will.

"I confess," she said ruefully, "I began not to know what to think for the best; in London it seemed plausible to incline towards England and for so many things it suited me best to be linked with my brother's power. Yet, I could never forget James had always welcomed the French as old allies and my personal remembrances of you made me wish to see a return to the days when you had been Regent. Where did I go wrong?"

"Dearest." (It was the first endearment he had used towards her and the foolish

401

tears came again into her eyes.) "You are but yet a young woman and the diplomacy needed to deal with Wolsey's wiles could only be gained by years of practice in a hard school. Do not reproach yourself too harshly. Come, tell me of some of the more pleasant and successful achievements of your stay at Henry's court; what did I hear about your efforts to save the young apprentices who had rebelled against a new law and had terrified the citizens of London with unruly behaviour?"

"My sister-in-law and Mary and I only did what any woman would have done when she saw the young being called upon to pay too high a price for their bid to state their case. If Wolsey had had his way all the ringleaders would have hung and this seemed to us too terrible punishment for a moment's folly. We pleaded with Henry to pardon their offences and I am happy to say he listened to us and the foolish boys went free. How did you know of the matter?"

Margaret knelt up to face him, her elbows across his knees. John stroked her cheek and he touched her forehead lightly with his lips.

"A brave action stirs the heart of most people and the story of the three queens seeking justice fired even the imagination of the most stolid French emissary at the English court."

"I cannot abide bloodshed."

"Neither can I, but there are times when it is unavoidable; you are thinking of the Homes?"

"Yes, and the subsequent assassination of de la Bastie. You will find there is much for you to settle in Scotland at this moment; Angus cannot abide Arran, as you well know, and while we have an ally there their violent dislike of one another makes your task more difficult."

"I am not afraid of any of them and while I am here in Scotland I shall compel them to recognize my authority."

"Do not tell me you are not here to stay for the rest of our lives?" Margaret could not hide the anguish his words caused her. "I can only live if you are with me!"

"Then you shall return with me to France; when I have managed to persuade the Pope to grant your divorce from Angus you should be able to come with me and I shall find a house, gracious and warmed by the southern sun, where you may dwell in peace and security."

"I cannot believe I would be permitted to follow my own desires," she said as the optimism she had known since his arrival burst like a bladder the village boys used for football.

Albany, his heart aching for her misery, tilted her face and kissed her mouth very gently.

"The fates hold all our lives in their hands; you and I know full well it is of no use to plan this or that for the future. It is sufficient to live for the hour and take the happiness so charily meted out to us; what more would you ask than this night when I, who love you in a way I had not believed it possible, am with you and want nothing but to carry you to yon bed and taunt those fates with our joy. Look at me, Margaret, trust me to have your interests always close to my heart. Tomorrow we shall go to Edinburgh where I shall present you to your nobles and extort their loyalty to you and the little son who I shall bring to your side to remain there until he is old enough to reign alone. Tonight is ours and we are alone, deeply in love — can you ask for more?"

Margaret looked up into his eyes and seeing the tenderness of his passion, shook her head and smiled.

"I ask no more and am fortunate to be allowed so much! Hold me close for within the circle of your arms I am safe forever!"

Epilogue

MARGARET TUDOR, eldest daughter of Henry VII and the Princess Elizabeth of York, died at Methven Castle on 18th October, 1541.

During the twenty years she lived after the events related in this book she was again to know much misery and discord in her connections with those whose lives were entangled with her own.

Her Victorian biographers are not always kind to her and there was much in her character to be decried; however, it is easy in the light of her unhappy marriages and close kinship with Henry VIII, to point at her weaknesses and forget the enormous strain under which she lived.

Bearing in mind mankind is less hardy today, how many women (Victorian or of now) are forced, at fourteen years of age, to marry men they have never met and suffer the personal tragedies of six or seven miscarriages before they have reached the pathetically young age of twenty?

Margaret was undeniably foolish in marrying Archibald Angus and it may be fairly claimed she brought all her ensuing troubles upon herself by this mistake; yet Scottish nature being what it was at this time in history it is reasonable to suppose the jealousies and rivalries of the powerful families would have divided sooner or later into parties either favouring England or France.

The love affair between Albany and Margaret is founded on fact and forms a really happy interlude in her troubled life, although much was made by Dacre and Walsey, for their own ends, of the Regent's desire to obtain a divorce for the Queen from Angus. It is true also that Albany and Margaret denied all rumours of their intention to marry for Anne de la Tour d'Auvergne was rich and dominating and Margaret had already tasted the bitter fruits of a headstrong union.

Margaret Tudor was capricious, wilful, perhaps greedy and spoilt but she was also courageous, compassionate and loving. The fact she was as well the grandmother of both Mary Queen of Scots and Lord Darnley compels interest for the qualities she passed on to these two highly dramatic persons.

TO FIGHT THE WILD
Rod Ansell and Rachel Percy

Lost in uncharted Australian bush, Rod Ansell survived by hunting and trapping wild animals, improvising shelter and using all the bushman's skills he knew.

COROMANDEL
Pat Barr

India in the 1830s is a hot, uncomfortable place, where the East India Company still rules. Amelia and her new husband find themselves caught up in the animosities which seethe between the old order and the new.

THE SMALL PARTY
Lillian Beckwith

A frightening journey to safety begins for Ruth and her small party as their island is caught up in the dangers of armed insurrection.

CLOUD OVER MALVERTON
Nancy Buckingham

Dulcie soon realises that something is seriously wrong at Malverton, and when violence strikes she is horrified to find herself under suspicion of murder.

AFTER THOUGHTS
Max Bygraves

The Cockney entertainer tells stories of his East End childhood, of his RAF days, and his post-war showbusiness successes and friendships with fellow comedians.

MOONLIGHT
AND MARCH ROSES
D. Y. Cameron

Lynn's search to trace a missing girl takes her to Spain, where she meets Clive Hendon. While untangling the situation, she untangles her emotions and decides on her own future.

NURSE ALICE IN LOVE
Theresa Charles

Accepting the post of nurse to little Fernie Sherrod, Alice Everton could not guess at the romance, suspense and danger which lay ahead at the Sherrod's isolated estate.

POIROT INVESTIGATES
Agatha Christie

Two things bind these eleven stories together — the brilliance and uncanny skill of the diminutive Belgian detective, and the stupidity of his Watson-like partner, Captain Hastings.

LET LOOSE THE TIGERS
Josephine Cox

Queenie promised to find the long-lost son of the frail, elderly murderess, Hannah Jason. But her enquiries threatened to unlock the cage where crucial secrets had long been held captive.

THE TWILIGHT MAN
Frank Gruber

Jim Rand lives alone in the California desert awaiting death. Into his hermit existence comes a teenage girl who blows both his past and his brief future wide open.

DOG IN THE DARK
Gerald Hammond

Jim Cunningham breeds and trains gun dogs, and his antagonism towards the devotees of show spaniels earns him many enemies. So when one of them is found murdered, the police are on his doorstep within hours.

THE RED KNIGHT
Geoffrey Moxon

When he finds himself a pawn on the chessboard of international espionage with his family in constant danger, Guy Trent becomes embroiled in moves and countermoves which may mean life or death for Western scientists.

TIGER TIGER
Frank Ryan

A young man involved in drugs is found murdered. This is the first event which will draw Detective Inspector Sandy Woodings into a whirlpool of murder and deceit.

CAROLINE MINUSCULE
Andrew Taylor

Caroline Minuscule, a medieval script, is the first clue to the whereabouts of a cache of diamonds. The search becomes a deadly kind of fairy story in which several murders have an other-worldly quality.

LONG CHAIN OF DEATH
Sarah Wolf

During the Second World War four American teenagers from the same town join the Army together. Forty-two years later, the son of one of the soldiers realises that someone is systematically wiping out the families of the four men.

THE LISTERDALE MYSTERY
Agatha Christie

Twelve short stories ranging from the light-hearted to the macabre, diverse mysteries ingeniously and plausibly contrived and convincingly unravelled.

TO BE LOVED
Lynne Collins

Andrew married the woman he had always loved despite the knowledge that Sarah married him for reasons of her own. So much heartache could have been avoided if only he had known how vital it was to be loved.

ACCUSED NURSE
Jane Converse

Paula found herself accused of a crime which could cost her her job, her nurse's reputation, and even the man she loved, unless the truth came to light.

A GREAT DELIVERANCE
Elizabeth George

Into the web of old houses and secrets of Keldale Valley comes Scotland Yard Inspector Thomas Lynley and his assistant to solve a particularly savage murder.

'E' IS FOR EVIDENCE
Sue Grafton

Kinsey Millhone was bogged down on a warehouse fire claim. It came as something of a shock when she was accused of being on the take. She'd been set up. Now she had a new client — herself.

A FAMILY OUTING IN AFRICA
Charles Hampton and Janie Hampton

A tale of a young family's journey through Central Africa by bus, train, river boat, lorry, wooden bicycle and foot.

THE PLEASURES OF AGE
Robert Morley

The author, British stage and screen star, now eighty, is enjoying the pleasures of age. He has drawn on his experiences to write this witty, entertaining and informative book.

THE VINEGAR SEED
Maureen Peters

The first book in a trilogy which follows the exploits of two sisters who leave Ireland in 1861 to seek their fortune in England.

A VERY PAROCHIAL MURDER
John Wainwright

A mugging in the genteel seaside town turned to murder when the victim died. Then the body of a young tearaway is washed ashore and Detective Inspector Lyle is determined that a second killing will not go unpunished.

DEATH ON A
HOT SUMMER NIGHT
Anne Infante

Micky Douglas is either accident-prone or someone is trying to kill him. He finds himself caught in a desperate race to save his ex-wife and others from a ruthless gang.

HOLD DOWN A SHADOW
Geoffrey Jenkins

Maluti Rider, with the help of four of the world's most wanted men, is determined to destroy the Katse Dam and release a killer flood.

THAT NICE MISS SMITH
Nigel Morland

A reconstruction and reassessment of the trial in 1857 of Madeleine Smith, who was acquitted by a verdict of Not Proven of poisoning her lover, Emile L'Angelier.

SEASONS OF MY LIFE
Hannah Hauxwell
and Barry Cockcroft

The story of Hannah Hauxwell's struggle to survive on a desolate farm in the Yorkshire Dales with little money, no electricity and no running water.

TAKING OVER
Shirley Lowe and Angela Ince

A witty insight into what happens when women take over in the boardroom and their husbands take over chores, children and chickenpox.

AFTER MIDNIGHT STORIES,
The Fourth Book Of

A collection of sixteen of the best of today's ghost stories, all different in style and approach but all combining to give the reader that special midnight shiver.

DEATH TRAIN
Robert Byrne

The tale of a freight train out of control and leaking a paralytic nerve gas that turns America's West into a scene of chemical catastrophe in which whole towns are rendered helpless.

THE ADVENTURE OF THE CHRISTMAS PUDDING
Agatha Christie

In the introduction to this short story collection the author wrote "This book of Christmas fare may be described as 'The Chef's Selection'. I am the Chef!"

RETURN TO BALANDRA
Grace Driver

Returning to her Caribbean island home, Suzanne looks forward to being with her parents again, but most of all she longs to see Wim van Branden, a coffee planter she has known all her life.

SKINWALKERS
Tony Hillerman

The peace of the land between the sacred mountains is shattered by three murders. Is a 'skinwalker', one who has rejected the harmony of the Navajo way, the murderer?

A PARTICULAR PLACE
Mary Hocking

How is Michael Hoath, newly arrived vicar of St. Hilary's, to meet the demands of his flock and his strained marriage? Further complications follow when he falls hopelessly in love with a married parishioner.

A MATTER OF MISCHIEF
Evelyn Hood

A saga of the weaving folk in 18th century Scotland. Physician Gavin Knox was desperately seeking a cure for the pox that ravaged the slums of Glasgow and Paisley, but his adored wife, Margaret, stood in the way.

DEAD SPIT
Janet Edmonds

Government vet Linus Rintoul attempts to solve a mystery which plunges him into the esoteric world of pedigree dogs, murder and terrorism, and Crufts Dog Show proves to be far more exciting than he had bargained for . . .

A BARROW IN THE BROADWAY
Pamela Evans

Adopted by the Gordillo family, Rosie Goodson watched their business grow from a street barrow to a chain of supermarkets. But passion, bitterness and her unhappy marriage aliented her from them.

THE GOLD AND THE DROSS
Eleanor Farnes

Lorna found it hard to make ends meet for herself and her mother and then by chance she met two men — one a famous author and one a rich banker. But could she really expect to be happy with either man?

THE SONG OF THE PINES
Christina Green

Taken to a Greek island as substitute for David Nicholas's secretary, Annie quickly falls prey to the island's charms and to the charms of both Marcus, the Greek, and David himself.

GOODBYE DOCTOR GARLAND
Marjorie Harte

The story of a woman doctor who gave too much to her profession and almost lost her personal happiness.

DIGBY
Pamela Hill

Welcomed at courts throughout Europe, Kenelm Digby was the particular favourite of the Queen of France, who wanted him to be her lover, but the beautiful Venetia was the mainspring of his life.